# The Saga of Dirt and Poncho

**Clayton D. Baker & Michael H. Kuecker**

Thank you for purchasing our book and giving it a chance. Please note that we aren't the best at editing, as we pride ourselves on our story telling more than punctuation. So if you notice anything that doesn't make sense or is just plain wrong please contact us at dirtandponcho@gmail.com and we will make the required changes. There shouldn't be many.

Cover by Justin Kuecker

Published Clayton D. Baker and Michael H. Kuecker

Michael would like to thank all the usual people, namely family and friends for not thinking this was a pipe dream.

Clayton would like to thank the same people, along with Red and Bobo.

They would both like to thank our proof readers and editors, you know who you are and we appreciate the hell out of it. Especially Sally and Truett who were the first two test subjects. Special shout-out to Justin's garage.

# Prologue

My name is Frank and this is the story about how everything I thought I knew got smashed to bits by two insane assholes. They truly opened my eyes for the first time in a very...very long time. In doing so they sacrificed more than anyone will ever know.

*That's pretty fucking rude Frank. Honestly if you are talking about the two of us that's not cool at all.*

Calm down, I'm trying to explain this whole mess and you aren't helping.

*Explain it to whom? And telling your 'asshole' friends to shut up is a dick move Frank. You're better than that.*

Anyone who will listen. Now will you please let me tell our story?

*Yeah tell your story Frank. But there isn't anyone else here but us man, just the three of us. The three amigos. The three musketeers, which actually works pretty well. But you have to be the fourth third musketeer, because he was the new guy.*

**How're there four musketeers, if there were only three of them?**

*Don't worry about it big guy, I'd explain it to you, but you know how you get with numbers. And anyway, the best you came up with was, "How were there four if there were only three of them?" That's not good buddy, you need to work on that. Frank just called you an asshole, why are you worried about the number of Musketeers?*

**That's pretty harsh, but fair point.**

Holy shit, shut the hell up! I'm trying to frame this story so folks will know what they are about to read.

*Read what?*

This!

*I don't follow, it sounds like you're talking to someone else, but like I said, there isn't anyone else here.*

Never mind. Just let me do this and we can go get some beers.

*Now you're making sense. You go ahead and ramble to the nothing and I'll sit here and pretend you don't sound like an insane crazy person. And I'll try my best to overlook the asshole part.*

Like I was saying, my life was pretty normal until I met these two... guys. They sent me on a journey of self-discovery and adventure that would...

*Hahahahaha! That sounds dumb as shit man. Seriously where is your purse at. You might as well say it was a coming of age tale about how you fell in love with a sparkling vampire. But your Pa was against the whole thing so you two dudes ran off to one of those silly communes.*

God dammit! Can I please tell my story? This is important to me!

*Sorry Frank, really. I'm sorry. Please continue telling your story, kind sir.*

An adventure that would... Stop laughing.

*I'm not!*

An adventure that would change everything, if you can call it an adventure, that is. It was more like a bunch of loosely related events that made little sense and culminated in further madness. The two gentlemen that caused this, reintroduced me to a world I could never admit was real. They brought my past back to me and exposed the errors of my ways.

*We didn't expose you to anyone, that's some low-brow shit, man. What kind of story are you telling about us Frank? Seriously, if you make us look like nerds I will have a friend of mine beat you senseless.*

**You don't have any friends.**

*Who needs friends? Especially ones that keep telling their imaginary friends that we are 'exposing' them to people.*

I mean expose in the sense that you made things known to me that were otherwise unknown or long forgotten.

*Oh, well that wouldn't be hard. You were kind of a square. Plus your memory is shit. Just let me know who the fuck you are talking to and I will just tell them the story myself. You know I am awesome at making things sound better.*

I met people, killed some of them, and most of them tried to kill me. It was an eye-opening experience to say the least. I constantly questioned what was real and what wasn't, ultimately wishing that none of it was, and that I could go back to my ordinary, uneventful life.

*Well, it's a good thing none of it is real then, Frank. Hell we aren't even real; we're just voices in your crazy head. Like those jerks you're talking to right now.*

**I'm pretty sure I'm real.**

*Well we aren't. Frank made us up to cope with his stupid life.*

**Oh.**

I didn't make you up, you idiots are real. I'd be dead if you weren't real.

*That's what we want you to think. You're crazy brain made us up and now it has also convinced you that we are real, tangible beings that can affect your world.*

I've seen you affect this world, in pretty big ways.

**Yeah, I'm with Frank on this one. I'm pretty sure we're real.**

*Then it's worse than I thought, we're fragmenting and the hallucinations can't even decide what we are now!*

**Shit.**

*Shit is right big guy, Frank is losing it!*

I'm not losing anything, you guys are real.

*How can you be so sure of that?*

Well for one thing there is no way I could drink as much as you do without dying, so I can't be the one drinking all the beers I find around the house.

*Fair point.*

**I think he has you on that one.**

*Yeah, I guess we could be real. But that could mean that Frank is made up and we are the crazy ones.*

It doesn't. We are all real.

**Good, I like being real.**

*I knew we were real Frank, can't you take a joke? Shit man, it's like every time you start talking to nothing about some crap or another you get all serious. It doesn't suit you.*

Sometimes I wish you really were just voices, it would mean none of this happened and I'd just be committed somewhere with padded walls.

*Bullshit Frank, you love all this.*

Maybe I do, but now everyone can see what I'm dealing with.

*Who can?*

God dammit! Here is my story, I hope it explains things.

*Explains what? To who? What the shit is going on Frank?*

**Let it go brother, it's probably not important.**

*Fine, but I'll figure out what Frank is up to. One way or another. Oh shit, I think I get it. Frank make sure to tell them how you were a shit private eye when this started, and that you didn't even wear that cowboy hat. Oh shit...tell them about how Neph almost killed you for thinking she looked hot in the leather I made her wear. People love hot chicks in leather. Honestly, you are messing this all up Frank. As much as you talk, you should be way better at telling stories. Shit, just tell them it is a story about the end of the world. People love that shit.*

Fuck it. This is a story about the end of the world.

# The Bar

I was at my favorite bar enjoying an ice cold Tallboy, a small reward for another job well done. It's the kind of hole-in-the-wall bar with no name. Just some crappy old neon sign in the window that reads "BAR" when the place is open for business. At least I think so, I have honestly never seen the place not open.

I don't drink often, but I feel obligated to when I've just wrapped up a case. Even if it was as simple as taking pictures of some mid-life crisis afflicted man and his far-too-young mistress and sending them to his wife. It may not sound glamorous, but it does pay the bills. That, and it's really easy. Plus one of the perks of being a self-employed Private Investigator is that you get to make you own hours so drinking at noon on a Wednesday is no big deal.

Right as I was thinking how much I was actually enjoying my obligatory Tallboy in my crappy bar of choice, a shitstorm, in the form of two homeless-looking gentlemen, walked in. Sometimes you can tell by how a person carries themselves that they're nothing but trouble. These two carried themselves like their shit don't stink and they were convinced that you would like the smell.

The big one, and I mean big, like flip-over-a-Volkswagon-big walked to the bar and just stared at Jim, the seventy year old bartender, while rolling his shoulders slightly. He looked like a guy who was just waiting for a fight. To his credit Jim, who I am 60% sure is actually named Jim because he is nearly impossible to understand, didn't look as terrified as I'd have been in his situation. Poor old bastard probably didn't even know what was going on half the time, which right then was a good thing for him. Without so much as a word old Jim grabbed a bottle of whiskey off the shelf and slid it over to the big bear-of-a-man.

The other gentlemen, who, after separating himself from his giant pal, was average height and build with a careless smirk on his scruffy face, sat down at the only nice'ish' booth with a few men in cheap suits who were presumably having a liquid lunch break. It seemed like they knew each other because he chugged one of the beers on the table, while they laughed like they were all old friends. He must have been their "fun but always broke" friend because they gave him all the cash they had on them, which seemed like a decent amount. The oddest part was they all seemed happy to be doing so.

As I was watching this odd exchange I felt the familiar sensation you get when you are sure someone is watching you. I shifted slightly on my stool and saw the big one, bottle in hand, staring directly at me. I glanced behind me making sure there wasn't someone back there he could be looking at. No one. I turned back to look at the giant, surprised to see that he had not bitten off the top of the bottle and consumed its contents, glass shards and all. This man was, as I mentioned, huge. Not in the way a bodybuilder is huge, with toned muscles, and muscles on top of muscles. No, he was huge in the way some people are just born with, the kind that still looks functional. The way he was dressed didn't help to alleviate my tension, black biker boots, jeans, and a tank top are not exactly the most imposing clothing options. When you put them on a very large man with long hair, a hobo beard, and arms the size of tree trunks covered in indecipherable tattoos, it does strike an unsettling image.

He appeared to be just staring for the hell of it, so I decided to avert my gaze, in an effort to look un-intimidated.  I doubt it worked.

I turned back to his companion, keeping him in my peripheral vision in case I needed to tactically retreat in a hurry. He was still chumming around with the disheveled business man types, which made me more curious. He was dressed in flip flops, cargo shorts, and a dirty shirt. Not fitting in with his pals at all. Like his friend, he had long hair, not dark like his, but blondish, or dirty blond, or maybe just dirty. I couldn't decide. He was also adorned with facial hair, it was just patchier. He was still drinking their beers and joking, they seemed to be having a great time.

For some reason I felt like I should approach them and join in the merriment, but I dismissed this thought when the mass in the corner of my eye started to move. Towards me.

At this point I decided that this was my bar and I'll be damned if some asshole is going to make me leave without so much as a word. I would chalk this up to bravery; however, it has more to do with my "fight or flight" being stuck right in the middle. I'm more of a "wait and see how this plays out" kind of guy. It's not glamorous and you never get the girl, but I'm still alive, so I figure it's working.

I tried to look as relaxed as possible, and luckily I couldn't see myself, because I was sure I would have been disappointed. He did not seem to notice my discomfort at being walked down, or more likely didn't care, and sat down at my table. He didn't speak, just took a pull from the bottle that made my eyes water just seeing that quantity of alcohol ingested at once. Much to my surprise I managed to raise a questioning eyebrow at him. He grinned showing his perfectly white, and noticeably not filed to jagged points teeth, and said "You must be Frank."

This is probably a good time to mention that in the past several years I have built a reputation as a P.I. that can almost always get evidence on a suspected cheating husband. Through personal experience, almost every woman who believes her husband is a cheating tool is right. I have had a few ex-husbands, who lost a lot in the resulting divorces, threaten me. But this might be the first time one of them has hired a goon to perform

Novocain free dental work on me, that or I'm just far too pessimistic for my own good. Whoever hired this guy must have found him in the yellow pages under "scary motherfucker." While weighing the possible damage I could inflict if I caught him off guard, he broke the silence.

"Frank, before you act on some stupid impulse to hit me with a beer bottle and run out of the bar, you should know a few things. One, it won't hurt. Two, you can't outrun me. And three, me and my associate are here to hire you, not assault you."

I relaxed my "smash bottle into face and run" grip on my bottle and asked, "Associate"? I scanned the bar for another potential member of the Hells Angels.

He nodded toward the bar, and I saw the dirty man he had come in with, of course, how had I forgotten? He had moved from the table and was now behind the bar and appeared to be serving drinks to a couple of coeds. Jim was carrying on as if he didn't notice a thing out of the ordinary, which was peculiar, because Jim never let anyone behind the bar, and I don't think I had ever seen college girls in this part of town. It looked a lot like Jim had no idea at all that there was an interloper behind his bar hogging up all the pretty girls. And when Jim walked right past him without flinching I started to think that him not noticing was exactly what was happening. For some reason Jim had no idea he was there, or I was just going crazy and they knew each other, or any other hundreds of plausible explanations that didn't involve invisible hippies.

This is when my hindsight had kicked in and it reminded me that the big one had walked in looking like murder incarnate and nobody seemed to care. Had it been a western movie, the music would have stopped abruptly and everyone would have glared at the swingy saloon doors sizing up this new stranger in town, only to look away upon seeing the murder in his eyes.

"Excuse me for a moment Frank," said the big man. He got up leaving his bottle behind and stalked over to the bar.

Upon his arrival the dirty hippy grinned and raised his hand in what looked like a "high five me" gesture, and after a few seconds of not receiving one he lowered it dejectedly. I couldn't hear what they said to each other, but the big one made sharp hand motions in my direction, followed by the dirty one making some of his own. His were directed at the women, the bar, an ash tray, and finishing with what I was pretty sure was the sign for traveling in basketball transitioning into the nose tap that usually had something to do with partaking in cocaine. When his flailing came to an end, he crossed his arms over his chest confidently. The big one said something that looked serious. And the dirty one slumped his shoulders in what could only be resignation.

Bouncing back from his verbal defeat quickly, he hopped over the bar and landed flat on his face on the other side. My suspicion that nobody was noticing them was confirmed when there was zero reaction from anywhere inside the bar. I held back a chuckle, because let's be honest, when people fall down its usually pretty funny. He bounced back to his feet quickly though, with a showman's grin that said "I did that on purpose!" He dusted himself off, turned around, and grabbed three tall beers off the bar and headed toward my table.

The whole situation seemed so surreal, and I attribute my lack of a reaction to that fact. Maybe I was just curious enough to see how this all played out, or maybe I just needed the work. I filed these thoughts away for future analysis.

The dirty one sauntered over and set one of his three beers in front of me, one next to the giant's whiskey bottle, and left the third in his hand.

"Hey Frank," he said, "my name is Dirt, and my large friend here is Poncho."

I almost burst into laughter, the one I had been calling "dirty" was actually named Dirt. It didn't seem real. And the giant scary man was named Poncho? This had to be a trick.

Dirt was casually sipping his beer, while Poncho's had apparently consumed itself and he had transitioned back to whiskey. He also had a look on his face that implied he was terribly amused by something, in a bloodthirsty way that is. This is when I remembered that after you meet people you are supposed to say things back, so I cleared my throat and said, "Hi."

Still waters run deep they say.

"Can I help you?" I managed.

"We find ourselves in need of a man with your particular skill set, Frank" said Poncho.

"We have money" said Dirt idly looking around the bar.

So they were trying to hire me, not murder me and leave me in a gutter, but this confirmation of Poncho's earlier claim did little to alleviate my suspicion. Why would two people, who can clearly take care of themselves, need the help of a small time Private Investigator? I decided to use my internet training for its intended purpose.

"My particular skill set being what exactly?" I asked.

"Spy shit, Frank," said Dirt. "Creeping around in the bushes taking pictures of assholes doing shit they aren't supposed to be doing skills."

"Any idiot can do that, it's literally the easiest thing about this job."

"Not the way you do Frank, you..."

Poncho cut him off, "He is being dramatic, we just need anybody, and you are anybody, so you'll do."

Dirt looked crestfallen and consoled himself in his beer glass. I was a tiny bit upset that I was just anybody to them, not hand-chosen from some secret stable of P.I.'s, but a job's a job.

"Ok, so what kind of job did you have in mind?" I asked.

Dirt perked back up immediately and almost as quickly lowered his head conspiratorially, "Oh nothing." He paused to glance around furtively. "Just save the world is all." To top off his performance he put his index finger to his lips and made the universal gesture for "shhhh" winking with the exact opposite of subtlety.

Poncho rolled his eyes and said, "Nothing that grand at all Frank, we just need you to take some pictures of a guy and see if he is up to no good, Dirt just has a flair for the ridiculous."

"I do not!" Dirt said sounding hurt.

Poncho said nothing, just glared at Dirt until he gave up his mock defiance.

"He is a vampire though." Dirt said pretending to hold a cape up in front of his face.

"If he was a vampire why would we need Frank to take pictures of him? We would already know he is up to no good and this would be a waste of time."

"No, you suspect he is, I know he is. I saw a Costa Rican flag at his house and everything." He said this as if it made perfect sense.

"I've told you a thousand times, the fact that he has been to Costa Rica has nothing to do with him being a vampire," Poncho said, rubbing his temples.

Dirt looked offended this time. "Everyone knows that all vampires come from Costa Rica, it's in books, it's like their fatherland."

"Sure, but that doesn't mean that all people from Costa Rica are vampires," Poncho said.

"You can't be sure of that," Dirt responded.

This whole exchange seemed normal for them, and this made me very uncomfortable. I hate taking jobs from crazy people, but if they actually pay me it could be worth my time. I never know when to walk away before I get too deep.

Poncho rubbed his eyes in frustration, he looked like he would love to continue arguing and was having a hard time deciding what to do.

"Look, we have to stay on track and hire Frank, he doesn't want to listen to this," Poncho said.

I took a sip from my beer, glancing between them. A little part of me wanted to see how this played out, but a bigger part just wanted to leave them to their squabbling. Indecision won out and I waited.

It was Dirt's turn to sigh, "Listen man, how can we expect Frank to accept this job without telling him the facts up front? The major ones being: he is Costa Rican and therefore a dirty whiny vampire. He drinks blood, which kills people Ponch. That's bad. He has great big wings, pointy teeth," he floundered a moment, "laser eyes, turbo boosters, all that shit that makes vampires bad fucking news."

"Vampires don't have turbo boosters, shit head."

"Shit head!?" Dirt yelled. "Which shit head lived in Costa Rica during the great Panamanian vampire invasion? This guy, I saw things there that would ruin your fucking day."

"Well, we both did," Poncho answered calmly, "and that only lasted three days. I hardly see how it's valid as to whether or not all Costa Ricans are vampires."

Dirt appeared to be deep in thought, "I get what you're saying, not all Costa Ricans are vampires because some of them are Panamanians. I'm an idiot."

Partly true. I wasn't sure how that made any sense, and I was pretty sure it was all bullshit anyway. So I continued to drink my beer and bystander to the best of my ability.

Poncho nodded, somehow accepting this as a reasonable conclusion.

"So Frank," said Poncho, "we need you to go follow a guy and find out if he is a vampire. We have money and it will be easy."

"Super easy" added Dirt.

I decided to see how far they were willing to take this crazy excuse for employment.

"So does this vampire have any magical vampire powers I need to be worried about?" I resisted the urge to air quote the word vampire. "Besides laser eyes that is."

Poncho started to say something, but Dirt cut him off. "I'll field this one."

Dirt leaned back on his stool and stretched his arms wide, cracked his knuckles and neck, then chugged the remainder of his beer. He set the glass on the next table over and grabbed the fresh one that was not sitting there a second ago. Or maybe it had, I wasn't really paying attention.

"The thing you have to know about vampires is that almost everything you have seen in movies or read in books is one hundred percent real. Even. No. Especially, the stuff that is straight up contradictory. Because there are different kinds or whatever. Also they just bitch and moan all day long about being cursed and having to drink blood and boo hoo. It's really annoying. And..." he paused apparently lost for words. "They are all stupid," he finished looking incredibly satisfied.

"God damn it Dirt," said Poncho. "Stop filling his head with this shit, it isn't helping. All he needs to do is take pictures, nothing else."

"Well they do complain a lot," Dirt said sullenly.

"True, but irrelevant."

I cleared my throat and they both looked at me.

"If all that stuff is true then you can't see them in mirrors, and I assume they wouldn't show up on film either. How am I supposed to photograph this nefarious vampire's deeds?"

They exchanged glances that told me they had not considered this possibility.

"That part is just an urban legend," said Poncho.

"Magic!" shouted Dirt at the same time.

Now I was certain I was being lied to, but the way they were going about it made me very curious. I surmised that this was some elaborate prank and the cameras would burst out of the walls and I would be properly shocked. I wasn't sure if that show was still on though. Despite their constant stream of nonsense it all seemed harmless, and I deduced that the quickest way to end it was to ask for the money.

"I'm gonna need a retainer for this."

Dirt grinned again, "Oh ye of little faith! I told you we had money!"

He pulled a stack of money out of his cargo shorts and waved it in my face. I had seen enough movies to recognize a ten thousand dollar stack of hundred dollar bills. That and I was once the manager of a poor performing local bank. It was clearly fake, people don't carry around money in those quantities unless it's in a movie. Dirt started flipping through it, relishing the smell of brand new money, or just making a show out of it. He pulled out two crisp one hundred dollar bills and set the stack on the table. That figured, I thought, it was only slightly less than I would take for a job like this if it wasn't a bag of lies. But it was just little enough for me to turn down this particular circus.

Dirt put the two hundreds into his pocket and slid the remaining ninety-eight hundred dollars in front of me.

"That should cover any expenses you have for a job this simple," Poncho said.

Even if it was fake money, it was still a shit load of fake money, and it was hard not to be impressed. This is probably why I almost choked on my beer when he did it.

I regained my composure and said, "That's quite a bit of money for a job this simple."

"You don't like money Frank?" asked Dirt.

"He thinks it's fake," said Poncho staring fists into my soul.

"What?" Dirt said confused. "It's right there in front of him, how could it be fake?" he poked it cautiously. "It's real."

What the hell was wrong with these guys, who doesn't know what counterfeit money is?

"He knows it's there stupid, he thinks it's fake money, not legal tender."

"Fake money," Dirt said, rolling the words around his mouth as if it was an entirely new concept. "What makes it fake?"

"I think only certain people are allowed to make money, like they have a permit for it or something. If anyone else makes it, it doesn't count."

"Why not?" Dirt seemed properly offended with this news.

"Think about it, if anyone could make money then there would be too much money and..." He stopped. "I don't fucking know."

"That's stupid, it's real money Frank, straight from the money building this morning."

I was still pretty sure that it was fake, but I could check on that later. I was pretty sure I still had one of those bank markers that show up a different color if you mark on counterfeit bills. I put the stack of fake money into my pocket and waited. Dirt still looked like the fake money thing was bothering him, but snapped out of it when Poncho kicked his stool out from under him. This was a pretty severe reaction to being distracted and I expected a fight. A short one-sided beating of a fight, but a fight.

Instead of coming up swinging Dirt just hopped to his feet, righted his stool and sat down. He reached into his pocket once again and pulled out a photo that looked to have been folded into oblivion several times.

"All you need to know is on this," he said as he slid it into my shirt pocket and patted it. "Get proof he is a vampire and we will be in touch in a few days." He tipped an imaginary hat at me and got up to leave. Poncho nodded and heaved his bulk off the no doubt grateful stool and made for the door.

I heard Poncho saying on their way out the door, "You know Costa Rica doesn't have an army right?"

"Of course not," he replied, "They all died in the war, or worse."

Poncho said something else, but they were outside and I couldn't hear it, and despite everything that had happened I kind of wanted to know how it all played out. Once they were outside I could still see them through the dingy clear'ish' thing on the front of the building that Jim called a window.

They stood on the sidewalk, lit cigarettes, and walked off in opposite directions. I finished my beer, still watching the street, and saw Dirt go sprinting past in the direction Poncho had gone, and I was positive he was wearing a hat now.

"Shit," I said out loud. Garnering hostile looks from the suits at the table, of course they start noticing what's going on around them now.

Take pictures of a guy who isn't a vampire, because vampires aren't real, and they were lying to me about something, so that had to be it. Do this for a couple of lunatics with a stack of probably fake money, more than I have ever been paid for a single job.

Why not, what's the worst that could happen?

# The Vampire

Despite my better judgment, I decided to take the job. Particularly after I determined that the money was real, or the marker I kept from the bank was busted, it had been a slight shock. When I had taken the money at the bar I was just keeping it safe. From muggers. Honestly I hadn't been sure if I was going to take the job or not, but when the money turned out to be real, I didn't really have a choice. It was too good to be true, all that money to take a picture of a guy not being a vampire.

I was skeptical about the whole thing, but the guy definitely wasn't a vampire, mostly because they aren't real. But one thing was for sure, Dirt and Poncho were lying to me, I just wasn't sure about what.

I started to get my supplies together and change my clothes, you can't go on a stakeout in blue jeans, that would be silly. I decided against the dark suit in favor of a classic brown, brown is the best stakeout color; dark, but not too dark. This may seem odd, but I once read that having suits that are not black makes other people believe that you own more than one suit. I left the tie and put on comfortable shoes. Running is always a possibility in these situations and it's almost impossible in dress shoes. The suit jacket was just loose enough on the sides to hide the bulk of my trusty sidearm in its shoulder holster.

The coat had some extra pockets, for all the extra shit I carry that I never need. Batteries, flashlight, notepad, typical Investigation supplies. I put the digital camera in one of the pockets as well, the one thing I was sure I would need. I still miss the bulky real film cameras, but the digital is just so much easier to carry and you don't have to deal with developing film. And last, but not least, my slightly battered fedora. Cliché I know, but call it a guilty pleasure.

I checked myself out in the mirror to make sure I was pulling off the grizzled private detective at the end of his rope look. I had the pre-requisite wrinkles, tired eyes, and the five-o-clock shadow that was almost always present. I noticed the gray at my temple creeping ever higher in an evil attempt to make me old. I wondered if I should have grown a mustache.

I practiced my "I'm a hard mother fucker" look a few times. It was still missing something; I shrugged and headed out the door.

About an hour later, I was parked across the street from the target's house and it would be dark soon. My old model Chevy didn't really mesh in a neighborhood this fancy, but I've found that the people who live in such cookie cutter areas tend not to notice much that isn't themselves.

The house looked empty and there weren't any cars in the driveway, so I assumed that the target wasn't home. More evidence that he wasn't a vampire, driving around in the sunlight was probably against the rules.

I had no idea why Dirt and Poncho wanted me to spy on this guy, the real reason anyway, not the vampire shit. But the money was real, and in the end that's all that mattered. I couldn't shake the feeling that something fishy was going on; I put it down to the peculiarity of the way I was hired.

I pulled the photograph out of my pocket again as if I could glean more information from it than last time. It was still a picture of an unremarkable man sitting in a car, it appeared to be taken from the street at a stop light. On the back was the address I was currently at, and a name; Dracula. Seriously, and it was written in what looked like red permanent marker, complete with little red droplets drawn coming off the bottoms of the letters.

I sighed and stuffed it back in my pocket, still no help.

Just about the time I had decided to drive off and leave this mess alone I saw Dracula's BMW turn onto the street from my rear view mirror. I ducked down and while he pulled into the driveway I got my camera ready. I popped back up to snap a few of the 'getting out of the car action shots' people like so much, and followed through with some 'unlocking the door shots'. I was disappointed that he didn't turn into mist and flow through the seams of the door, maybe the seal was too tight.

After he was inside the house I didn't really know what to do next, this wasn't a cheating husband so there wasn't a mistress to wait for. I decided to just take a few more photos through the kitchen window and call it a night.

The sun finally set and it was only a matter of time before hell bellowed out onto the world, or Dracula made ramen noodles. That's right, house one wing short of a mansion, 7 series in the driveway, and he was cooking the food that costs less than a quarter. Ramen noodles, the great equalizers of the classes. I got a few photos of Dracula cooking his noodles and deduced that this was surefire evidence that this guy was no vampire. Easiest ninety-eight hundred dollars anyone has ever made.

I was about to start the car and go get a victory drink when a van pulled in behind the Beemer. The plot thickens as they say. It had no markings, and was the typical white van you see all over the place. It was probably a private delivery company dropping off his coffin and soil from his homeland. Turns out I was half right, it was a delivery company. Not coffin delivery, but hooker or possibly stripper delivery. That is a seriously fine line when you're being dropped off at someone's house. For arguments sake I will just call them hookers, because who needs five strippers. Five mid-grade hookers shuffled out of the van, I say mid-grade because as anyone will tell you; high class hookers don't show up in vans. Hell I'm pretty sure even middle class strippers don't show up in vans.

They were not the svelte, elegant types in expensive evening gowns either. They were clad in an overabundance of leopard print, fishnets, and ill-fitting tube tops. I could almost smell the hair bleach and sadness from across the street. More than one of them had the dead look in their eyes that said, "I stopped doing this to pay for college a long time ago."

They headed for the door and the van took off, while I snapped a few more photos. I wasn't sure if this affected his vampire nature, but it couldn't hurt. Before any of them rang the doorbell they huddled together, I couldn't tell what they were doing, but by the drastic change from shambling husks to bubbly party girls, I assumed that good old fashioned cocaine was involved.

I kept on photographing them while they rang the doorbell and were invited inside to surely be exsanguinated. Why did he need five prostitutes? I could understand two, maybe three in a pinch, I guess I'm just not the dynamo in the sack that the undead are.

After the door closed and the music started throbbing through the walls and into the streets I started to wonder about something. I wondered how I was supposed to prove that this guy was or wasn't a vampire. I hadn't been given any specific criteria on how to determine this fact. He was out in the sun, but they never said if that was real or not. Hell, they never said which part of the bullshit was real bullshit or fake bullshit. My closest point of reference was Dirt's rant about movie vampires, which was useless. I had seen my share of vampire movies, as anyone who has ever seen a movie has. There are thousands of those things and no two of them have the same rules.

Some can go in the sun and have no ill effects, unless looking like a glitter dusted toolbag is an ill effect, while others burst into flames in an instant. Some vampires are great big whiny pussies and some are no nonsense killers. That part may be a personality issue, so I put it in the maybe category of my bullshit list. Some vampires are super-fast and some are normal speed, but most lean towards fast. Some can fly, some can't, seemed silly to me to make a vampire that couldn't fly. Shape shifting was a big one too, bats, rats, wolves, mist, other people, and who knows what else.

I took a quick tally and confirmed my decision that vampires weren't real, and I was just stalling. I wasn't sure if it was because I was sure Dracula was just a normal hooker loving rich guy and I didn't need to take pictures of him because deep down I was afraid he might actually be a vampire.

Nah, vampires still aren't real. It was settled, I was going to head into the bushes and take some pictures of Dracula and his hookers.

It was dark enough that sneaking into the bushes would be pretty easy. Any peeping tom will tell you, hiding in the foliage isn't the hard part though; it's getting to the hiding spot that gets tricky. Lucky for me the rich folks in this neighborhood must have to get up early and Dracula's house was the only one with any lights on. After going down the street to the nearest crosswalk, which is honestly a chore in a neighborhood like this, I strolled toward Dracula's house looking casual and confident, just in case that kind of thing worked.

I looked around to see if I was being watched and ducked into the bushes bordering the yard. It was almost too easy, except having to get all the way to the backyard in a crouch, I was noticing my age a little during that part.

The bushes must have been designed to conceal spies, because once I hit the backyard there was a perfect place to sit down and see directly through the glass patio doors into the living room. It looked pretty much like I figured it would. The walls were adorned with gaudy paintings that were probably art to some people. With the various pointy statues and ancient looking vases it looked like a horrible place to live. Even the couches looked uncomfortable, which is just masochistic.

The center of the room had a glass coffee table with a pile of white powder on it. Dracula must have been baking and spilled flour...in the living room...in a neat little pile. Clearly it couldn't be drugs, there was just too much. It made the mountain of cocaine in *Scarface* look like; well actually it was considerably smaller than that. But it was sure as hell a lot more than I had ever seen before. It had to be worth, a shit load I guessed. I really have no idea how much that stuff is worth, it always seemed to be an expensive hobby.

As my shock wore off I noticed more of what was going on inside. There was a lack a black candles, pentagrams, and bloodletting, and an abundance of cocaine snorting, terrible dancing and immoral touching. Nothing to worry about, the only things this guy was guilty of was drugs and whores. I felt fairly stupid worrying and snapped some photos in case by Dirt and Poncho's logic this constituted proof. I keep saying 'snap' but digital cameras don't snap, resisting making the noise myself was difficult.

As I was looking through the view finder I spotted something that I surmised to be irregular. It was the sight of two of the hookers being stabbed in their necks. Dracula was on his knees alternately stabbing them, not ripping them apart with fangs and claws, just stabbing. One of the hookers was kneeling at the coffee table inhaling large quantities of powder, doing a fine job not noticing what was going on behind her. The other two were nowhere to be seen, maybe they ran away when they saw the stabbing start and were calling the police.

I was still taking pictures, possibly out of reflex. When the two on the floor were good and dead, the oblivious one turned around and froze. I could see her loading up what was sure to be a blood curdling scream when a fire poker was jammed through her chest, Dracula attached to the handle. She looked down in confusion as he yanked the poker from her chest, the scream she had wound up coming out as a fine spray of blood.

I stopped taking pictures and gaped, slack-jawed, at the massacre inside. Surely this wasn't happening and I had gone insane. Before I could make any sense of it the other two hookers rounded the corner and walked head-first into the carnage. They must have been in the bathroom. I wanted to shout a warning to them when I saw Dracula slip behind them, he had moved before they came back and they hadn't seen him. I shouted no warning, my flight or fight being caught in the middle is a constant problem.

He hefted one of the large pointy statues, or maybe it was a sculpture, over his head, and before either one could scream, he brought it down on the closest one's head. The sound of her head caving in was drowned out by the horrible bass coming from the stereo. The remaining hooker managed to scream making Dracula wince, he dropped the statue and wrapped his hands around her neck. He dragged her to the ground by her neck and straddled her, maintaining the choke.

Seeing her not fight back, snapped me out of my stupor and I made up my mind to save her. Better late than never, I just hoped I wasn't too late. I drew my .45 and rushed the patio door, it was unlocked. When I opened it, the bass thundering out giving me pause, but I charged forward. Dracula was still choking the hooker on the floor and didn't notice me. I couldn't help but wonder if hookers had a security deposit. I was neck deep in the murder of four, possibly five, marginally innocent women when this crossed my mind. Despite the fact that there was zero chance he could have heard me I tiptoed toward him anyway, old habits die hard.

I was about to step over the two that had been stabbed in their necks, when he looked up at me, clearly startled at my abundance of clothing. Dracula...was startled to see me. Or maybe he was startled to see a .45 semi-automatic pointed at him. He started to speak, but the music drowned him out. He frowned and slowly started reaching for a remote on the arm of the couch. I shook my head and tilted the barrel of the gun up a bit in the 'hands up' motion. He got the point and stopped, he put his hands up for good measure too. I reached out with my free hand and turned the stereo down, keeping the gun pointed at his chest.

"What?" I asked.

"Who the fuck are you?" he sneered back at me without moving, not moving was important. If he had moved I might have shot him, I don't point guns at people very often and I was trying hard to hide my jitters. I doubted it was working. The girl I had been so valiantly trying to save wasn't moving, and her eyes were open and glassy. I hadn't seen a lot of dead bodies in my time, but enough to know one when I see one.

I considered pistol whipping him multiple times, but I like my gun too much to put it through that kind of abuse, plus it actually takes more technique than most people realize. Instead I held my ground and said, "None of your goddamn business." My throat was dry and the smell of blood was choking my nostrils.

"Why did you kill these women?" I asked, not really wanting to hear the answer.

Dracula was looking more comfortable with the situation, which meant I was losing my surprise control. "Because it's fun, you the cops? You look like a cop."

I didn't see how it mattered if I was with the police or not, it probably didn't. It was just most people's first reaction after being caught doing something they aren't supposed to be doing. It did bring up a good point; I needed to not be in that house any longer. Time to wrap it up and get the hell out.

"No, I'm not the cops," I answered. "Which means if I shoot you I don't have to fill out all the paperwork. Are you a fucking vampire?" I don't normally brag, but I said this with an amount of anger I didn't know I possessed.

His eyebrows shot up and he started laughing, "Oh shit." he said. 'Oh shit' is what I thought, no way this guy actually thought he was a vampire, but why else would he be laughing? I guessed he could just be a crazy person and stuck with it. I was in the process of having a mental breakdown trying to decide if he was crazy or a vampire, when he coughed his way to a stop.

"Sorry" he said, "I should have known those two assholes were behind this."

Of course he knew them, I masked my surprise with a clever, "Huh?"

"Whatever those two shit birds are going by these days, the savage and the drunk, they are always pulling shit like this." He furrowed his brow and continued, "They told you I was a vampire? That's a new one, you are a great big idiot. Or..."

I cut him off with my foot, to be precise with my foot impacting his face. Normally insults don't get under my skin, but as it turns out, insults from guys who just murdered five people do.

He rocked back a little, but stayed on his knees, spitting blood on the floor. "You have no idea what's going on do you? They just gave you a pile of money and sent you on your merry way huh? Those two are using you to..."

This time I cut him off with four bullets in his chest. It wouldn't occur to me until later that hearing him out could have saved me a world of trouble, but at the time my blood was running quite high and I wasn't in complete control of myself. I turned the music back up in hopes to mask the gunshots and looked down at the man I had just killed. To my surprise, he didn't seem all the way killed yet, I needed to get a hold of some of those movie bullets that kill people right away. He coughed up bright red chunks of something that should still be inside him and managed to sputter some last words.

"Those guys are the worst," and was cut off by more coughing. I cut off his coughing with a bullet in his head and started heading for the patio door, dammit Frank, listen to people's dying confessions.

I looked back over the carnage and noticed the red, white and blue squares of the Panamanian flag hanging over the entryway to the kitchen. I looked it up earlier, which seemed much less crazy now. As I closed the door and headed back to my car a thought occurred to me, if he was from Panama he damn sure wasn't a vampire.

# ~Dirt~

## *Fucking Vampires*

The great Panamanian vampire invasion wasn't all the fun and games you'd think a war against the unholy spawn of the night would be. It was way more fun than that. Me and Ponch were banging around Costa Rica minding our own business, yelling at howler monkeys and things like that.

Then this guy runs up, says, "Watch out! There is a civil war going on!" then runs off.

We look at each other and nod. We know what's really going on.

Fucking Vampires.

But we knew what to do, we made for the Cartago as fast as we could. It turned out that the god damn Costa Ricans were all vampires and they tried to invade Panama, but the Panamanians said nuts to that, and reinvaded Costa Rica in the daytime. They used the guise of Costa Rican rebels to stay under the rest of the world's radar.

So everyone thinks it's a civil war, and there aren't any vampires, and the Panamanian freedom fighters posing as Costa Rican rebels are fighting their asses off *against this demonic vampire force, and actually not doing too bad. But me and Ponch figure they can use any help they can get.*

*So we get to Cartago and there's this guy named Jose planning to sack the place. Turns out he just steam rolled up the Pan American Highway, taking towns along the way. But Cartago is a big one, and some guy has hunkered down pretty good.*

*We offer to help fight the vampires, but Jose isn't too sure about us, and he pretends that he never heard of any vampires. Pretty good cover that guy had. I give him a wink and offer to help win freedom or whatever he wants. He still isn't convinced, so Poncho convinced him for us.*

*After that we had to come up with a plan. Normally with this many vampires we would just burn everything down and call it a day. But Jose was pretty insistent that we only fight the armed ones, he would 'take care of' the 'civilians.' Whatever that meant.*

*After that we roll in and tear the place up, it was pretty brutal. I must have killed like two hundred vampires that day, Poncho just hung back and offered witty remarks and clever commentary. Not as clever as mine, but he tries really hard.*

*A few days go by and we win. Jose is happy that the good guys won, but he isn't too sure about us. I think he thought we were vampires too. Which is stupid because we were out in the daylight.*

After the fall of Cartago we head for the capital, where some other clowns are holed up. Some stuff happened, and Jose won, and he got to be king of Costa Rica. We all partied pretty hard after that.

Problem was though, Jose was a vampire too, and he used us to take control from the other vampires so he could for real invade Panama with his loyal vampire army. Also I think they could go out in the daylight. Either way we got the hell out of there, all those alleged civilians we didn't burn were surely going to be press ganged into his army, and we couldn't fight a nation. Not after the last time we tried that without an army behind us.

So we left the country and kept an ear out for news about the future slaughter of all those canal people. But it never happened, it was a secret invasion. They took over slowly and quietly. Nobody even noticed that the population was being replaced with vampires and their brainwashed lackeys.

So that's why it costs so much to cross the Panama Canal.

Fucking Vampires.

**Pretty much how I remember it Dirt.**

# The Bar 2

The next day I found myself sitting in a corner booth at the bar. People who sit in corner booths by themselves in the middle of the day, in a poorly lit bar as shitty as this one, are usually doing it for one of two simple reasons. One, they are planning to do something extreme, and two, they just did something extreme and they are having a rough time dealing with it. I was in the latter category.

I had murdered a man less than twelve hours ago, and I had left fingerprints on the door and shell casings on the ground. Probably footprints in the blood too. I wasn't sure what sort of investigation would take place, but there was enough potential evidence to make me nervous. Granted the man I had murdered wasn't a good person by any stretch of the imagination, obviously a full-on serial killer even if what he was doing wasn't his usual behavior. And to cap it all off I almost got smoked by a car crossing the street on my way here. If I worked a nine-to-five I'd be sure it was a fucking Monday.

No matter how I churched it, one thing didn't change, I had killed an unarmed man. The part that worried me the most was that I wasn't that shaken up about it, I should be a mess of worry and guilt. But mostly I was just indifferent, except about getting caught, that still worried me. My method of reaching some future catharsis involved drinking and frowning.

The only thing I was truly sure of was that Dracula was not a vampire. Partly because he didn't do anything magical, he died pretty easy, and those two assholes were lying to me. If they ever showed up I hoped I would be able to get some answers, assuming they even came back after getting me to do their dirty work.

I had just finished my basket of greasy bar fries and started my second beer when they walked in and headed straight to my booth.

"Good to see you Frank!" said Poncho, he slapped my back and sat down next to me.

"Frank, my man!" said Dirt excitedly, "High five killer!" He raised his hand expectantly and grinned. I did not reciprocate, and after a few seconds he shrugged, high fived himself and sat down on the other side of me. I was now trapped by two people that any normal person would never want to be trapped by. On one side was the closest thing to a proper Viking in the flesh, and the other a grinning madman, who I'm pretty sure could hurt me very easily if he wanted to. I took a large swig from my glass and stared at the bottom. Unfortunately there were still no solutions there, but checking never hurts.

Jim came over and set two tankards on the table, at least I think they were tankards, and walked away without a word. I was sure I had never seen tankards in this bar before, this fact didn't faze Dirt and Poncho as they each took one and drank. Poncho slammed his down on the table after a lengthy pull splashing some of its contents and wiped foam from his beard in a decidedly Viking fashion.

"So how goes the job Frank?" Poncho asked.

I cleared my throat and preparing my resolve to demand answers and proclaim my disgust at being their pawn in some dastardly murder plot.

"Uh, done I guess," is what I managed.

Worthless, just worthless.

Dirt, who had been tearing a napkin apart with all the focus of the heavily medicated, perked up and shouted, "Alright Frank! You got some pictures of this shit bag sucking blood and stuff?"

Shit, I never printed out the pictures, it seemed pointless after killing him.

"Not so much," I said. "There were... complications."

Poncho nodded gravely, "We heard, you killed him, very impressive."

Of course they knew already, why wouldn't they? I was being played and they were holding all the cards. It was their move again and I was certain it would involve some kind of blackmail. I should have followed my instincts and told them to beat it, that much money for pictures, it was obviously a trap.

"Shit yeah!" Dirt said. "Killed a vampire, that's some hard shit man, those fuckers are slippery."

My anger at being tricked solidified my resolve a bit so I decided to try and get some answers.

"About that," I said. "He didn't seem like a vampire, with the super speed and blood drinking, He just killed some women with normal strength and speed, nothing fancy." I decided to put off finding out how they knew what happened that night until I could sort out the vampire lies.

"Come on Frank, he wouldn't blow his cover! That's not how they operate," Dirt responded.

"Wouldn't he blow his cover after getting shot in the chest?" I asked.

Dirt coughed. "He must have had a backup plan, all evil villains monologue a bit before they unleash their diabolical plan."

"Right," I said, drawing the word out to emphasize that in this instance 'right' meant 'bullshit'.

Dirt continued unfazed, "You just surprised him is all, when you shot him in the face."

Poncho choked on his beer a little and out of the corner of my eye I saw him shake his head back and forth while making the "stop talking now" motion across his neck. He stopped immediately when I looked his way, pretending he was scratching his beard instead.

They must have been watching the whole thing somehow, how else could they know how it played out?

"How do you guys know what happened?" I asked as slowly and deliberately as I could.

Poncho looked at his beer and mumbled to himself. Dirt froze like a deer in the headlights with his eyes darting back and forth rapidly before settling on the remains of his ruined napkin. I glanced between them smugly, I was quite proud of myself, I had taken them off guard.

Dirt scooped his napkin tatters into his hand and threw them on the floor. "We may have followed you a little."

Poncho squeezed the bridge of his nose and closed his eyes. "Only a little."

"Then why did you hire me?" I asked not very calmly. "Did you want me to kill this guy? Is this some sick joke?" I was shouting a little now. "What the fuck is going on!?"

There were only a handful of people in the bar and none of them even glanced our way while I was shouting. I was taking it for granted that people just didn't notice anything that was going on around these two. My theory was that they were afraid of pissing Poncho off, and pretended to ignore everything just in case.

Poncho leaned back and sized me up, "There are things in this world that would make you piss your big boy pants Frank, and some of them need to die. You've got a knack for it, we just needed to make sure you had the guts to follow through."

"Knack for it? Knack for what? I never killed anyone before, how could I have a knack for it?"

"Some people are just killers Frank, when you kill long enough you can spot it in a person easily." Poncho drank more beer, eyeing me over the rim.

He had more or less just admitted to being a killer, this verification of my suspicion turned my insides to water.

"Plus you still haven't killed anyone, *that* was a thing." Poncho added.

Monsters are real and they hired me to kill one on a trial basis, then watched me do it to see if I could. I still had no proof that Dracula had been a vampire, and it wasn't a stretch to think they hired me to kill a guy and made up this bullshit story to keep me quiet about it.

They seemed dumb enough to accept that as a legitimate plan, or maybe the stupidity was an act too. Either way, the man I had killed was a murderer, and in the long run I was fine with him being dead, vampire or not.

I looked at Dirt and asked, "That guy had a Panama flag hanging in his house, I thought that meant he wasn't a vampire?"

Dirt winked at me, saying, "Classic misdirection" and continued to look as if he wasn't paying attention. I sighed and rubbed my eyes, this wasn't getting anywhere.

"So what happens now?" I asked.

"Now you get another job!" Dirt said with sudden enthusiasm. "And you probably won't have to kill him!"

"What is it this time? Frankenstein? A mummy? The wolf man?" I asked dripping with sarcasm.

"Whoa," Dirt said sliding away from me. "Third guess, are you psychic too?"

"The wolf man?" God dammit.

"Sort of anyway, more like a werewolf, less man shaped, more eat your face with giant teeth," He paused, "also Frankensteins aren't real."

"Of course they aren't," I said shaking my head. Why me? I could only imagine what nonsense they had in mind as an explanation for this one. I should have gotten up and walked out, but curiosity is a bitch, and I'm the cat. "OK, what's the story?"

"That's the spirit Frank!" Poncho said grinning at me. I think it was supposed to be friendly, he managed terrifying.

Dirt worked his way out of his slouch and straightened an imaginary tie.

"Werewolves," he began, pausing for effect, "werewolves are hairy big fucking monsters and you should stay away from them at all costs. They will murder you for no reason."

Poncho nodded in agreement.

"Furthermore, they can smell real good and they know when you are around, this will cause them to tear you to pieces. They can't turn into wolves on weekdays unless it's a holiday, but they are always really strong so don't even go near one."

"What am I supposed to do then?" I asked, "Internet stalk him?"

Dirt stared blankly at me confused, or more confused than normal. "No, that's stupid, just follow him and see what he's up to."

"But you just said..."

Dirt cut me off, "I know what I said," he rubbed his chin and I suspected that he didn't. "It's the same as before, he won't break cover, so it won't be a problem."

"By break cover do you mean, not really a werewolf like the last guy wasn't a vampire?"

"You calling me a liar Frank?" Dirt half whispered grabbing a butter knife and sliding it onto his lap.

Poncho leaned forward to put out the potential serial scratching. "Calm down brother, it's a tricky concept for folks to grab onto, he'll get it in his own time. Or get his rib cage torn out."

Dirt exhaled slowly and set the butter knife back on the table, but well within reach. "That's true, I get carried away sometimes."

"I bet." I said. To myself. In my head.

"Anything specific about this wolf man that I need to know?" I asked, "Assuming I take the job that is." I added quickly.

"Normal stuff really, lives in the woods, hairy, stinky, and mean," Poncho said.

"Which woods?"

"No, witches live in witch woods." Dirt said throwing his hands up in exasperation.

"He lives in Wolf woods then?" I was getting the hang of this.

"Frank, you suck at this. Wolf woods isn't a real place."

Maybe not.

"Here, take this," Poncho said pushing a crumpled wad of cash at me. "Sorry, it got put through the wash."

I had a hard time believing these two washed their clothes.

"Oh shit!" Dirt slammed his hands on the table making me jump a bit, "Money laundering is illegal!"

I sensed another insane argument coming, but before I could think of a way to stop it they had started.

"It isn't illegal if you do it on accident, Glen can't be responsible for checking everything he puts in the machine."

Glen? There was a third one? Great.

"That makes Glen a criminal, and us accessories to crime!"

"How is it a crime to make your money clean?"

Poncho must have won this argument in the past, because it shut Dirt down fast. He sat there contorting his face in what must have been thought, it looked painful.

After a minute or so he simply said, "That makes sense, I don't know why movies make such a big deal about it."

They had no idea what counterfeit money was, or even what money laundering was. I was relieved that I couldn't possibly be working for criminals, unless they were the absolute worst at it. I saw a gleam in Dirt's eye that told me he had come up with a new point to argue, I decided it would be best to try and cut it off.

"How do I find this werewolf?"

They eyed each other, possibly making mental notes to complete the argument at a later date.

Poncho pulled a folded piece of paper out of his pocket and transferred it to my shirt pocket. "It's all on there."

"Good luck man," Dirt said. "Remember, just find out what he is up to, where he goes, what he pees on, who he eats, basic stuff."

They got up, Poncho nodded to me and headed for the door. Dirt just sauntered out without a word, maybe strolled, either way he made it casual.

Last night I killed a fake vampire, tomorrow I get to follow a fake werewolf. I put the money ball into my pocket, peeling off enough to pay for the beer, what I thought was enough anyway, I had no idea what a tankard cost. I put my hat on and got ready to leave, at least I wouldn't get eaten tomorrow, it was a weekday.

# The Werewolf

The Woods turned out to be the name of a seedy motel nowhere near any actual trees. The picture was an even bigger help, instead of an actual photo there was a drawing of a stick figure with a crude beard and speech bubbles over his head with gems like "grrr" and "snarl" written in them. There was a name as well, Pierre. The best part was the giant penis that I assume Dirt had drawn on his facsimile of Pierre, complete with a giant arrow pointing at it. Why was I doing anything these guys wanted? It had to be more than curiosity, I was a sucker for a good mystery, sure, but this was just crazy. Maybe a part of me wanted to see how far they would carry this charade before it fell apart, maybe I was bored. The money was good, that much was true.

I was still slightly worried about being caught for the murder thing, half expecting the cops to show up and haul me off at any moment. Between the finger prints, bullet casings, and my car possibly being seen, there was more than enough evidence to put me away for a long time, they would probably pin the hooker murders on me as well. The wolf man job was just a way to keep my brain distracted from spending the rest of my life in a cell, while attempting to not be a victim of some old fashioned prison rape.

I was waiting across the street from 'The Woods' motel on a bench. Across the street always seemed like the best place to spy on people. I brought a newspaper to read, because that's what people do on benches in the middle of the day. I failed to realize that nobody sits on benches reading newspapers anymore until much later, especially while wearing trench coats and fedoras. I was in for a long day, I was sure a lot of bearded people frequented this motel, and I doubted any of them were well endowed stick figure wolf men.

I was a few pages into the newspaper when an article caught my eye. It was a story about a house fire, in a neighborhood that sounded very familiar. I started to sweat a little as I read it, surely there would be mention of murder and subsequent arson to cover it up. As I read I calmed down, it was all fairly normal, as house fires go. By the time the firefighters showed up the house was too far gone to be saved. Upon investigation of the wreckage, multiple human remains were found, burned too badly to be identified. They were suspected to have died of smoke inhalation.

The part toward the end was surreal, no foul play suspected. That means when they found the bodies they didn't find the casings. Dirt and Poncho had done this, I was sure of it. I didn't think it was farfetched to believe that after I left they went in, took the casings and burnt the place down. Despite being a Private Detective, I didn't really know anything about police procedure, but I was somewhat certain they could autopsy the bodies and find out they were good and dead before the fire started.

Murder and arson, I was fucked if any of this ever got found out. Dirt and Poncho were setting me up as some kind of sick game.

I broke from my contemplations of incarceration when a large bearded man without a shirt walked by. He wasn't skinny enough to be a stick man, and not wolfish enough to be a wolf man, but he was close enough and I needed the distraction.

I pretended to read the paper and watched the potential Pierre head toward to motel. It was the kind of place that still gives you an actual key to your room, not the programmed cards that most places use these days. You could probably rent rooms by the hour at a place like this, hell maybe even in fifteen minute increments. Pierre jogged across the street towards The Woods, mullet flapping majestically in the breeze. If Dirt thought the rich, well dressed guy was a vampire, then it makes sense that this dirty hairball is what he would think a werewolf would look like. Close enough.

Potential-Pierre went to one of the rooms with the doors facing the road and went in. Damn, if he was just getting there I could be in for a wait. Before I could hunker down to wait he came back out, now wearing an off-white wife beater and relighting a half smoked cigarette. He must have been on his way to do evil in a place that had a strict 'shirt' rule. He turned and walked off in the opposite direction he had come from. I considered breaking into his room to look for clues, but that wasn't part of the job, and I didn't know how to pick a lock.

I folded my newspaper under my arm, pulled my hat down over my eyes and got up to follow him. I followed him at what I determined to be a good distance, I was guessing really. There were enough people around so I assumed I wasn't being too obvious, this wasn't my usual kind of thing after all. It was a good thing it was a nice day out, all the homeless people and gang types were out enjoying the weather, or whatever they did all day.

It occurred to me that I was in a terrible part of town, I was regretting leaving my murder weapon at home. I decided it was best to avoid having potential evidence on my person until I was sure I was in the clear for the whole murder-arson-tampering situation. Luckily my car wasn't likely to be stolen, it wasn't new enough, or nice enough, to turn a profit if stolen, or I wouldn't have left it parked at the motel. I did have my trusty pocket knife though, just in case I needed to unscrew something with its broken tip, or eventually craft a spear with its dull blade.

I tried to avoid places like this whenever I could, but I was no stranger to them. I squared my shoulders and tried to look dangerous, which mostly involved glaring and scowling. I learned this trick from a half dozen previous office jobs, if you walk around with a purpose, looking angry, people assume you are busy and leave you alone. It kept me from getting fired from more than one job, for a while anyway.

As I followed the supposed werewolf I realized how stupid this all was, again. I was essentially taking jobs from madmen, checking up on fairy tales. It was more than money, more than curiosity, I just couldn't pinpoint what my reasons were. Perhaps I was bored and subconsciously the danger excited me, maybe I was just broken inside. This kind of self-examination wouldn't get me anywhere, it was probably just the money. I should have just walked back to my car and pretended none of this had happened, but I took the money. I should at least see this current job through, and be done with Dirt and Poncho afterwards.

I didn't decide to become a P.I. to kill people, I never wanted it to be like the movies. Ex cops fed up with the bureaucracy, setting off on their own to make a difference, saving the day and getting the girl. I'm not sure if those even exist, truth be told, I'm not even licensed as a real Private Detective. You have to have some kind of experience I think, and go to a class and take a stupid test. I looked into it a little bit, but it seemed like a big pain in the ass. It's not like you need a fancy education to take pictures of people doing shady shit, and I never told people I wasn't registered, and luckily they never asked. I guess I just slipped through the cracks as far as anyone caring went, which was fine with me.

I only took small time jobs, cheating spouses and the like, it paid the bills. The rest is just looking the part and keeping your head down. Best job I've ever had, no boss and the deadlines are whatever I want them to be.

My mind wandered as it always does when doing the boring parts of watching people, but I didn't mind. I was still doing my job, and I didn't even have to pay much attention, can't beat a job this easy. Follow someone around and see what they do.

Then my mind wandered right back to the burned down house full of dead people. Sometimes all this thinking can be bad for a person.

I shook myself out of it and focused on my mark, he was still just walking down the sidewalk doing nothing suspicious. Unless you count going into public with a mullet as suspicious. I wished he would do something, anything to keep my mind off the other night.

I had been following him for five or six blocks, while keeping my distance. I didn't know if there were procedures for tailing somebody, but I figured I was doing ok. He never looked back or bolted around a corner, so I must be invisible to him, like a shadow, always there. I was getting bored again.

Then he turned! It was getting exciting now. He turned and entered a bar, at least it was something. I was getting thirsty anyway. It started to dawn on me that I had picked the wrong beard to follow, this guy was relatively normal. I should have waited until a full moon to follow him, or just the weekend, to see if he turned into a monster. More likely I should stop entertaining nonsense about monsters and go into this bar and get a drink so I could mull it over in air conditioning. Believe it or not, wearing a trench coat and a fedora in the middle of the summer is really uncomfortable.

The bar was more of a bar-restaurant hybrid, the kind that start off as a bar and eventually serve food. Not the kind of food that is wise to eat, but drunks are never picky. It was dimly lit and looked sticky, it was a lot like my favorite bar, just nicer.

The werewolf was sitting along the side wall looking at a grubby menu and generally minding his own business. I sat at the bar so I could see him in the mirror behind all the liquor bottles. We were the only two people in the place, it was the middle of the day, and even around here the hard drinking probably didn't start until early afternoon. I noticed a third person in the form of a matronly old lady with a perpetual scowl on her haggard face. Honestly she made old Jim look like a fucking cheerleader. She brought a beer over to the wolf's table and presumably took his order. She looked like the type of woman who doesn't take shit from anyone, and makes sure you know it.

She scribbled something on a pad of paper in response to his pointing at the menu and shuffled back to the bar. Pierre must have been a regular, as they never exchanged words. She took the paper containing the order and passed it through the window to the kitchen, soon the sounds of swearing and pan rattling emanated from within.

When she headed my way I ordered the light version of the two beers they had on tap. She grunted, filled a glass and placed it contemptuously down on the scarred wood of the bar, splashing beer carelessly. She added another grunt and went into the kitchen, presumably to check her ginger bread trap for fresh children.

I took a long drink of the beer, relishing the frosty beverage. It was way too hot to be wearing an overcoat and hat, and I was sweating underneath it, but a little ice cold beer would soon put out that fire. I savored my drink and avoided looking directly at the wolf, he didn't seem to notice my avoidance to notice him, I was still incognito. I considered looking into getting my license again, I appeared to have a knack for it.

A few minutes and three quarters of a pint later the werewolf got up and headed straight for me. I started to tense up, he was onto me, I was made as they say in P.I. talk. My mind raced trying to come up with a believable reason to be following him, or that it was all just coincidence, and came up with jack shit. I was about to smash my glass into his face preemptively, when he continued right past me and into the hallway past the bar. The very same hallway with the giant "Pissers" neon sign above it. Nailed it, stayed calm and collected, and he didn't even notice me. Fight or flight is so overrated.

A few more minutes and the rest of my beer went by and he still wasn't back, his food was waiting at his table getting cold fast. Nobody ever pays attention to how long someone is in the bathroom unless you are waiting for them, then it's always an eternity. He must have been working out an epic growler. I left a five on the bar in case things got weird and I had to bug out and headed to the toilet.

The bar wasn't large, but it still had the kind of bathroom multiple people can enter at a time, the kind that has a trough along the wall filled with unhappiness. I went in, doing my best to act like I had to go, not like I was following a guy around suspiciously. I was confronted with two things right off the bat, it smelled like a trash fire, and it was empty. There were no stalls to hide in, just one sit down toilet with no walls that no respectable person would use outside of an emergency.

Shit, he must have slipped out when I wasn't looking. I went back into the hallway, he wasn't back at his table, he must have gone the other way. I passed the ladies room, doubled back and checked inside guiltily, also empty. Continuing down the increasingly dark hallway I found a rear exit off to one side. It must exit to the alley, I thought. The son of a bitch figured it out and bolted, I was the worst at this. I didn't think he would still be out there, but there's no harm in looking.

I opened the door and was hit with too much light, then I was hit with equally too much blunt object. I didn't walk into something forcibly, it was directed at my skull with intent, by a truck of some sort. I did the only sensible thing a person can do when struck on the head, fall down and slumped against a wall. I should have opted for unconsciousness, but my head must be thicker than I thought, because the sweetness of the dark eluded me. I put my hand to my head to see how much of my brains were exposed and brought it back in front of my still unfocused eyes. No gray matter, just good old fashioned head blood. What a relief, I could feel its warmth running down the side of my face, finally free from the prison of my body, I would miss it.

I looked up to see what kind of truck hit me, and saw a man. The same man that I had been following, he had a length of 2x4 in his hand and was looking at me with disappointment. He flung the board away in the nearby trash cans and pulled a gun from the back of his pants.

"Why are you following me?" he asked, pointing the barrel at me face.

My brain was still reeling from the hard reset, but I still managed to say, "Huh, what? Ow." All in one word, it was very impressive, and sounded like a simple grunt. My eloquence wasn't as disarming as I had hoped and the werewolf clubbed me in the head, not very hard, but enough to send my head spinning again. I must have blacked out for a second, because when I looked back at him he was going through my wallet. I remained immobile and tried as hard as I ever have in my life to hold back vomit.

Pierre rifled through my wallet snorting contemptuously at every new thing he pulled out and inspected. To my surprise he didn't scatter its contents on the ground, he placed them all back carefully where he had found them. That was awfully considerate of him, assuming I survived this ordeal I wouldn't have to worry about getting a new library card.

He laughed when he got to the cash, "Only eight dollars Franklin? I hope you were getting paid to follow me." He didn't take the money either, just put it back and tossed the wallet back at me. I put it in my coat pocket in a daze. My head still hurt, but I was less dizzy, still defenseless, but thinking clearer. Did he call me Franklin? Right, that's what my driver's license says, so a little clearer, just not 100% yet.

If he was going to kill me I might as well make it personable. "People just call me Frank," I mumbled.

He aimed the shiny gun back at my face and said, "I thought that second hit might have done you in, I intend to rectify that shortly. Now, why were you following me?"

"I wasn't following you." It was worth a shot. I touched my bleeding head again, there was a nasty gash over my right eye, about five or six stitches worth. Nothing that would kill me, head wounds always bleed like bastards and look like hell. Although, him hitting me in the head was the reason I had a gun pointed at me with no way out. So maybe in a way it would kill me.

"Bullshit Franklin, what kind of idiot doesn't notice an old man reading a newspaper on a bench in the middle of summer. Around here the only people on benches are under the newspapers." He looked around making sure the alley was still empty and continued his speech. "Then you follow me down the most un-crowded streets and into an empty bar. A blind person could have spotted you. With their eyes."

So I wasn't very good at tailing people, or it was because he had super werewolf senses. Neither choice was something I wanted to believe.

"I hope whoever put you up to this wasn't paying you very much, because I might feel obligated to track them down and give them their money back." He thought for a second, "And to kill them I suppose."

I decided to give him some information in the hope he would let me live, my reasons for following him were pretty lame, and maybe he would appreciate the silliness of it all and let me go. I realize it was weak, but it was all I had.

"I was just supposed to see if you were a werewolf or not." I slurred.

This took him off guard and he burst out into laughter. Now we were best friends and he would surely let me go. He stopped laughing after a bit, still shaking the remaining chuckles you get from truly funny things from his system.

"Here I was all worried about who sent this inept triggerman," he was still working through the giggles. "Lonny would have sent someone competent, but now I see." He stopped, choking back more laughter.

"Who's Lonny?" I asked, stalling.

"Lonny is none of your fucking business, your business should have been picking your employers better. That way you could have avoided getting shot in the face."

I struggled to think of a way out of this that didn't involve a body bag. Having a gun pointed at you tends to limit your creativity somewhat, and all I could come up with was further distraction. I wasn't sure if I was trying to distract him from shooting me, or distract myself from the thought of being shot.

"If you are going to kill me anyway, at least tell me who those two assholes are?"

Pierre put his free hand to his lips and thought, then he scratched his head with the barrel of his gun. Holy shit, I thought, my cleverly crafted plan was working! But no matter where he pointed that thing he could still kill me before I could get to my feet. Times like these made me wish I had a plan B.

He settled the gun back at my now fully bloodied dome, coming to a conclusion.

"No, I'm not telling you." He said with childlike defiance. "These two jerk offs are nobody's concern, nothing but a thorn in the world's side. Whatever they are calling themselves these days, they are nothing more than a nuisance." He moved close and put the barrel against my skin, I closed my eyes and waited to die. It was a good run, I couldn't be too upset about dying now.

I heard a loud noise, I was surprised to hear the shot that killed me. Curious, I opened one eye and saw a truck pulling into the alley, it must have hit a trash can. Pierre jerked back and tucked the gun under his arm, obscuring it from view. I live for a few more minutes! Unless he decides to kill the truck driver too.

The truck pulled up to us and an ordinary delivery man stepped out with a clipboard. He looked at me bleeding on the ground, then at Pierre.

"Hey guys," He said nervously. "Everything ok back here?"

I opened my mouth to say something, maybe yell for help, I hadn't really thought it through. Pierre beat me to the punch.

"Yeah man, everything is cool. My friend here just had a little too much to drink and fell on his face." He looked down at me. "It looks worse than it is. You know how these head wounds bleed like a stuck pig."  .

The delivery man didn't look convinced, but as any working man can tell you, it isn't his job to care.

"Alright, as long as you're sure he's ok, I've got a couple of cases to drop off and I'll be out of your hair." He started for the back of the truck and I saw a way out. I dragged myself off the ground with Pierre glaring at me the whole way.

"Hang on, I'll give you a hand," I paused trying to think of a believable reason. "It will help me clear my head."

The delivery man looked doubtful. "I'm good man, you look like you cut your head pretty bad. You should see a doctor."

"Nah," I said stepping closer to the truck and life. I checked out his name tag, John. "Listen John, it's like he said, looks worse than it is, plus the bleeding has pretty much stopped. Just a scratch."

John looked at Pierre who was glaring menacingly at us, deciding if he should just kill us both and be on his way. He sighed and said, "If you're sure you're ok." Like any working class man, he had a hard time turning down free help.

"No problem," I said less convincingly than I intended. We headed to the back of the truck to unload with Pierre trailing behind brooding.

John was obviously nervous, but he played it off well. "Not the first time I've seen someone bleeding in an alley," he said chuckling, "But it's damn sure the first time the bleeding fella offered to help unload the truck."

I laughed with him attempting to ease the tension, Pierre lurking behind us intent on maintaining it. John opened the back of the truck and pulled a dolly out, he checked his clipboard and started taking cases of cheap whiskey out and setting them on the cart. I pulled one off, the weight surprised me and I almost dropped it, I was still dizzy.

"How many of these do you need?" I asked.

"Only five, shouldn't have to come back here for about a month either." He sounded relieved.

I pretended to understand why and nodded, Pierre lurked. I put the last case on top and 'accidentally' ripped the top of the box open.

"Shit, sorry about that," I said, as I pretended to fumble with the top.

John grabbed the handles of the dolly, "No worries man, happens all the time with these shitty boxes."

I kept my back to Pierre and he didn't see me grab a bottle by the neck, and he damn sure didn't see me whip around and smash it into his face!

John's will broke and he disappeared out of the alley as fast as his legs could take him, without so much as look back. He must have been a subscriber to the flight mentality.

Pierre hit the ground in a mess of blood, glass, and whiskey. He dropped the gun while reaching up, trying to hold his blood in. I dove for the ground snatching it up, and came up with it pointed square at his chest. I could have just reached down and grabbed it, Pierre wasn't concerned with it anymore, but with the adrenaline it seemed like the right move.

He stopped moaning after he realized what was happening and looked up at me, eyes pleading.

"Don't shoot, Frank," he said through his bloody clasped hands. "I can..."

Between the adrenaline of a near death encounter, the blood loss, and the possible concussion, I couldn't tell you why I shot him. But I did, and I didn't feel particularly bad about it. He stopped twitching as the puddle of blood from the hole in his head spread towards my feet. Later I would ponder whether I am too impatient to listen to dying confessions, or If I just enjoyed killing the people that had answers. I was pretty sure I shot him because he hit me in the face with a board though.

# Bar Lady

After my first back alley murder I didn't really know what to do, there had been a witness, I had the murder weapon, and the cut on my head would have made anyone ask questions. I stood in the alley, for what felt like forever, waiting for the police to show up, but my rescue came in the form I least expected. The stern old lady came into the alley and looked at me, at Pierre, and at the delivery truck. I didn't say anything for fear that she may scowl me to death before the authorities could take me away.

"Bout time someone took care of that rascal," she said, her face softening a touch. "Let's get him off the street before someone sees him. Throw some cardboard on that blood before some drunk slips and breaks their damn neck."

I started to tuck the gun into my pants and she shook her head, holding her hand out like a mother would waiting to be given whatever contraband you were caught with. I handed it over, I wasn't sure why, but I was too tired to argue, or think for myself. She took it and deftly unloaded it and disassembled it like a pro, stuffing the pieces into her apron.

We set about dragging Pierre's corpse to an outdoor cellar entrance and unceremoniously dumped him down the steps.

"What are you going to do with the body?" I asked.

"Don't you worry about that young man, no one will ever find him, that's all you need to know."

I stared blankly as she padlocked the door shut, I had no idea why she was helping me, but I wasn't about to turn it down.

"Let's get you inside and have that head looked at, can't have you dying on me."

After engineering a walkway of cardboard from the pool of Pierre's blood to the cellar stairs I dumbly followed her into the bar, through the kitchen and into an office. She sat me down on a dingy looking couch and set about collecting supplies. The bandages were in the desk drawer, which she swapped for the gun parts. The alcohol was in a flask between the couch cushions, and the suture kit was behind a stuffed owl on a shelf. I wasn't about to knock her organization skills, not many people were willing to help a guy who just murdered a person in your back alley.

"Names Opal," she said wiping the blood off my face.

"Frank," I replied, "Why are you doing this?"

"You look like a Frank," she said, ignoring the question. "Take a few of these, they'll dull the pain. You don't have a concussion, that's good."

I swallowed two of the white pills not really caring what they were and washed them down with whatever heaven she had in that flask. It was easily the best liquor I had ever tasted, and I was immediately relaxed. I didn't even notice when she started with the stitches. She said nothing more while she worked, just hummed a tune I couldn't place. When she was done stitching, she put a bandage over it and gave a satisfied nod.

"Are you a nurse?" I asked in my stupor.

"No sonny, you just pick these things up after a while. Now you run along home and don't worry about a thing, I'll take care of that bugger in the basement."

"Opal, ma'am, I am pretty sure that delivery man John might be back in a little while, and, I'm pretty sure that he might have a few questions." I couldn't quite formulate how to explain that he might be the last person to see Pierre alive and if questioned might have a few details about a guy in a fedora smashing a cheap bottle of whiskey in his face.

"Oh honey, don't you worry about li'l Johnny. He wouldn't tell the cops his own birthday if he didn't have to."

I was thoroughly confused at this point and took her word for it.

"Thank you, how can I repay you?"

She gave an irritated grunt, "Don't go fussing about that, just helping out a nice young man. If you ever get into trouble again you just come see me and I'll see if I can't get you sorted out." Then she shooed me out into the street, slipping an unmarked bottle of pills into my hand.

"If your head gives you trouble just take a couple of these," she started to go back inside, turned back to me and continued, "You be more careful from now on sonny, it's a dangerous place out there." She disappeared inside the bar, and I was left on the street feeling great, but confused.

# Frank's House

I don't really remember driving home and I was pretty glad I didn't get pulled over. Whatever was in those pills had me more relaxed than I'd ever been in as long as I can remember, that or what was in the flask. No matter what the reason, I was happy my head didn't hurt. The encounter with Opal had me a little confused, but I wasn't really all that concerned with it at the moment. I just settled on the couch with a six pack and relished the calm. My time under the employment of Dirt and Poncho had seriously altered my drinking schedule.

My house wasn't nice by any means, but it wasn't a dump either. I never got around to redecorating after the ex-wife left, so it was pretty bare. It was home and it was cozy, that's all that mattered to me. It helped that the house was paid off too, it's part of the reason I could be a Private Investigator who doesn't really have that much demand. Not having a ton a bills makes the necessity of constantly working fall by the wayside.

I never knew why my ex-wife hated me so much that she had to up and leave so suddenly. I wasn't cheating on her and I never hit her, I guessed she just got tired of me and my lack of ambition. She didn't take anything in the divorce, just cut and run. We got married when we were too young and in love, we were happy for a long time. I bounced around from job to job, never being poor, but never really succeeding at anything. When I got the job at the bank it looked like things were going to pick up, it paid well and I didn't really have a lot of responsibility. Call it a dream job.

One day when I came home from work she was gone and there were divorce papers on the kitchen table. The papers made it clear that she wanted nothing, and all I had to do was sign them, after fifteen years of marriage, that's how it ended. No discussion, no counseling, just a lawyer and papers. I loved her enough to sign the papers and let her go, never knowing why and never speaking to her again.

I kind of fell into a slump after that, showing up late to work, and generally being shitty to everyone. One day my boss pulled me into the office and told me to fix my shit or I was fired, I didn't really care, and was intent on making him fire me. He didn't get the chance though, because later that week the bank got robbed. I won't get into the details, but during the robbery there was some shooting with the police and I got grazed by a bullet. Nobody knew if it was the robbers or the police, but I got a decent settlement out of it and quit my job. It was enough to pay off the house and that's when I decided to switch to self employment. That was the day I bought my first fedora, which is a really lame mid-life crisis purchase. No wonder the old lady left.

I didn't think about the divorce much anymore, or the bank. I used to dwell on it often, but now my reminiscing was rare to the point that none of it seemed real. I had decided a long time ago that she left me because we couldn't have kids and left it at that. I didn't blame her, but I did miss her sometimes.

Fuck these white pills!

Actually I don't mean that, and I am sorry.

Before I could slip into full "woe is me" mode, my door opened with Dirt and Poncho strolling in like they owned the place. I wasn't all that concerned about it-- probably the pills. How they got the deadbolt open was a mystery though.

"Hi Frank!" Dirt exclaimed waving like an idiot.

Poncho nodded his usual nod, sat down on the couch, and put his massive biker boots on the coffee table. Dirt just kept on walking right into the kitchen.

"Grab me a beer while you are in there," might as well get some use out of him. I pointed at Poncho questioningly, he nodded. "Two beers!"

"Roger!" he yelled from the kitchen banging something around.

"Rough day, Frank? Your head's all busted" Poncho said not looking very concerned.

I should have been mad, should have ripped into them, but mostly I was calm, and glad to be alive.

"You could say that, that guy you wanted me to follow about knocked my head off."

Poncho took his feet off the table and leaned forward. "Holy shit Frank, we didn't think he would be dangerous."

"You told me he was a fucking werewolf, how does that not make him dangerous?"

I stared at Poncho while he formulated a response, Dirt was still banging around in the kitchen.

"You were just supposed to follow him, not try to fight him," Poncho said, although he didn't really sound worried.

"I did follow him, I followed the shit out of him, then he ambushed me!" I said pointing to my bandaged head.

"Maybe you aren't very good at following people if they ambush you and hit you on the head."

I had to laugh at that, maybe it was the pain killers, but he had a point, and it was pretty funny. Poncho grinned, I flinched involuntarily, and he leaned back putting his feet back on the table.

"You made it back in one piece though, that's good."

I couldn't fault his logic, I was mostly fine, battered but living.

Dirt appeared from the kitchen with a plate of nachos and a case of beer. I was certain he hadn't brought anything with him, and I knew I didn't have that much beer in the fridge, let alone the supplies to make nachos. I wasn't in the mood to worry about it though. He set the nachos on the table and handed me and Poncho a beer, settling into the easy chair and cracking one open for himself.

"He didn't bite you did he?" asked Dirt, "If he did, you sir, are fucked."

Right back to crazy town, and I felt like I had just left. It was starting to feel like familiar ground, that was probably a bad indicator for my sanity.

"No he didn't bite me. He did hit me in the face with a 2x4 right before he threatened to shoot me in the face," I said.

"You sure he didn't bite you? We're going to have to check you for bites anyway. Being bitten automatically turns you into a liar, like with zombies. People always say they aren't bitten, but they are, then they turn and bite everyone else and nobody has a merry Christmas after that." Dirt dug into the nachos, keeping one suspicious eye on me the whole time.

Poncho lit a cigarette, I started to tell him not to smoke in the house, but thought better of it. I was still kind of scared of him, but mostly I was just certain he wouldn't care and would keep doing whatever he wanted.

"So what exactly happened?" Poncho asked.

"You mean you didn't spy on me this time?"

Dirt spit out a mouth full of nachos and looked incredibly offended, then picked up his mouth nachos off the table and continued pretending to not pay attention. I was still trying to decide if everything he did was an act, or if he actually was that much of an idiot. Whichever it was, it was working, because I still had no idea what he was up to. At least Poncho was somewhat direct.

"You wound me Frank," Poncho said putting his hand to his heart. "We knew you could take care of yourself after the first job, and you weren't supposed to fight the guy anyway."

Of course he was lying, he had to be. If the werewolf had just beaten me and warned me to stay away from him, that story might hold water. But the fact that he tried to kill me for following him wasn't the kind of thing a nice person does. This is not the kind of person you send someone to follow without expecting trouble. Unless they had sent other people and I was just the first one to survive.

It took another plate of nachos and what seemed like two more cases' time to explain to Dirt and Poncho the day's transgressions. I try not to think too hard on where the extra nachos and beer came from. By the end of the detailed story, plus more questions than I care to remember, the coffee table was awash in empty beer bottles, cigarette ash, and all the nachos Dirt spilled each time he asked me to reassure him I hadn't been bitten.

I'm not sure why I left out the part about Opal fixing my head, but they never asked, so I let it be.

"Now that was solid thinking Frank!" Poncho said almost breaking my arm with a friendly punch to the shoulder. "Bottle to the face! What did it look like? His face I mean." He got a disturbing gleam in his eyes as he said it.

"Gross, I guess." I didn't know how else to explain it, but Poncho looked satisfied by my answer.

"You should have just finished your drink and went out the front door, he could have bitten you in that alley." Dirt reminded me for the tenth time. "You should have at least listened to his story, it could have been awesome."

"That reminds me, who is Lonny?"

"Some guy, I don't know," said Dirt.

"He really isn't important, an acquaintance of his I suspect," Poncho added.

"So how did he know you two?" I asked.

"Lots of people know us Frank, we are kind of a big deal," Dirt said.

This actually made sense somehow, if you are worth having people follow you then I supposed you would have a list of people you suspect. And since they had hired me to follow him they obviously knew him from somewhere. Still not good enough.

"Enough of this shit, the job is done and I have done everything you fucks have asked. I can't do this anymore, I think I've earned the truth. Tell your next dupe all the lies you want." The combo of beer, painkillers, and bullshit had finally put me over my limit. "So tell me the truth or get the hell out of my house."

"Whoa, be cool Frank! We have never lied to you, maybe we did withhold a few minor details from you, but not lies!" said Dirt.

Poncho gave an awkward look and added, "Frank we could really use your expertise with one last job."

"No way," I said with as much defiance as I could muster. "No more jobs until I get some answers."

Poncho looked thoughtful for a moment and sighed. "Fair enough Frank, what do you want to know?"

"Yeah Frank, you ask and we will answer. No bullshit this time." Dirt added.

This was too easy, but I had to try. Trouble was, I couldn't think of a question, so I stalled with beer drinking. After a thoughtful drink I asked, "Why are you sending me out to kill these people?" Sounded simple enough, until nachos came flying out of Dirt's mouth again.

"People!?" he shouted incredulously, "Monsters, Frank. You didn't have to kill anything either, that was all you. They would have for sure killed you given the chance, but you put yourself in harm's way!"

That did make a sick kind of sense.

"And monsters are bad frank, that's just common sense," he added.

Poncho looked like he had nothing to add, so I resigned myself to fish for information from Dirt's madness.

"OK, so they are monsters, why didn't any of them do anything supernatural?" Dirt started to say something and I cut him off, "Taking into account not wanting to break cover."

Dirt calmed down a little, "Well the most likely reason is that their powers take a while to wind up from normal mode to monster mode."

"Like a diesel engine," Poncho added.

"So when you catch them off guard like you did, they don't have time to turn that shit on." Dirt sat back looking pleased with his explanation.

"The supposed werewolf knew I was following him for quite a while before he jumped me, wouldn't that have been enough time to turn his werewolf powers on?"

Poncho looked at Dirt with an amused smirk, he was clearly getting some enjoyment out of this.

Dirt didn't miss a beat though, "Werewolves are tricky sons of bitches man," he paused to let his pun sink in, not receiving a positive reaction he continued unperturbed. "He probably had his heightened senses on, that's how he knew you were following him. When he cracked you in the head he must have had his strength on, and was just a great big pussy most of the time. That's why your head is still on. Plus it was a weekday and he couldn't have all his powers on at the same time."

Poncho was full-on grinning now.

"So his super strength was probably just like normal peoples strength, relatively. You just got lucky he was a weakling," Dirt finished with a flourish.

"There are a lot of probablys in there," I said.

"Well yeah, I wasn't there was I? But I'd put a paycheck on it."

More lies, I doubted very much that Dirt got paychecks. Poncho seemed amused by these descriptions and it didn't look like he was going to be helping his buddy out with them. I decided to push on.

"Why pick me then?" I asked. "Pretty sure my resume doesn't have monster killer on it."

Dirt leaned forward, fingers steepled like a movie villain and said seriously, "That's just it Frank, we are monster hunters, and we've been at it a long time. We can spot talent, even latent talent like you have."

This time Poncho had no reaction, and I still decided it was bullshit.

"No. Fuck you guys, I'm done. I don't believe you and I won't be murdering anyone else for you. Get the fuck out of my house!" I was shocked at my resolve.

Dirt looked hurt, Poncho looked like he'd been expecting it.

"What about the next job Frank? These monsters don't just kill themselves you know!" Dirt almost shouted.

"You're the monster hunters, you go kill them. I'm done."

Poncho got up and stretched, "Come on, the man asked us to leave."

"We are just undermanned Frank! We need fresh new faces to round out the employee pool! We need manpower!"

Poncho started dragging him to the door.

"Come on Frank!" Dirt pleaded, "The next one is the worst of them all! She is a Fae creature, they live on tormenting mortals! Like a lot!"

Poncho was pushing him toward the door, using his mass as an impenetrable shield of meat to stop Dirt's retreat back into the living room.

"Don't talk to her Frank, just kill her! We need you man," Poncho finally had him outside where he immediately stopped struggling, and opted to stand there dejected.

Poncho leaned in and set an envelope on the table by the door. "In case you change your mind," he said.

I almost jumped up and threw it in his face, but my balance was shaky just sitting. They didn't close the door or walk away, they just stood there having a silent argument. There was a lot of gesturing and muttering until Dirt appeared to have remembered something.

He leaned in, grabbed the door handle and said, "See you later Frank, stay in the crosswalk!" and slammed the door.

I went from piss drunk to stone sober in zero seconds flat. I bolted up, rushed the door, and whipped it open. There was nothing, they couldn't have gotten away that fast, I walked outside and still nothing. This was impossible, or I was going mad. I wandered back inside and shut the door, my brief adrenaline induced sobriety wearing off fast.

I hadn't thought about it at the time, but the morning after the vampire job I noticed a book on the end table on my way out of the house. Scrawled across the front was *Stay in The Crosswalk.* It didn't seem important even after I almost got hit by that car, but now it did.

One thing was for sure, I was going to find out what the hell was going on. I took the envelope off the table and checked inside. It was a picture of a pretty girl with devil horns crudely drawn on her head. The back said "Fae chick, don't talk to her. 5th and Elm at 4pm every day. I drew the horns, but she does have huge jugs."

Maybe she had some answers.

# Fae Chick

The next morning was brutal, and I mean morning in the loosest sense possible, considering it was past noon when I dragged myself out of bed. I still had plenty of time to clean up and talk myself out of being downtown by 4 o'clock.

A few hours later I was downtown at the corner of 5th and Elm. Turns out I'm terrible at winning arguments with myself. As much as I hated to admit it, this was the best way to find out what Dirt and Poncho's game was. I wasn't going to be able to get a straight answer out of them, so talking to a pretty girl they didn't want me talking to was the next rational step. Rationality being relative once again. She might try to kill me, sure, but if I didn't provoke her what's the worst that could happen?

My head still hurt, either from the hangover or the head wound, or both. But the painkillers were taking the edge off pretty well. It was approaching 4 o'clock and I was scanning the crowd, there weren't that many people out, but enough to keep me busy looking. I decided that randomly looking at my non-smart phone was exponentially better than the newspaper and park bench tactic this time. After all, Pierre had marked me for a tail within seconds.

I spotted her across the street, she looked much better without the devil horns. She was a pretty, blond girl, showing just enough skin to let people know she worked for that body, but not enough to look scandalous. As I was admiring her figure she stepped into the street and proceeded to jaywalk without a care in the world failing to see the dump truck trying to beat the yellow light barreling towards her.

I took a step into the street to try and stop her, but the fresh warning from Dirt blaring in my head, in addition to the odd book eating at the back of my head stopped me cold.

"Stay in the crosswalk," Thundered through my head long enough for me to do nothing. The impact of the truck hitting her was a blur. The next thing I saw was her crumpled form in the street, broken and bleeding. Omens be damned, I ran out to try and help her, realizing it was futile when I got close. She was going to die, her brain just hadn't gotten the message her body was sending it yet.

I didn't know what to do, so I started to say something, anything, but she beat me to it.

She coughed, blood spattering unnoticed onto her already soaked clothes, "You were supposed to save me Frank."

Then she died.

# Dirt and Poncho's House

After the official parties took my statement and hauled the body off I had made up my mind regarding my next course of action. I was still shaken from the accident, but I was certain of two things now: I hadn't killed any supernatural monsters, and whatever Dirt and Poncho were up to, I was going to get to the bottom of it. My path was clear, find them, and hopefully see them do something nefarious. I went to the bar after a quick stop home for my gun, it was probably safe to carry it since the crime scene had burnt down. Damn, I forgot to ask them if they burnt the house down, I made a mental note for later. Although I am sure that would turn into another bag of lies.

I bribed the guy at the auto garage across the street from the bar to let me park in one of his stalls. They were always empty, my hunch was that it was a front for something illegal. Not that it mattered, I wasn't the cops, and I had the twenty dollars the guy wanted. I could see the front of the bar from the shadows of the mechanic's stall, and settled in for a wait.

My mind went back to analyzing the past few days' events. I had killed two men and failed to not kill a woman. The first two were troubling, but the last one gnawed at me. Out of the three jobs, this one knew my name, meaning she had to be in on whatever Dirt and

Poncho were planning. About which I was clueless. They were obviously some kind of criminals, maybe some big heist had gone wrong and I was the dupe they hired to silence the others involved. I am pretty sure I've seen that movie, and the dupe always gets fucked in the end.

That didn't explain why she thought I was supposed to save her, unless I was supposed to be silenced saving her and the truck was a plant too. Maybe she thought I wasn't going to go through with it, and saving her meant keeping her away from Dirt and Poncho. None of these reasons explained the need for the lies about monsters though. Whatever was going on, I was starting to think I was one of the bad guys.

I wondered what Dirt would say about his last words that night and her last words on earth. Smart money was on some bullshit about being psychic.

I was prepared for this stakeout to take several days, but that wasn't the case. Dirt and Poncho walked out of the bar not ten minutes after I parked my car. Either I was very good at guessing when people would be the places I needed them to be, or I was lucky. Luck seemed to be somewhat absent lately, so it was obviously the latter of the two.

They stood on the sidewalk smoking and making all manner of hand gestures, I deduced that they were conversing. After the hand gestures told me they had come to a conclusion they turned and surveyed the assortment of cars parked on the road. It wasn't an extensive selection, but the three cars present appeared to confuse them. It made a certain sense that they wouldn't be able to remember their own car. They must have determined that the multi-colored firebird was theirs and got in. Poncho in the driver's seat, Dirt jumping through the open window on the passenger side. I pictured Poncho as more of a Harley guy, and Dirt as a hippy van full of pot and hippies guy.

The firebird took off in a cloud of blue smoke and the rattling of a car on its last legs. I pulled out to follow them, my experience tailing people via car was as limited as tailing them on foot. Hopefully movies would be more accurate in this endeavor, stay a few cars back and ... that's pretty much all I remembered. I took solace in the fact that they were unlikely to kill me if they spotted me, unless talking someone to death is a real thing.

Following them was uneventful; they didn't drive fast or break any traffic laws, which struck me as odd. After several uninteresting blocks we went from bad to worse, as far as real-estate went. The nearest explanation I could give was gangland. I wasn't sure if I had the vernacular right, but I saw a lot graffiti in complex patterns, and similarly dressed youths peppering the area.

When Poncho finally stopped the car it was in front of what looked to be a nice house, well fifty years ago it was probably a nice house. I was still at the corner when they got out and walked into the house without knocking. I had found their house, of course it was theirs, it was a shithole house on a shithole street. I was working for criminals, my adulation at solving part of the mystery was crushed by my realization that I was a criminal too. Even if the people I had killed were in self defense I was still supposed to call the cops.

I decided to pull around to get the house address for some sort of further investigation. They were probably squatting, but it was worth a try. I parked behind the Firebird and checked the house out. Typical rundown house in a shit neighborhood, dead lawn strewn with trash, peeling paint; a real gem. It was Dirt and Poncho's kind of place that much was true. The house didn't have any numbers, neither did the neighbors, also I hadn't paid attention to what street I was on, I needed to work harder on paying attention. I'd just have to look for a street sign on my way out of there.

While pondering my inattention to detail, Dirt and Poncho stepped onto the porch, Poncho carrying a large military style duffle bag. I ducked down, not sure if they knew what my car looked like and waited. I heard footsteps outside the car, I hoped it was just the women of ill repute I had seen a couple blocks back. I heard my trunk open and I put my head up just as Dirt was opening the passenger door and sitting down.

"You shouldn't park your car around here Frank, this place is lousy with wampus cats."

The trunk slammed shut and Poncho was visible in my rear view mirror, minus the duffle bag. As he rounded the back of the car and let himself into the back seat I wondered how he had gotten the trunk open. The key slot was broken, and the only way to open it was with the indoor release, I also wondered if that was blood on Poncho's shirt.

"Good timing Frank, we were just about to come find you," Poncho said wedging himself into the backseat which was clearly not made for Vikings.

I again found myself confused, I was getting used to it with these two; however, it didn't stop me from being a touch irate about earlier.

"What the fuck is going on? I'm not going anywhere with you assholes til I get some goddamn answers." It came off more hostile than I intended.

Poncho frowned and I controlled my flinch better this time. "Seems to me you may be having a bad day, you want to talk about it?"

"You could say that," I said preparing my barrage, but before I could launch it Dirt cut me off.

"Let's go to our place and worry about it there, it's not a good idea to stay here for very long," Dirt said looking around nervously. He had a beer in his hand, I was starting to accept this as normal.

"Yeah, you drive and tell us all about it," I couldn't tell if Poncho was mocking me or not. "When we get there we can sort it all out over beers."

I knew they were avoiding something, they were rarely this coherent, something to do with being international crime lords I guessed. As long as they were in my car I could at least gather more intel, and the trunk was teeming with incriminating evidence, or laundry.

"Wasn't that your house?" I asked like an idiot.

"Nope, that was just a ... business associate, nothing to worry about ... anymore." Poncho cracked his knuckles menacingly, was that blood on his hands too?

Dirt fiddled with the radio and pointed down the street, I took it as a signal to drive. As I pulled away I asked, "What about your car? Doesn't seem like the best place to leave it."

Dirt looked at me, clearly confused, or normal faced, I couldn't tell them apart anymore. "We don't have a car Frank."

Great, add accessory to grand theft auto to my ever increasing list of crimes. As we drove I received instructions on when to turn and I told them what happened at the street corner. It wasn't a long story, but I addressed some of my previous arguments from the past few days hoping for some answers. Much to my surprise neither of them spoke, as I ranted about what I had been through the past few days. I failed to notice the scenery change as we drove from dilapidated crack dens, to mowed lawns with actual grass and friendly looking people.

I pulled into the indicated house and my suspicions rose even further. We were in a nice suburb, and I was convinced I was about to get mixed up in something horrible. My instinct was to wait for them to get out, peel away and never look back. I was in too deep though, and I didn't want to have to move to a new town or anything, plus they said they had beer. I shut the car off and got out, it's amazing the things you can convince yourself of when the alternative seems like too much work.

"Home sweet home," Dirt said.

Poncho said nothing and headed for the door, I expected him to kick it open and start ransacking the place. Instead he took a key out of his pocket and unlocked the door like a normal person, I was a little let down. I lingered by my car, they left the duffle bag in the trunk. I considered grabbing it, but decided that finger prints on something likely to be key evidence in court was a bad idea.

I entered the house at Poncho's behest, the interior was not the destroyed wreck I had expected. They must have a maid in addition to a lawn service; no way these guys were this orderly. I briefly entertained the notion that they were undercover cops using me to bust some enormous crime syndicate, making me a hero. I dismissed this theory when Dirt attempted to slide across the hood of my car and landed in a bush. It was an awesome fantasy for the three seconds it lasted.

Poncho directed me to the living room and gestured for me to have a seat on the couch; he sat opposite me and said nothing. Dirt finally came inside after untangling himself from the bushes--leaving the front door open--he stood at the bar-style nook near the kitchen facing us. None of us said anything for what felt like forever, just as I was about to break the silence a voice came from the kitchen.

"Hey guys, didn't expect to see you back so early today!" the voice said.

The voice's owner appeared on the other side of the bar in the kitchen, and looked nothing like what I'd expected. He was middle aged, clean cut, wearing an expensive polo shirt and khakis. Not the kind of person I expected to be hanging around these degenerates, but I was hanging around them, so what did that make me?

"Hey," said Poncho.

"What's up Glen?" Dirt said excitedly.

"Just heading into the office to take care of some things, you boys need anything before I go?"

"We could use some drinks if we have any Glen," Dirt replied.

Glen smiled and went to the refrigerator, returning with three bottles of expensive looking craft beer. He set one down in front of each of us, caps removed.

"I picked these up at the shop by the office you guys like so much, there's more in the fridge if you need any." He looked suddenly ashamed. "You didn't introduce us!" His eye twitched a little. "I'm..." He glanced at Dirt, "I'm Glen." He drew out his name like it was unfamiliar to him.

"Frank," I shook his offered hand.

"Nice to meet you Frank, I hate to be rude, but I have to get to work. I ordered a pizza, it should be here soon, you guys help yourselves."

"Thanks Glen, you're the best," said Dirt.

Poncho nodded.

Glen left, closing the door Dirt had left open. I took a tentative sip of the beer, thinking I would need the help to get through the conversation to come. It was quite good, you can never be too careful with craft beers, sometimes they can taste something awful.

"I don't like it when you call him Glen," Poncho said, "His name is Thunderaxe and you know it. It only confuses him."

"He doesn't look like a Thunderaxe to me, he looks like a Glen. He is goofy like a Glen would be, and way too nice for a Thunderaxe, right now."

"That's why his name is Thunderaxe, he needs to be tough. Do you really think he will toughen up if you keep calling him Glen?"

"Glen wouldn't hurt a fly. Why does he need to be tough?"

This could go on forever if I didn't stop it. "Why did that girl say I was supposed to save her?"

Dirt and Poncho exchanged glances, Dirt exchanged glances with the wall, then his own hand. I turned to Poncho hoping for a sensible answer. He sighed and downed half his bottle.

"It's a tricky situation Frank, not everyone can handle it," he replied after wiping his mouth.

"So you feed me bullshit about vampires and werewolves instead?" I asked. "That's pretty fucking hard to believe too."

Dirt started to say something but Poncho stopped him.

"It's time we told you the truth."

"That would be nice," I said fully expecting more outlandish lies.

"Basically we are immortal, and the ones you killed were as well."

"And psychic," added Dirt.

I said nothing, waiting for the punch line. It was the kind of silence that gets you answers in movies.

Poncho continued, "We can be killed, before you ask that."

I was wondering that, but psychic?

"We just don't die from old age or sickness."

More bullshit, but hey, I kind of wanted to see how far this went.

"So why have me kill these other immortals?" I asked.

"That's what we do, we kill the bad ones so they don't do bad shit to all the mortals, and it helps to outsource from time to time."

"If you are all psychic why did they let me kill them? Wouldn't they have known?"

"Whoa, just us two are psychic!" said Dirt.

My burgeoning ego was crushed yet again.

"Yeah, just us," Poncho said not very convincingly.

If any of this shit was actually true, it did make a few things add up, or just stop making as little sense.

"So where did the book on my end table come from, the one that said stay in the crosswalk?" I asked.

"We put that there," said Dirt proudly. "So you would know that we knew you should stay in the crosswalk. So you wouldn't save the fairy chick, cause if you did you would have died, that's why I said it that night, so it would be fresh, and you wouldn't die." Dirt was rambling. "Because we like you Frank, and we don't want you to die."

"Something like that," Poncho agreed.

"Did you guys also try to hit me with the car that day too, and did you burn down Dracula's house?" I was all questions now.

"You probably almost got hit by a car because you weren't in a crosswalk, the book was very clear." Dirt stopped, awaiting more questions, before remembering the second half of my query. "Yes, we did burn the house down, can't have you getting caught Frank!"

That made sense, I was glad I wouldn't be caught for murder and arson, and the realization that they had actually done it settled some demons. It did mean that they were willing to burn a house down to hide what was going on, that didn't alleviate any additional stress.

"How did she know I was supposed to save her if you are the only ones who can see the future?"

Dirt pretended not to hear me and took an overly long drink from his bottle, stalling for time. Poncho did nothing, as usual, aside from general menacing.

"We are the only ones Dirt knows for sure are psychic, it stands to reason that there could be others," Poncho clarified.

Dirt took the bottle out of his mouth, it looked to have been empty for a while. "Yeah, that's it!"

"If she could see the future and saw that I was supposed to save her, why didn't I?" The answer came to me before I finished speaking. "Never mind, something like more psychics seeing something, and intervening changes it, right?"

Dirt and Poncho exchanged a surprised look. "Sounds good to me, let's go with that," Dirt stated.

I had just given them their own bullshit answer, worst P.I. ever.

"But if she knew she was going to be hit by a car, why go into the street in the first place? Why take the chance that I would save her?"

Poncho leaned toward me with his serious face on. "She knew that if you saved her, you would die instead. We didn't want you to die, so we warned you. She took the chance because the opposition wants you dead."

Now there was a supernatural hit out on me, any minute there could be vampire ninjas jumping from the rafters to kill me.

"Opposition?" I asked.

"Opposition is a bad word. It's more like anyone trying to do bad shit to people. We know they want you gone and we would like that to not happen."

"We just don't know why," Dirt added.

"Could it be because you hired me to kill some of them?"

Dirt and Poncho shrugged, these guys were useless.

"Let me get this straight. An unorganized group of generally bad people--sorry, immortals--want me dead. You two have known about it since before we met, long enough to leave a cryptic message on my nightstand, even though I would likely ignore it all together until you didn't try to hit me with a car. Then closer to the actual event of my possible death you show up to further put me in danger by sending me to kill what you pretended to be monsters. Then warn me again without any explanation, thereby tricking me into possibly dying to save a person you wanted dead. She put her own life on the line in the off chance that I would save her and forfeit my life in the process. And despite your psychic powers having deduced all of this you still don't know why this group wants me dead?" I took a breath. "That about sum it up?"

Dirt and Poncho looked at each other again and said at the same time, "Pretty much."

"I hate you guys."

"You don't have to be a dick about it Frank, we're friends," said Dirt.

"We did kind of save your life," Poncho said.

The saddest part of all of this mess was that these idiots were the closest thing to friends I had at the time. That made me reevaluate how I had spent my entire life.

"You allegedly saved my life, use your fancy mind powers and tell me what happens now that I'm not dead."

"I wish," said Dirt. "But it doesn't work like that, it's all changed now. So until we get more visions and stuff, we are in the dark just like you."

"There weren't any vampires, werewolves, or faeries?"

"Yes," Dirt said.

"No," said Poncho at the same time.

Dirt attempted to glare holes in Poncho, failing miserably. "You can't prove they weren't."

"You can't prove they were, so let's just drop it," Poncho replied, then looked at me shaking his head and mouthing "No."

"When Frank sprouts hair and starts ripping out your god damn neck meat don't come crying to me about werewolves being real," Dirt said on his way to fetch more beers. On his way back the doorbell rang, he tucked the bottles in one arm and answered it, coming into the living room with a pizza box in his hand.

Whatever was happening with these two, I was going to find out. It wasn't the smart choice, but I was fairly confident that no matter what I did, I wasn't going to be able to get away from it. I downed the remainder of my beer and grabbed the fresh one Dirt set in front of me.

"Fuck it, I'm in. What's next?"

Dirt opened the pizza inhaling deeply, "Next we go after our book of prophecies!" He took a bite of pizza and past his mouthful of food said, "After this pizza and some more beers of course."

# Book 'o Prophecies

Dirt and Poncho were in no rush to retrieve the so called "Book of Prophecies." After the pizza was gone and a few too many beers later we got on our way. I was in no shape to drive, at least not safely or legally, and was about to mention this when Poncho yelled "Driver," and ran out the door. Dirt jumped to his feet cocking an imaginary shotgun and ran after him. It looked like I was riding in the back of my own car, because when I got outside they were both sitting inside waiting.

I climbed into the backseat and asked, "Where are we going?"

Dirt was thumping the dashboard in excitement, to a tune unknown to me.

"Not far," Poncho said pulling into the street.

That was the most description I was liable to get from them, so I leaned back and closed my eyes. Maybe it was the remnants of the head injury or the large quantities of alcohol I had consumed, but I was soon asleep.

I awoke to the sound of arguing, I had no idea how long I was asleep or where we were. I never was a fan of car ride beer comas.

"I don't see how it matters," said Dirt.

Poncho had the seat as far as it would go back with one slab of an arm hanging out the window, still managing to look cramped.

"It matters because Frank is human, and some heavy shit might happen, no sense in him getting hurt."

They didn't seem to notice that I was awake, so I stayed still, hoping they would slip up and let some of their lies out.

"Frank can take care of himself," Dirt said. "He wrecked those other clowns, and this guy is kind of a bitch."

"A well connected bitch who always has a bunch of goons hanging around," Poncho explained.

"I'll just condor punk them, that always works."

"What the fuck is condor punking?" Poncho questioned.

"You ever watch one of those nature shows where some vultures are picking at a corpse, then a condor shows up and punks them all out?"

"No."

"Well, these vultures are all around this corpse having a grand time eating its butt and stuff, then a condor sees it and want a piece. Everyone knows condors are seriously the most badass flying dick birds in the world, except bats, but some clowns say bats aren't birds so I won't count them. So the condor flies down and puffs his feathers out and chases them all away. After they fuck off he eats until his fat greedy ass is full. The best part is, before he flies away he goes and punks them out some more, just to make sure they know who the boss of all birds is."

"That sounds dumb, how would that work against goons?"

"You just run at them flapping your arms! They will run away for sure," Dirt explained while making his best imitation of condor punking. Which pretty much consisted of him flapping his arms and bobbing his head like an idiot.

"I'm not doing that, and if you do I'll let them beat your ass into the ground. Hell, I might even help them."

I could imagine Dirt's upset frown. "Fat fucking chance, you'd never get past my red panda defense."

"I don't want to know what that is," Poncho said.

"As if I'd give up all my strategies to you," Dirt scoffed.

"Whatever man."

"Back to the point, that's what you're for, just go in there and beat some ass, Frank will be fine."

"I expect I will have to hand out some beatings, but it's way easier without other people getting in the way, also more fun."

"What about me? I'm not a kung-fu badass like you, and I don't get in your precious way."

Poncho let out a laugh. "Not anymore, but you used to be a huge pain in the ass."

"Lies!"

"No lies brother, you remember that time in Europe?"

"Which one?"

"The one on top of Africa, next to the cold one."

"Ok, which time?"

I was fairly sure that was supposed to be a joke, but it went screaming over Dirt's head so fast he never even had a chance.

Poncho shook his head slightly, disappointed that his joke was missed. "Any of them."

Dirt scoffed, "That wasn't my fault, I was drunk." It looked like he had a beer in his hand at the time too.

"You got the wrong continent."

Dirt scratched his head and drank more, "Oh that Europe!" he said snapping his fingers. "That wasn't my fault, I wasn't drunk."

"Yeah, and we sorted that problem out, you and sobriety don't get along."

On that note Dirt crushed his beer can and threw it on the floor to rattle around with what sounded like many others, then opened another.

"We just need to get Frank more drunk, then he can come!"

"Frank will just pass out again if we get him more drunk, and I don't want him stumbling around getting in the way. You know caution isn't really my thing."

Dirt sighed, "Fine, Frank wake up and get the fuck out!"

I ended my clever sleeping ruse but, I'll be damned if someone is going to make me get out of my own car, especially after commandeering it. I was about to say so when Poncho pulled the car over and murder stared at me. It wasn't so much a glare, or a scowl; murder stare is about the only accurate description.

"I'll have you know," I said getting out of the car, "that I do this under protest."

"Noted," said Poncho.

Dirt looked at me apologetically and said, "Sorry man, it's out of my hands."

Then they drove away, leaving me on the street to fend for myself. I had no idea where I was, but judging by the wrought iron fences and gargantuan houses I was unlikely to be robbed and killed finding my way home. I also had no idea how I was going to get home, so I started walking the direction Dirt and Poncho had gone hoping to find a familiar street name.

A block later I saw my car parked in front of one of the monolithic houses that lined the streets. They must have changed their minds and decided to let me come along for the ride, assuming they wouldn't just pull away when I grabbed the door handle. After one or two tries they would let me in and we would continue on our idiotic mission. As I approached the car I saw that they weren't inside, maybe they left it for me and found their own ride through whatever sorcery they employed to make odd things happen.

They were standing by the gate that in movies has a buzzer that only lets in the right people. I was still far enough away that they didn't see me, and Dirt was talking to the box while Poncho stood waiting. Dirt must not have been making any progress because Poncho nonchalantly kicked the metal gate sending it crashing to the ground. I was fairly certain that this was impossible, but my list of things I found hard to believe was quickly getting smaller when it came to these two. They rounded the bend onto the mansion property and I ran up to peek around the corner. I couldn't help but wonder if they had dropped me off within spitting distance of their destination on purpose, or if their idiocy was that monumental.

What I saw on the property grounds was not a lawn strewn with bodies and Poncho covered in blood like I had imagined. He was instead, standing in front of a group of men who were dressed in polo shirts and looked very much like a bunch of frat boys. They were having a conversation and I crept forward to try and hear what was being said without being noticed. Dirt was milling around off to the side kicking aimlessly at the ground, not paying much attention.

"Just walk away guys," I heard Poncho say as I got into earshot. "Then you won't have to worry about keeping your blood inside your bodies with all your bones being broken."

The frat boys didn't budge, but most of them didn't look much like they wanted to be there anymore. The lead goon was more confident, and didn't seem fazed by Poncho's threat, I was threatened by it and it wasn't even directed at me.

That's when Dirt made his move, rushing the group flapping his arms and bobbing his head like he had in the car. I couldn't believe my eyes when everyone but the lead man cowered with their hands over their heads, clearly terrified. Holy shit, condor punking worked, but not on the lead man, he looked more irritated than anything.

"Caw, caw, caw, run motherfuckers!" Dirt yelled circling the paralyzed group of goons.

"Knock that shit off man, and go do the thing, I'll handle these dicks," Poncho told him.

Dirt looked upset, then proud, after proving his condor punking theory in action. He waved at me and walked casually into the house, the goons seeming to have forgotten about him.

"Handle us?" the lead goon said. "What are you going to do big man? We outnumber the shit out of you bro."

"Numbers," Poncho chuckled. "Numbers don't mean shit, there are only…" he paused for a few seconds and appeared to be doing some complex calculations, "less than ten of you."

There were exactly six of them, I was now sure that Poncho was an idiot.

"I've beat the shit out of less than ten people plenty of times," he continued.

All but the lead goon were sufficiently intimidated, and had only just recovered from the fearsome condor attack. They didn't look like they wanted to fight, but were also too scared to run.

"Fat fucking chance man," said the tough guy, to the cowering goons. "Come on, he can't do that much damage against all of us."

The others didn't seem convinced and continued hanging back.

"But what about my bones?" one in the back asked.

"And my blood, I need my blood man," Added another.

"Fuck your bones, and fuck your blood, the boss will do way worse if you pussy out. You know what he is like," the lead goon said. So it wasn't bravery, it was misplaced fear that motivated his bravado.

Mention of the boss solidified their resolve and the shuffled a little closer, still not convinced.

"Any time, ladies," Poncho said sounding bored. "I don't have all night, so get your purses out and let's get this tickle fight over with." He crossed his arms across his chest and waited.

The lead goon rushed him yelling like a lunatic with the others reluctantly hot on his heels. The leader got to Poncho first, and in a blur of motion he was laying on the ground with his arm going the wrong way. The rest of them didn't stop like I would have thought, but were

bolstered on by either fear of vengeance and attacked
Poncho in a flurry of punching and kicking.

I'm no fighter, so I can't accurately describe what
followed. Poncho was far too fast for someone so big and
moved in a way that defied reason. Those goons couldn't
lay a hand on him, and he looked like he was toying with
them. He had a giant grin on his face and madness in his
eyes that told me he was enjoying himself. He was tossing
them around like ragdolls, not really hurting them, they
just kept coming at him caught in some kind of battle lust.
Even the goon with the broken arm was back at it,
complete with the crazy gleam in his eyes.

I tore my eyes away from this and noticed that I
could see Dirt through the massive window on the front
of the house. Through it I could see a grand central
staircase and most of the front room, foyer? Whatever
people call the big room inside the doorway of big
houses.

He was walking up the stairs with a bag of chips,
stuffing them into his mouth and looking aimlessly
around. At the top of the stairs he stopped to wipe chip
dust off his fingers on a curtain that probably cost more
than my car. He moved to the left and looked behind the
first painting he came to, apparently finding nothing he
moved onto the next, wiping more chip dust on the front.
Dirt kept doing this until he was out of sight.

"Frank!" Poncho yelled. "Get the fuck inside and help Dirt find that book, I'll be right behind you." He punched one of the goons in the face, sending blood flying. "Right after these guys run out of gas, or blood."

They looked pretty out of gas to me, most of them were bleeding and a few of them were navigating with broken bones. None of them were trying to get away though, one whose legs looked broken was even crawling towards him.

I nodded and ran to the door, avoiding the melee, it wasn't something I wanted to get mixed up in. As I opened the door a body slammed into the wall next to it, I had no business outside anymore.

I went up the stairs at a slow jog, not really wanting to know what Dirt was involved in. When I reached the top I heard a gunshot from the direction I had last seen Dirt going. Against my better judgment I went towards it, my instincts were becoming worrisome. I ran down the hall past the chip stained curtains and crooked paintings, and ended up in an office. It was the kind you see crime bosses operating out of in movies, a lot of old books, stuffed predators, and everything was made out of probably endangered wood.

The only difference from a movie crime office was the dead body sitting in the high backed chair behind the large desk. He had blood in his mouth and there was blood spattered on the wall behind him, you didn't have to be a crime scene investigator to see that he shot himself in the mouth. Dirt was standing in front of the fireplace eating chips and staring into the fire. I couldn't believe that that this man had committed suicide out of fear when he saw Dirt walk in munching chips.

I decided to do something unthinkable and ask Dirt how things played out.

"What happened?"

"He threw the book into the fire when I walked in and shot himself in the face," Dirt said past a mouthful of chips.

"That's it?" I asked, surprised at his straight forward answer. "No ghosts or other supernatural junk?"

"Yep."

I looked down at the fire, there was a book that looked very familiar burning to ash, too far gone to be saved. Shit, this turned out to be a big waste of time.

"Threw the book into the fire and shot himself?" Poncho asked coming into the room.

"Yep," I said.

"Well duh, he couldn't shoot himself in the mouth and then throw a book into the fire," Dirt said. "He isn't a fucking poltergeist."

"You know what I meant asshole."

Poncho stared at the fire with us.

"Did you kill those guys outside?" I asked Poncho after I saw the blood all over his clothes.

"Nah," he said disappointed. "They should be fine after the cops show up and put some new blood in them."

"Cops!" Dirt yelled, chucking the partially empty bag of chips into the fire. "We need to burn the evidence and get the hell out of here!"

He ran to the desk grabbing whatever documents were handy and threw them into the fire, including paper weights, pens and anything else not nailed down.

"What are you doing?" I asked.

"Evidence!" Dirt yelled, not stopping his scrambling.

Poncho didn't move, and I had no idea what evidence he was referring to. Maybe the documents he was burning had business transactions with Dirt and Poncho that they needed to get rid of. I dismissed the thought immediately: no way those guys had business transactions.

"What evidence?" I asked.

"The incriminating kind, like the security tapes!" Dirt said frantically.

Oh shit, security tapes, that kind of evidence. I hadn't seen any security cameras on the way in, but I hadn't been looking either.

"Check the computer," Poncho said.

"Computer, yes!" Dirt grabbed the laptop off the desk and brought it over to the fire. He looked at the computer, then at Poncho, for support. Poncho shrugged and Dirt tossed it into the fire distastefully.

I didn't know if burning computers was the best way to destroy them, but the inferno caused by all the other flammables Dirt had thrown in was making short work of it.

"That should do it," Dirt said dusting his hands. "Let's bounce."

As we made our way outside, I pondered what would keep the goons that saw us all from identifying us to the authorities. When we passed the broken and bleeding bodies of said goons, I mostly wondered how they were still alive. The scene on the lawn made war footage look like a Saturday morning cartoon. Them identifying us was secondary to getting out of this place, and I was certain that nothing would come of it, nothing ever made sense around Dirt and Poncho.

"We'll see you tomorrow Frank, we are going to take one of his cars," Poncho said.

They walked to the open garage while I stood and did nothing. A few seconds after they entered the garage they drove out in a super car that probably had some fancy Italian name. Dirt waved at me from the window and they screamed off down the road.

"Wait!" I shouted. "My keys!" They had driven my car here and never gave me my keys back. I contemplated being stranded at the site of a massive fight, a suicide, and some arson, when I patted my pockets down and found my keys.

"How the fuck?" I said to no one in particular. I went to my car shaking my head. I hate those guys.

# Lonald Forandalo

I didn't sleep much that night, mostly because I was having some problems rationalizing everything that had been going on recently. I fell into a fitful sleep in the early hours of the morning, but still woke up early. Despite this, I laid in bed until noon. As a normally early riser, this was kind of a big deal, usually I only get out of bed that late when I drink too much or have recent head wounds, or both. I didn't get up early because I was a morning person, but more out of stubborn resolve. When you get up early you can hurry up and get the day out of the way.

But not today. Today I was involved in a war between immortal madmen, the stakes of which were never made clear. That was something I had to address, Dirt and Poncho never told me why they were doing any of this, other than to kill "bad shit" as they put it. I didn't know why I hadn't taken my money and moved to somewhere warm, where all the drinks have umbrellas in them and the girls are never wearing much. Maybe it was my curious nature, maybe it was because despite the craziness of it all, it was kind of exciting.

I left the soul searching for another day, and dragged myself out of bed. I didn't know what the day held, so I decided to start it with a trip to the bar.

An hour later I was at the bar, hoping to see Dirt and Poncho. It made me a little sick at the thought of actually wanting to see those two, perhaps I was going mad. This thought started to fester, and I was moments away from becoming very depressed when the door opened spilling light into the dim interior. The light was blocked out by a mass that could only be Poncho, Dirt was right behind him carrying a duffle bag. They ambled over to my table and sat down, Dirt set the bag down in a scheming fashion on the floor between us.

"Crazy night, huh Frank?" Dirt said winking and glancing oddly at the bag. "We picked up your 'laundry' for you."

When he said laundry he did the air quotes that let everyone within earshot know that it definitely wasn't laundry. Dirt slid the bag over to me with his foot while pretending to look at a menu.

I'm not sure what I expected to find in the bag, but I was suspicious none the less. Upon opening the bag my suspicions were justified as well as alleviated, the bag was full of money. I had never seen an entire duffle bag full of cash before, so I had no estimation of how much it contained. There was no rhyme or reason to what manner of currency it contained either, there was brightly colored money that looked foreign, and I was pretty sure I saw some coins and jewelry.

I closed the bag, "What's this for? Do you need me to buy a literal ton of cocaine for you?"

"I told you it was too much money," Poncho said.

"It isn't too much money!" Dirt said. "It's the right amount, I counted it myself."

"No you didn't," Poncho said.

"Well I put a bunch in there, so basically I counted it."

I frowned down at the bag.

"We can pay you in drugs if you want," Dirt said, trying to be helpful. "We just figured you would want options."

"That's not what I mean, it's just way too much money. What am I supposed to do with it all?" I asked.

"Do you want some of those money cards you people like so much? We can do that instead." Poncho said.

"What?" I asked

"You know, those plastic things that work like money, you show them to a guy and he gives you the things. Money cards," Dirt offered.

Oh, they meant credit cards. These guys were seriously out of touch with how money works. I didn't want to find out where they would get ahold of credit cards, and the trail it would leave.

"No, that's fine," I said. "Are you guys bribing me or something?"

"It isn't a bribe Frank, you can do whatever you want with it," Poncho said.

"But why so much?" I asked. "You paid me for the first two jobs, and I haven't really done much since then."

"Call it a bonus, plus a retainer for future collaboration," Poncho said.

"You're paying to put me on retainer, for what, more killing?" I asked, suspicious.

"For whatever we need you to do Frank," Poncho stated, matter-of-factly.

"So I'm a slave?"

"Slaves don't get paid," Dirt said sliding a beer towards me. I didn't see him get up to get any beer, and Jim sure hadn't brought them, but this was becoming common place.

"Besides, you can quit whenever you want, no strings attached. You can take your money and disappear someplace warm," Dirt said.

"Little umbrellas in your drinks and everything," Poncho added.

Maybe they were psychic after all, probably just a lucky guess.

"But we all know you won't do that, you want to see what this is all about," Poncho said knowingly.

I wanted to protest, but he had me dead to rights, I was in this for the long haul. "What's next then?" I asked.

"Next we hit the streets, sweat some sources, find out the word on the street," Dirt said.

"What?" I asked, not sure if he was being serious or just trying to sound like he was.

Dirt appeared unsure of himself and looked at Poncho for help.

"He means we don't know, give us a few days and we will have something," Poncho clarified.

"What do I do in the mean time?" I was going to have a hard time with a few days off after the recent excitement.

"Just lay low Frank, relax, watch some TV, get a hooker, whatever people do when they aren't working," Dirt said.

They finished their drinks and headed for the door. "We'll be in touch," Poncho said and went outside.

Dirt pointed his finger at me in the shape of an imaginary gun and winked, then stepped outside to join Poncho.

I finished my beer, finding myself a little relieved to have some time off after all. I had time to sort out some of the bullshit anyway, that was something. I left a twenty on the table, unsure if I really needed to bother with paying. I shouldered the bag and made for the exit.

Little did I know that my RNR was going to be moved down my schedule a bit. Parked outside the bar was what my brain told me was an impossible car. The front looked like one of those new electric cars, so did the back, but the part in the middle was the spitting image of a stretch limo. While I was trying to wrap my head around this unexpected sight a large man with one eye stepped out of the driver's seat, his face was a mess of grizzly scars all originating from one milky white eye, disappearing beneath the collar of his finely tailored suit.

My first instinct was that this clearly had nothing to do with me and I should ignore it completely, but the last few days had shattered my cleverly crafted cave of naiveté. I was proven correct when the cyclops bruiser made a bee line towards me. I was about to make an exceptionally witty comment in an effort to appease this well dressed enforcer when he opened the door to the stretched part of the car and said, "Get in."

Feeling bold and perhaps a little reckless I asked, "Why?"

His one good eye glared at me. "It wasn't a request," He growled.

I doubted that I would be murdered in a stretch limo in the middle of the day, it stuck out pretty bad and more than a few people were ogling this rare sight. At least if they did kill me there would be witnesses, it was a small consolation. When post death retribution seems like a viable backup plan you know you aren't making good decisions anymore.

I shrugged and got in, what's the worst that could happen? The last few days had increased my acceptable levels of wacky shit I can put up with. Inside the limo was pretty nice, having never been in a limo before my standard was probably skewed though. I sat facing the back of the car, another treat you don't get in normal cars, across from a clean cut, well dressed man with no noticeable evil aura. He was sitting cross legged wearing flip flops, the giant smile on his face looked genuine, and it put me at ease slightly, only slightly. His posture and lack of closed toe foot wear didn't mesh with his suit, but I know precisely dick about fashion, he seemed to be pulling it off, which I guess is all that matters. His face wasn't a mess of scars like his man outside, his was more kind. I'm not sure how I would describe it to a sketch artist, but he just looked like a nice guy.

I set the bag between us and waited.

"Hi Frank!" he said. "Sorry about my associate out there, no matter how much you pay someone you can't buy manners it seems." He smiled, then looked embarrassed. "It seems my manners have taken a brief hiatus as well, I'm Lonald, Lonald Forandalo. How do you do?" he said sticking his hand out.

I shook it, it was one of those limp handshakes that make you feel dirty. "Wait, Lonald? Like Lonny?" I asked, remembering Pierre's comments in the alley.

"Oh you've heard of me then?" he said excitedly.

"A man with a gun to my head mentioned you."

"That's terrible! But I see you are ok, who was it that put a gun to your head? If you don't mind my asking," Lonald said concerned.

"He went by Pierre, I think," I answered.

"OH! that man is just no good at all! A brute of the lowest sort. He used to work for me, but his violent tendencies were unacceptable. I had to terminate his employment, he was not happy about it."

"Yeah, he didn't seem like a happy guy," I said.

"What happened to him? After he had a gun to your head I mean," Lonald asked.

There was no way I could put this delicately, but I was pretty sure he wasn't the cops, and I was very sure he had a hand in what Dirt and Poncho were up to. So there wasn't any harm in telling him.

"I got the upper hand and shot him in the face, pretty sure he's dead," I said.

"Oh my! That is just dreadful! But, he wasn't very nice, and someone was going to do it sooner or later." He didn't appear all that broken up about it, but he did look a little sick at the thought.

I had solved a tiny part of the mystery; how Pierre knew this man. This information meant exactly nothing, a lot of people know people, but at least it was one less thing eating at me during the night. I decided it was time to see what this peculiar man wanted.

"So what's this about? I doubt you wanted to talk about murdered past employees."

"Oh no! Certainly not! Before we start, do you want a drink? I have some all natural vegetable juice and..." He rummaged around the mini fridge, "and some reverse osmosis filtered water..." He was still looking when I stopped him.

"No thanks, I'd rather just talk about why I'm here if you don't mind." I mostly didn't want whatever was in that fridge, rich people never have normal drinks.

"Straight to business, I like that," Lonald said, looking very much like he didn't. He adjusted his tie and said, "I'll be frank." Then immediately fell into a fit of laughter, holding his stomach and wiping his eyes like it was the funniest thing he had ever heard. "I'm so sorry Frank!" he said still wiping his eyes and chuckling, "You be Frank, and I'll just tell you why I need you."

"Right," I said, drawing it out, this man was insane, I was on familiar ground again. Familiar ground in no way meant that I knew how to handle it however, I was just used to it. I was also sure that his inability to act normal put him in the same category as whatever Dirt and Poncho were.

Lonald cleared his throat and regained control of himself, "I'd like you to come work for me Frank."

Great, one more lunatic wanting to hire me to do something horrible, this would be easier if I was some kind of ex-military special forces mercenary type.

"Last time someone approached me for a job I got wrapped up in something way over my head, and I got the feeling your job won't be any different," I said matter-of-factly.

"Ah yes," he said rubbing his chin, "You must be referring to those gentlemen," he paused. "Grit and Honcho was it?"

"Dirt and Poncho," I corrected.

"Quite right, I can never keep names straight anymore."

"So you know them I take it?" I asked, hoping in vain for some answers.

"Oh yes, we have a long history, you might say."

"You are like them then?"

He looked wary, "In what way?"

I decided it wasn't worth beating around the bush, and at the worst he would think I'm crazy and we could part ways.

"You know, immortal psychic guys?" It sounded a lot dumber out loud.

Had he been drinking I'm sure he would have spit it all over the car, instead he just choked on air, coughing uncontrollably and settling into laughter.

"That's what they told you? Immortal psychic guys?" He asked after he caught his breath.

"Not in those exact words," I said sheepishly.

"Those guys are just precious, they always did know just what to say to make me laugh."

At least I knew they were still full of shit, unless this guy was full of shit too.

"So what are you guys and why do you need me?" I asked.

"One thing at a time Frank, I want you to work for me because you are an outlier in our twisted little endeavor. You can go places unrecognized and avoid unnecessary conflict," he said.

"Conflict huh?" I said disbelieving. "You should know that the first two jobs I did for those assholes ended in conflict."

"Well I knew about the first one, it was hard to miss with the fire and so on. But Pierre just disappeared, nobody has heard from him and we assumed he just ran off, no one knew you killed him. But those two were bad news, and any interaction with them was bound to end in violence no matter how you approached them." He curled his lip in distaste at the thought. "But you survived! Making you quite a valuable employee, and the jobs I have for you won't be nearly so offensive."

"What kind of jobs?" I asked, getting uneasy.

"What I need you to do is simple, I need you to recruit."

"Recruit for what?" My uneasiness creeping into worry.

"There are certain individuals I would like to have on my payroll, I can't have me, or any of my associates approach them. There is sometimes bad blood between us that could make showing up unannounced bad etiquette. So I need you to go talk to them for me!"

"And they won't try to kill me?" I wasn't sure why I was asking, it was a bad idea to even consider this, but as long as he was willing to talk maybe he would tell me something useful.

"I should hope not!" Lonald exclaimed.

"Ok, let's say I agree to this, what's in it for me?"

"What do you want?" He asked as if it didn't matter how I responded.

That was a loaded question, I want lots of things, but answers was the first thing that came to mind.

"I want to know what's going on with you people, like what are you, and what you are up to, all that stuff," I said, not very eloquently.

"I'm sure that can be arranged, but you have to understand that I'll have to hold that information hostage for now."

"Why?" I asked, sure that I already knew the answer.

"If I tell you what you want to know before you see what an excellent employer I am, you may decide to leave. So one job and I'll tell you anything you want to know."

"No bullshit?" I asked.

"No sir!" he replied.

I was going to regret this, I was sure of it. "Ok, what's the job?"

"Hang on there, first things first. I'd like to pay you for your trouble in addition to your answers, what have those rascals been paying you?"

They didn't really have a formal pay system, so I just pointed to the duffle bag on the floor.

Lonald raised an eyebrow. "May I?" he asked.

I shrugged and he set about opening the bag and inspecting its contents. Frowning, he turned to the telephone in the armrest, dialed some numbers and waited.

"Yes, hi. I need you to meet me at the agreed upon place," he said into the phone. I couldn't hear the voice on the other line.

"Yes, the bar."

Pause.

"Also I need you to round up some currency."

The person on the other end said something loud, but still undecipherable.

"I don't know what kind, let me check," he rummaged around in the bag and pulled out a wad of brightly colored bills. "I don't think this country exists anymore." Further digging, "This is fake jewelry... These are chocolate coins wrapped in foil... American... Is this taffy? A flask... Frank do you want this?" He handed me the flask, and I put it in my coat pocket, I would likely need it later. He continued looking in the bag. "A deck of cards... Euros... gems... rocks...?" He pulled his hand out of the bag. "I can pay you in drugs if that's easier."

"No thanks, not really a drug person." What was it with these guys and drugs?

"No drugs then."

The phone said something he must not have liked. "I don't know how you're supposed to find all that stuff, that's your job!"

Another pause while Lonald frowned.

"OK, hold on, I'll ask." To me he asked, "Do you just want American money?"

"Works for me," I said nodding.

"He says American money is fine." Pause, "Ok, I'll see you then." He almost hung up and remembering something, quickly added, "And put it in the nice bags!"

There was a pause, "Two of them I suppose." More speaking on the other end. "I don't know, just fill them up. Ok, bye."

With that settled he hung up the phone. He looked as if he was about to say something and stopped, reached into his coat pocket pulling out a handful of credit cards. "I can just pay you in money cards if you want, I know how you people love those."

Where did these guys come from, If they truly were immortal why couldn't they figure money out?

"No, that's ok," I said.

He looked a little disappointed and put them back in his pocket. This is around the time I realized that the limo hadn't moved. I thought these clandestine limo meetings always involved driving around and dropping people off at inconvenient locations.

"We aren't going anywhere?" I asked.

"Oh no, I didn't want you stranded someplace if you decided to storm off in a huff. People do that sometimes. This way if you wanted to leave, your car is right outside, it's only polite," he smiled his far too happy smile. At least it settled the not moving part.

"So what's the job?"

Lonald handed me an envelope, "All you need to know is in here, just go see him tomorrow and bring one of the bags my associate will be dropping off."

"See him and say what?" I asked, thinking whatever I had to say would be with bullets.

"My card is in the envelope, give him that and tell him I would really enjoy speaking with him about possible career opportunities. Please let him know that the bag is a gift and he has no obligation to contact me."

"Sounds easy enough." A sucker is born every minute. "What's the catch?"

"No catch! Promise!"

As I was contemplating how to express my disbelief of this statement there was a knock on the window.

Lonald clapped his hands, "That'll be Neph with your money!"

We stepped out of the car into the blazing light of the un-tinted outdoors, once my eyes adjusted I saw a woman wearing a scowl with two large canvas-looking bags at her feet.

"Neph, this is Frank," Lonald said.

"Nice to meet you," I said offering my hand.

She looked at my hand like it was possibly tainted in some way and crossed her arms in front of her chest. My keen detective instincts told me that she didn't like me very much, they also told me that when she crossed her arms she didn't approve of my glancing at her breasts. Her scowl became more severe and I looked down ashamed. She was quite pretty despite her attempt to make her face as hostile as possible, she was of some kind of Asian descent, but I couldn't place it.

It had only been a few minutes since Lonald had spoken on the phone about the money delivery and it was already here, this lead me to believe that she was also one of them. That or it was all an elaborate ploy to make me think so, either way thinking about it too much was going to give me a headache.

Lonald noticed the tension and broke it, "Oh, you did use the good bags, excellent!"

She said nothing and I had no idea what he meant by the good bags, so I pointed my confused face at him.

"These bags are great Frank!" He was very excited. "They are made from 100% renewable resources, completely biodegradable. If they ever tear or anything you can just put them in your compost! It won't happen though, just look at that stitching! Top notch craftsmanship. If they do break somehow you can just take a picture of the broken bag and send it to the company, they send you a brand new one! Free! The best part of course is that when you buy one the company donates 80% of the cost to poor kids!"

"That's gre..." He cut me off.

"And! And, they give the kids a bag too, it's just great!"

"Cool," I said after a slight pause to see if he had more to add. I didn't know how to respond to any of this, I'd never seen someone so excited about bags before.

"It is cool," Lonald replied, beaming.

Then an awkward silence descended upon us, the kind that happens when one person doesn't care, or know, what the other person is saying, and the other person is certain that anyone within a city block couldn't help but be interested.

Neph came to our rescue, "There is a catch."

"Catch? What catch? I told Frank no catches!" Lonald said, frustrated.

I could only watch smugly, I knew it after all, nothing is ever simple with these people.

"The catch is that I couldn't get the bag for the job, it has to wait until tomorrow," she said.

I was a little let down, this catch wasn't the great debacle that would send my world crashing down around my ears. I would get over it.

"That's no problem," Lonald said clearly relieved. "Frank, you don't have a problem waiting until tomorrow do you?"

I didn't have an answer, mostly because I was having a hard time caring about things anymore, so Lonald agreed for me.

"It's settled then, Neph will drop by your house tomorrow with the bag and give you a ride to the job."

Neph didn't looked pleased with this turn of events, but nodded.

"Tomorrow then! Good luck!" Lonald stepped into the limo and tossed my duffle bag out carelessly. Neph got into the passenger side in the front, I guess she didn't bring the bags in a separate car. They were probably in the trunk of the limo and she was just waiting in the front the whole time.

I stood on the sidewalk like the confused idiot I felt like, wondering how I was going to carry all those bags to my car. I had just decided to put Dirt and Poncho's bag on my back and drag to other two when the driver's door of the limo opened. The large one-eyed man got out cracking his knuckles, I guess Lonald had decided to have him beat the message into me after all. But he didn't pummel me, he walked up to me and picked up all three bags like they were nothing, carried them to the back of my car, and threw them on the ground. Then he walked back to the limo, making sure to bump my shoulder on the way, letting me know that it wasn't his idea to carry them over there. He got back in the car and they drove off silently.

I went to my car and stuffed the bags into the trunk, it was a tight squeeze with the bag Poncho had put in there earlier. I managed to get the trunk closed after a few attempts, I was really going to have to find a place for all this stuff. Not today though, today was reserved for going home and getting more than a little drunk in preparation for a new bloodbath tomorrow.

# Marvin

I woke up early the next day, maybe because I was excited about the idea of finally getting some answers. Or maybe it was because Lonald never told me what time Neph was going to show up, and I didn't want to answer the door in a state of undress. 8:00 AM all dressed and ready to go, and I was immediately bored. Waiting on people is the worst thing there is, especially when you have no idea when to expect them.

So I busied myself around the house, cleaning up the beer cans from when Dirt and Poncho were here, swept, vacuumed, dishes, dusted, laundry, the works. Once all that was done I looked at the clock, 10:00 AM. It was going to be a long day if she didn't get here soon. While I was cleaning I had the feeling that I was forgetting something, but I couldn't put my finger on it, until I almost tripped over it. Three bags filled with money on the floor by the front door, I wasn't sure how I missed them in all my cleaning, probably a mental block against decision making.

I didn't have a clue what to do with them, going to the bank was out, depositing money over certain amounts was risky, and safe deposit boxes always seemed like a lot of work. I didn't think people still stuffed their mattresses full of cash and I didn't have a safe. Digging a hole would take too long, and if I ever needed it I would just have to dig it back up. I wasn't about to start ripping up floorboards either. I decided to toss them in the attic and deal with it later, I would probably be dead in a few days anyway.

Then I was bored again, but a plan started to develop. I was hungry, and if I started making some lunch Neph would show up right in the middle making it all very inconvenient. I set about making an elaborate meal, I heated the oven, unwrapped the frozen pizza, put it in, and set the timer. She would be here any minute now.

I started to question my logic on the matter a few minutes into baking. This wasn't the kind of nonsense I thought would ever work. Dirt and Poncho's logic was rubbing off on me, and that scared me. If I ever truly started acting like them my sanity was doomed. I took the half cooked pizza out of the oven and threw it away, I hated wasting food, but I hated being crazy more. I wasn't hungry anymore anyway.

Waiting all day for Neph to show up was quickly becoming something I wanted no part in, she would probably track me down somehow no matter where I was. I got my gun and coat and headed for the door, mind made up. As I opened the door to brazenly step out and not wait for Neph, I saw her hand was inches away from the doorbell. Goddamn sorcery.

She was unfazed by my timing and retracted her hand. "You're ready then? Let's go."

"Yeah, sure," I said, hiding my annoyance at being a victim of magic. It did occur to me that had I continued cooking she would have showed up right as it was getting done. So my plan technically worked, I should have left it and seen if she wanted to have lunch with me. Surely the gesture would soften her serious behavior and we could be friends. Doubtful, I never was very good with the ladies, especially ones that were thousands of years old.

I locked the door and followed her to the street where her car was parked. It was a non-descript black sedan, the kind that is so non-descript that it sticks out like a windowless van outside a playground.

"I take it..."

Neph cut me off, "I'm driving," and she got in the car.

It was going to be a fun drive. I got in and she took off.

"What's the plan?" I asked. "The only thing in the envelope was Lonald's card, I was under the impression it was supposed to have information on the job."

"And it would have, but now I get to ferry you around instead. So all you need to know is that we are going to a place to see a guy, you will give him the bag and the card and we will leave." She paused, "Then I will take you back to Mr. Forandalo for your answers after. Also no talking, I'm not here for fun."

This woman was a barrel of laughs. "Ok," I said, might as well play it her way.

"I said no talking."

I almost said something again, but pushing her seemed like a terrible idea, so I shut my mouth and nodded. It would have been nice if she turned the radio on.

We rode in silence and I couldn't help but fall back into dwelling on what I had gotten myself mixed up in. I hadn't done anything to gain entry into this strange circle, but I hadn't really done anything to get out of it either. Dirt and Poncho had approached me for seemingly mundane reasons, not that I had super powers or anything. Then Lonald Forandalo, another fake name, had found me, surely because of my affiliation with Dirt and Poncho. Shit, maybe I was special, or just a pawn. Hopefully once I was done self-defense killing this next guy I would get some answers, real ones this time. And hey, maybe I'd get lucky and Lonald would be on the level and straighten this all up, and this next guy wouldn't try to kill me, and Dirt and Poncho would never come back! Fingers crossed.

After a few minutes of driving we pulled into a cul-de-sac in front of a very ordinary house. There were bikes laying in the neighbors' driveways and other children's' things strewn about. This worried me, I didn't want to fight a guy to the death in a place where kids play. Neph looked at me and nodded toward the house in mild irritation.

"You sure this guy won't try to kill me?" I asked.

"No," She said matter-of-factly.

I sighed and checked my holster, in case my gun had mysteriously flown away, or just as a reassurance.

"Bag is in the trunk," She said hitting the trunk release.

I got out of the car and warily made my way to the back, expecting danger to come from all sides. I retrieved the bag, it was the same kind I had been given the day before, and started for the house, stopping by Neph's window. I was going to ask her anything I could think of to stall for time, but she was reading a book and didn't even glance at me. At least she hadn't sped off laughing, that was a good sign.

I made my way down the stone-lined sidewalk to the front door. The direct approach was bound to work, my failed attempts at spying the last few times had taught me one thing; people don't like being spied on. I rang the doorbell and braced myself for a flurry of violence to smash through the door and tear my liver out.

What came to the door instead of my doom, was a pudgy, balding man with reading glasses.

He looked at me cautiously and asked, "Can I help you?"

So far so good. "My name is Frank, Lonald Forandalo sent me to talk to you."

His eyes got wide and I braced for impact, his hand shot towards me and I started to recoil for my counterattack. Instead he just clapped me on the shoulder and dragged me inside. "Lonald sent you? That's wonderful! How is he?"

That was unexpected. "Uh, good. I guess," I said.

"My name is Marvin, can I take your bag?"

Before I could respond he continued, "Where are my manners, would you like a drink? I have tea, water, maybe some soda." He paused, "And it's a little early but I might have brandy around here somewhere."

"Tea is fine, thank you," I said. I was too confused by him not attacking me that I just picked the first thing he said.

"You can just set that bag anywhere, Frank was it? Have a seat and I'll be back in two shakes with that tea." He shuffled into the kitchen whistling, undoubtedly to whip up some poison or release the hell hounds. But my reticence was wearing off and I sat down, put the bag on the floor by my feet and waited.

I briefly wondered what was in the bag, and just dismissed it, it was probably money. It was the bag potentially filled with money or the mention of Lonald that was keeping him civil right now. Without one or both of those things he would surely be trying to kill me.

Not a minute later Marvin was back with a tea tray, he must have had the kettle on before I got here. Or it was more magic, both were unsettling for different reasons. He poured me a cup and passed it to me on a saucer. He took his own and took a sip, sighing contently. Now that I knew it wasn't poison I took a sip as well, it was really good. I'm not a tea person, so I couldn't say what it was, but it tasted like good tea, and that was enough for me.

"Now then Frank, why did Lonald want you to come see me?"

I realized that I had no idea about the grand scheme of this visit, so I fumbled with my pocket and pulled out Lonald's card.

"He said to give you this, and he would like to discuss possible employment." I said passing him the card.

He cocked an eyebrow at me, took the card and set it on the coffee table.

I coughed, "Also he said to give you this, as a gift, even if you don't call him." I slid the bag to him.

Marvin set down his tea and looked at the bag as if it was filled with spiders. His expression quicly changed and he got really excited. "Oh my! Is this one of those compostable bags?"

"I think so," I said.

"These are just wonderful, you know they give a bag to a needy child every time you buy one?"

"I've heard that, yes."

"And the craftsmanship is just exquisite, look at that stitching!" He was shaking with excitement now. He also didn't seem interested in what was inside it.

"I think you are supposed to have what's inside it as well," I offered. Mostly because I was curious.

Marvin reached down and undid the buttons on the bag, and if there was ever a more excited grown man I've never met him, he all but bounced out of his seat. I looked down at what artifact could have made him so happy and saw more bags. The bag was filled with the same type of bags folded neatly. Marvin set about pulling them out and stacking them next to his chair.

"Goodness, this is just fantastic. These bags are hard to find, they just sell out so fast. Nobody can keep them in stock. Wonderful, I can't wait to..." He stopped and clapped his hands to his mouth the way people do when they see babies. "This is just precious," He said pulling out what looked like a jewel studded chalice. He got up and put it on the mantle over the fireplace, replacing a smaller, less jewel encrusted chalice. I had to admit, it did look really good there, really tied the room together, I have no idea why, it just seemed to fit.

Marvin went back to his bag and continued fishing around. He pulled out a scarf that looked hand knitted and put it on, grinning ear to ear. He also found a watch, some house slippers, and some other odd trinkets that he just set on the coffee table. I watched all this while sipping my tea, and when it was gone I set it down, not knowing how much longer he would be looking in the bag.

The sound of the saucer hitting the table snapped him out of his treasure hunt and he looked up at me. "I'm so sorry Frank, I lost myself for a moment there."

He grabbed the card off the table and put it in his shirt pocket. "Tell Lonald that I'll call him first thing tomorrow, and thank him for me. This was just the best gift."

"I will."

Job done, I decided it was best not to linger, just in case he was some kind of trinket demon that gained a killer bloodlust from odds and ends. My fears went unjustified as we said our goodbyes and he thanked me profusely. When I was finally out the door and back in the car I breathed a mental sigh of relief, and a physical one, why limit myself? Lonald hadn't lied to me about this job being a milk run, so maybe he wasn't lying about my answers.

I couldn't help but wonder why they needed me to deliver the card and bag of goodies, Lonald and Marvin seemed like old friends. If they truly were immortals fighting each other since the beginning of time, I supposed that there could be a large amount of falling outs to be had. I've seen old friends on the street that I couldn't remember if I hated them or not, so with thousands of years to build and destroy friendships anything could be possible with these people.

Neph started the car and we headed to Lonald's place, one way or another it would be an illuminating experience.

# Answers

The ride to Lonald's house was as exciting as the ride to Marvin's. Neph said nothing and my attempts at idle chit-chat were ignored entirely, I couldn't even manage an annoyed glance from her. I considered some flirtatious comments to see how she would react, but decided that I didn't really want to be murdered, so I kept my mouth shut.

The scenery on the way to Lonald's house was nothing to write home about and I was starting to get bored. As I was about to hassle Neph with more questions that would receive no answers I noticed something. We were in a part of town I didn't even know existed, it wasn't outside the city limits and I was fairly sure it wasn't all that far from downtown. I'd just never been there, or even past there.

We drove through a heavily wooded area with decorative bushes and maybe trees, I don't know if trees can be specifically decorative or they just pick ones that grow that way. There were houses, I assume anyway, at the ends of all the driveways, behind large steel gates with stone walls topped with sharp decorative spikes. Aside from the wall spikes being decorative I was sure they were designed to cut you to ribbons if you decided to scale them. Then the roving packs of attack dogs would eat your corpse and your body would never be found.

We drove past several of these driveways to nowhere until she stopped at one that looked, as far as I could tell, the same as the others we had passed. Neph hit a button on the intercom and the gate slid open, not in the creepy haunted way, but the way that tells me this gate and its mechanisms cost more than my car. We made our way up the winding driveway passing what looked like old gas lamp light poles and large stone pots with strange plants overtaking them.

I fully expected to see tigers, jaguars, or even a dinosaur or two creeping around the brush. It looked less like a forest than it did a jungle, it was thick and even from the car I felt uneasy about what could be inside. I was pretty sure I saw a monkey and a few brightly colored birds, stuff that only lives in jungles. I need to read more books. How there was a jungle in the middle of a city I don't know, but if this guy was as rich as he seemed anything was possible.

We stopped in front of another gate, and behind this one I could see something resembling a house, if houses have towers, that is. We were buzzed through this gate and the car rolled into 100% crazy town. There were at least two dozen men in black tactical gear roaming around the place. They were on the wall patrolling, and on top of the house in specially made sniper nests scanning the jungle. The house itself was more of a fortress than anything else, the walls looked like they would withstand a nuclear blast, or at least several tornados at once.

The sheer amount of security at this place would make a SWAT team nervous, aside from the tactical gear they were all carrying military-grade rifles that I didn't recognize. They must have been some new kind that people don't know about yet. I guessed it was a private security contractor of some kind, basically just mercenaries. Until I noticed a few of them carrying swords and other more personal tools of death. That meant they might be immortals like Lonald and Neph, which was far more unnerving. These people were clearly dangerous no matter what they were.

We parked in front of the huge double doors between the ridiculous fountain and the house. Neph got out and walked to the door, none of the private army even looking her way, she must be a big deal. I got out and followed her, garnering hostile looks, and curious whispers to each other from nearby guards. This was probably a bad sign, they didn't appear to know I was coming, but were afraid to do anything. I got next to Neph by the door as quickly as I could, in case they decided that shooting me would win one of them employee of the month.

Neph opened the door and begrudgingly held it open for me to enter. I walked into a palace, it was the kind of house you see on those shows about people with way too much money and nothing specific to do with it. It was massive, which wasn't that surprising judging by the outside. Before I could fully take in the grandeur of it all, I think it would have taken days, Lonald Forandalo came out of a side room wearing a smoking jacket and a big smile.

"Frank!" he said, shaking my hand vigorously. "I told you working for me would be easy!"

He put an arm around my shoulder and led me to the room he had come from.

"Yeah, pretty easy." I agreed.

As he led me through the house I noticed even more security types wandering around, these weren't dressed for an assault though. The indoor security apparently had a strict formal dress code, they were all wearing suits with small sub-machine guns hanging from slings around their necks, and dark sunglasses. Not subtle, but somehow less terrifying, if only a little less so.

Lonald led me to what I would call a den, or a study, Neph had disappeared at some point on the way and I hadn't noticed. There were large comfortable looking chairs, an extensive bar, cigar boxes, and all the other old timey stuff you see in these types of rooms. He sat down and gestured for me to do the same in the chair opposite him. I sat and waited, Lonald gestured to one of his goons and he filled up a few glasses with some sort of whiskey, or scotch, something brown at any rate. The goon handed us our glasses and offered cigars out of a wooden box, Lonald took one, as did I, reluctantly. I never did like cigars all that much, they all taste the same no matter the costs or quality, but I was being polite.

"I have some spare smoking jackets if you want." Lonald said eyeing my overcoat.

"No thanks, not really my style." I wasn't sure if that was true, but I didn't want my first foray into smoking jacket attire to be a borrowed one.

"Fair enough," He said sounding a little disappointed. "I heard that everything went swimmingly with your job, that's good."

"It did."

"And I believe I promised you some answers didn't I?"

"You did," I said, trying to keep him on track. It was probably a lost cause on these guys, but it was worth a shot.

"So I did." Lonald tapped his fingers against his chin thinking. "It would be best to just come out and say it I suppose. We are involved in a conflict that pits good against evil, so to speak."

"Like God and the Devil, angels and demons kind of thing?" I asked.

"Oh no! Nothing so silly Frank. Well sort of. Not in those words though." He seemed to be floundering a bit. "No, not God and Satan, but angels and demons is closer. We aren't angels or demons, but it's a good comparison. There are good guys and bad guys, let's just say that."

God dammit, God fucking dammit. This was basically the same shit Dirt and Poncho were telling me. So it was either a great big lie by all of them, or the scarier option; it was all true.

"Ok, so why are you fighting?" I asked, I didn't have any better questions off the top of my head.

"That's just how it works, we exist to fight each other. We know as much about the meaning of our lives as humans do. We just have longer to come to terms with our lack of understanding." He smiled and lit his cigar.

"So Dirt and Poncho weren't lying to me?" It was the most ridiculous thing I have ever said.

Lonald chuckled sympathetically, "I highly doubt they are psychic."

"Why did they get me involved in all this?" If I could at least get an answer to this question it might make me feel better, or way worse.

"That I don't know, they see something in you I think." He squinted at me, "I don't see what it is entirely, but you do have a knack for staying alive, and I can use that."

"You can use me not dying?" I wasn't sure if that was reassuring or completely demoralizing.

"So to speak, your ability to not be recognized by our kind in addition to your ability to not be killed easily will help our cause immensely."

"Just to be clear, you are the good guys right?" I asked, just to be on the safe side.

"Of course Frank!" Lonald exclaimed.

I had a hard time not believing him.

"Why should I work for you instead of just walking away from all this?"

Lonald looked at me, calculating, "We both know you won't do that, you want to see what happens."

He had me, I was in too deep. I was also pretty sure they would kill me before I got out the door if I opted out.

"Frank, I don't want you to think you have to say yes. My men are not going to kill you before you walk out the door just for saying no."

Dammit, did I really look that uneasy? "I didn't mean, I mean of course you guys wouldn't kill me. That's stupid."

"So you're hired!"

I didn't think I had a choice, "Well I doubt I could live not knowing what this was all about, it's like that damn crosswalk thing."

"Crosswalk?" Lonald looked intrigued, and I instantly regretted saying it.

"Yeah, it's this whole thing with those guys, but..."

"It's settled then!" Lonald said cutting me off getting up and walking to the door.

Why he let it drop that quickly made me nervous, as most things these immortal types did.

"Neph has all the details." Lonald stepped out the door and peeked his head back in, "Make sure you get the good bags!" Then he left.

# Dirt and Poncho Sabotage

Neph gave me all the details on the ride back home, it was a simple go to a place talk to some guys job. She did warn me that things could get hairy on this one and to stay on my toes. I wasn't sure what that meant, but I assumed it was bad, and my regret was stirring again.

After a fitful night's sleep and a drive to another shitty part of town I was outside a shutdown night club of some sort. I was sitting in my car contemplating my avenue of attack when there was a knock on my window.

Shit, they made me already? I was seriously the worst at this.

But it wasn't some lunatic looking to kill me, it was a lunatic named Dirt. He waved when I looked at him, opened the door and got in. I looked around for Poncho, having never seen them apart and saw him standing by a trash can glaring at it.

"Hey Frank! What're you up to?" Dirt asked sitting down and lighting a cigarette. "Want to get some beers? I'll get the first round! Hell I'll get em' all!"

"What the fuck are you guys doing here?" I shouldn't have been surprised, but old habits die hard.

"Whoa, calm down Frank, we just wanted to hang out," Dirt said casually, as if this was a chance meeting. "Poncho must really want to hang out with you, he's always glaring at random shit when he's sad and he has been eye-fucking that trashcan for a solid hour. Seriously, if this goes on much longer I am almost certain that he is going to fight it. Let's just go grab some brews and cheer his ass up before he embarrasses himself."

"Do you think that trashcan could really beat him?" Dammit Frank how do you always fall into this nonsense, stick with the task at hand. "I'm kinda busy tonight Dirt."

"Hell no that trashcan can't beat Poncho, it's an inanimate object Frank. I meant that he will embarrass himself trying to fight a trashcan. Poncho is gigantic and way bigger than that stupid can, how could it win? That would look so stupid Frank." Dirt apparently remembered his original question at this point. "Busy doing what?"

I wasn't sure how much to tell him, but it probably didn't matter, I was sure he knew already anyway. I could tell them what I was up to over drinks, no harm in that, I wasn't given a timeline for this job either.

"I'll tell you when you get that first round." My willpower is shit.

"Atta boy Frank, I know an awesome bar right behind this shit building you are hanging out in front of." Dirt seemed taken aback. "Why are you hanging out here, this place has obviously been closed for a while man. Drinks now."

Dirt jumped out of the car before I could change my mind and ran over to dropkick the trashcan Poncho was clearly moments away from embarrassing himself against. Poncho seemed to take it rather well and they headed towards the alley besides the rundown club, stopping to stare in my direction long enough for me to open the door and head their way.

"Hurry up Frank, we are burning daylight," Dirt said, even though it was just after three in the afternoon.

I caught up to them just as they were entering what appeared to be a really shitty basement door, in an equally shitty alley, in an even shittier part of town. I was concerned that my vaccination record was not up to par for visiting this establishment. Let the good times roll, along with the hepatitis.

Poncho led the way through the heavy metal door into a typical basement bar. It was dark despite the many billiard lights hanging above no actual billiard tables. Everything looked filthy, but not unkempt, the grime had been there so long it had become load bearing. I was convinced that if this place was actually cleaned it would cave in on itself. My one hope was that the beer wasn't draft.

Poncho sat down at the bar and waved the bartender down for a drink. I expected a hostile cousin of

Jim to come over grumbling and hateful. Instead he looked more like Poncho's cousin, clad in leather and anger, and they seemed to know each other.

"Poncho! Brother! What are you doing here?" the bartender said, grinning and grabbing bottles of beer out of the cooler under the bar.

"Holy shit, is that you Clove?" Poncho looked properly stunned. "How the hell are you still alive?"

The man called Clove laughed, "I have my ways." Then he spotted Dirt. "Dirt? Both of you are here? Is it my birthday or something?"

"Oh, hey Clove." Dirt did not seem impressed.

"Don't be like that buddy, you still sore about that time I beat you at darts?" Clove asked.

"Yes! Why wouldn't I be? You swindled me, I hadn't even seen a dart before that day! You cheated me! Probably with black magic you son of a bitch sorcery-having asshole." I don't think I had ever seen Dirt so heated about anything before, except about werewolves, maybe.

"How about I buy you a drink little fella?"

"You buy us all drinks!" Dirt shouted.

Clove laughed again, apparently used to this. "Fine I'll buy you all drinks. I've never seen you pay for one anyway."

Dirt grinned and accepted the beer from Clove, "Deal! But you still owe me a rematch."

Poncho broke his silence, "You want a rematch against the guy who invented darts?"

"Goddamn right!"

"I'll play you in darts if you want, but when you lose don't be mad at me for another hundred years," Clove said.

"You're not the boss of me, just the boss of darts. You stick to that big shot." Dirt drank some beer, thinking. "Plus I know that people don't count as targets now."

"Let's get drunk first, you are way too sober for anything that requires coordination," Poncho said.

"Yeah I am!" Dirt nearly screamed and chugged the remainder of his almost full beer.

With the quickness of a professional bartender Clove had a fresh beer in front of Dirt, "Next round!" He looked my way and added, "Who's the quiet guy?"

"That's just Frank, he loves beer," Dirt said dismissively.

"Well get over here and drink some beers pussy!" Clove demanded, waving me over.

I don't like being called a pussy, but I do like beer, I figured they cancelled each other out and I sat down to drink my beer.

The next few hours passed with much drinking, laughing, and general drunken banter. Dirt and Poncho clearly knew Clove from long time ago and spent quite a bit of time reminiscing, I didn't follow most of it. They weren't big on details, so most of it was talk about random fights and inside jokes. Clove and Poncho seemed like old friends, brothers in arms types sharing war stories. To Dirt he seemed more like a casual acquaintance that he neither liked nor disliked. I thought Dirt liked everyone, so this came as a shock.

I wasn't sure how long we had been there, just how drunk I was, which was a shitload. It was probably a bad idea to follow through on my job in the state I was in, so I settled in to enjoy myself with my insane friends and their insane pal. As I was starting to put together the overall oddness of Clove working at a bar directly behind the address that Neph had sent me to I started to think it might not be a coincidence at all. Right about the time it started to really bother me, the enormous amount of beer and shots I had drank caught up to me and I decided to just have a good time and worry about the details in the morning.

Dirt and Poncho seemed to be really enjoying themselves reminiscing with Clove. This was the first time I can recall them letting down their guard.

"Alright you drunks, it's a few hours past last call. I have called it about a dozen times. Now get the fuck out of my bar before I kick your drunk asses out!" Clove screamed to the half a dozen drunks still in the bar. The mention of physical harm finally motivated the last few drunk patrons to stumble out of the bar.

"No way! You and me have a date with destiny Clovis," Dirt slurred out.

"Don't you call me that Dirt, I know another name for you that nobody wants to hear. Imagine the trouble that would bring into the bar tonight. I'm not sure you're drunk enough to wanna deal with that," Clove said in a tone that did not match his calm exterior.

Poncho gave Dirt a look of death, followed with some hand gestures that I was too drunk to follow.

"What! You promised me a rematch, and I'm not going anywhere until I get my satisfaction. Don't you go all sally on me now," Dirt replied.

"Darts, a destiny of darts. Why didn't you just say so Dirt? Let me lock up and we can head upstairs you drunk," Clove said seemingly calm again.

"Now this I can't wait to see," Poncho interjected.

Apparently locking up was all that closing this bar down entailed. No counting the drawer, cleaning the tables, or clearing the bottles off the bar at all. In a few seconds Clove was ready and asked. "Well that's it, let's head up. It's time for another beat down. You sure you're drunk enough this time Dirt?"

"Drunk enough biatch," Dirt replied.

We followed Clove up the stairs to what must have been where he slept. It was a large apartment that was just one big room with bed on one side and a pool table in the middle. Around the pool table were four dangerous looking biker types playing what appeared to be a game of eight ball.

What the apartment lacked in rooms was made up tenfold in decorations and empty beer cans. Every wall in the room was covered by what appeared to be incredibly intricate and likely expensive tapestries. These were not your run of the mill Persian rug designs either. Imagine one of the awesome 80's panel vans with hulking dudes, fire, and half naked women. Now imagine a whole room of those images on insanely large tapestries then add some dragons, smoke, stars, and epic battles and you get a tiny idea of the epic-ness of these. Best of all, the place was adorned with no-shit weapon racks filled with what appeared to be legitimate ancient weapons, or really good replicas. Above the fireplace was a collection of what had to be antique broadswords, below was what appeared to be a portrait of Clove all dressed up in Viking garb. Although I was certain that it was recently painted, the detail to the faux-age was impressive to say the least. Other than that I have no idea what was in the room, hell I'm only one guy. One guy with a dozen beers who could only focus on battle axes and half naked embroidered chicks covering the walls.

When Dirt and Poncho entered the room they almost screamed like little girls, almost.

"Fuck! Man I thought that Glen had awesome taste, but this is way more badass." Dirt almost giggled. He was literally fresh beer happy, which is saying something for him.

"No shit, Clove you have outdone yourself with this place," Poncho added.

"My casa is your casa, or something like that. I never got around to learning Spanish. I knew that you guys would love the place," Clove said with the same satisfaction of a proud parent. "You guys want some beers?"

Dirt, Poncho, and even myself, I am not ashamed to admit it, looked at him with disbelief.

"Yeah, stupid question. I get it," Clove said as he entered a door behind one of the tapestries.

This whole time the four guys playing eight ball didn't even acknowledge our entrance into the place, let alone greet us. Although I could swear I did notice some side long glances directed at us. Needless to say this did not sit well with Dirt who loves to be the center of attention.

"What is up gentlemen?" Dirt questioned in the groups general direction which garnered absolutely the same response as our entrance. "Hey you clowns, cat got your tongues?"

After another moment Dirt broke the silence, "I knew a cat that could do that once, it was creepy as fuck."

Dirt's attempts at getting a response continued to fail, so to me he seemed to start grasping.

Glancing at me he said, "Are you worried about Frank? Well don't, Frank is harmless, second nicest guy I know," He said this while Poncho was swinging a giant battle-axe at a target dummy I had somehow missed. He struck a far more imposing figure than me, especially considering I was having a hard time making the floor stay still.

About that time Clove came back with some beers.

"Hey Clove! What's with these assholes over there? Did you see that cat in here earlier?" Dirt asked warily.

Clove looked at the thugs playing pool and shrugged, "Don't worry about them, they hang out here all the time. They are just weird."

"By weird do you mean that they play pool out of order and can't make a straight shot to save their lives? Or by weird do you mean they looked like they had no idea there was a kitchen behind the tapestry right in front of the pool table they always hang out at?" Poncho asked after cleaving an arm off the dummy.

"Yeah, those things!" Dirt added.

Clove was clearly taken aback, his confident smirk was wiped off his face and he stammered, trying to come up with a response.

The response came from Poncho though, in the form of a battle-axe through the skull. Apparently Dirt was the only one that saw it coming, because he immediately dropped to the floor and combat rolled away from the blood spray. I can honestly say if I hadn't seen Poncho with the axe a second before I would have never believed that he threw it. I assume that he threw it anyway, but how it got there is irrelevant. Everyone else stood there looking stunned, I almost fell down.

What happened next can best be described as slaughter. Poncho pulled the axe out of Clove's skull, having crossed the room in the time it took me to realize what just happened, and rushed the frozen bikers. In the time that it took Poncho to cut the first two bikers in half with his recently claimed battle-axe the second two had taken cover between the pool table and Poncho. Which seemed like a reasonable tactic to me until Poncho flipped the table over on top of them. Before they could pull their random limbs out from underneath the slate trap Poncho hacked off everything that was still sticking out.

"Grabbed some new beers, Clove dropped those other ones, pretty shitty thing for a barkeep to do." While all of this seemed to take less than a minute somehow Dirt had made his way into the kitchen and was returning with three fresh beers right as Poncho finished taking off the last arm unfortunate enough to not be under the pool table.

"What the fuck just happened?" I choked out.

"Frank, you were supposed to be here by yourself tonight. Those guys would have killed you," said Poncho.

"I wasn't even scheduled to be up here tonight. That address was for the club in front of the bar."

"The same club that the doors behind the tapestries lead to, or some other club? Seriously is there another club here Poncho?" Dirt questioned while lifting back a tapestry covering the stairway to the first floor club.

"Oh shit, Lonald wouldn't set me up."

"Nah, he couldn't have known that Clove was so nervous about a few immortals getting murdered up."

"So what now?"

"Now you tools chug these cold ones and I'll go grab some roadies and tomorrow we can tell Lonald how you dominated everyone. Time to roll," Dirt answered while he handed Poncho the three fresh beers on his way back to the kitchen.

"What the fuck nerds, I said I would get beers and that it was time to go," Dirt said while returning from the kitchen in what seemed like less than five seconds. "Told you I wasn't going to lose at darts to that fuck again."

"Yeah you did Dirt," Poncho replied.

"You're right I did, Frank come up with a good story about how epically I threw those darts for later. Make it as good as the time I killed a dragon."

I honestly don't remember the ride home, but the morning was a different story.

# ~Dirt~

## *Poncho Kill'eth a Dragon*

*Dragons are real, and they're dickheads. They pretty much spend all their time hoarding gold and virgins when they aren't busy burning down villages. It's fucking annoying, you can't get anything done with a dragon around, unless you need a lot of fire that is.*

**Which is always.**

*Fuck off Ponch, this is my story.*

*Anyways. So me and Ponch are hanging around this village someplace, probably in Europe or France or something.*

**It was England I think.**

*Yeah, thanks Ponch, that's what I said.*

*Anyway we are in this village and Ponch just got done beating up the biggest guy in town. Village rules are like prison, you find the biggest guy around and kick his ass, or nobody will take you seriously. Problem was this village had different rules it seemed. They got real mad and came at us with sticks and torches and things. It was looking like a fight would break out and I'd have to kill the whole place.*

I can handle myself in a fight, but I didn't want Poncho to get hurt, so I tried to calm them down.

**I could have taken them.**

Sure you could have buddy.

"Hey! Calm down!" I says to them. "That was a bad dude my friend just beat the ass of. You should be thanking us."

That didn't work however, and they kept coming at us. It was pretty grim, and we were in for a fight. Then an explosion saved our lives, some building behind the angry mob burst into flames. They all jumped and looked at it, then they scattered into the night.

We never did figure out what started that fire, but it was pretty lucky timing. The end.

**You told them it was a dragon.**

Hmmm, yeah, I did.

Because it was a dragon! The same dragon you killed and they made us kings of Europe or France or wherever it fucking was! I remember now.

So the next morning all the village folks come out of their grass huts to see how many of them burned to death. It was none, which seemed pretty lucky to me. The best part was that their small idiot brains forgot about the *misunderstanding from the night before, and they no longer wanted to kill us with fire.*

*The chief or king or whatever comes up to me and says, "What horrible creature are you?"*

*Well that pissed me off pretty bad; it's not as if I would intentionally start a fight in this village knowing they would try to chase us out. But beforehand set up an elaborate distraction to make them think some magic was afoot when they did try to chase us off. And I would in no way then explain to the guy that it was a dragon.*

*So I tell him, "It wasn't me man, it was a fucking dragon."*

*"You are a dragon?" He asks me.*

*I tell you, these country types aren't too sharp.*

*"No stupid, a dragon set your shit on fire, not me," I tell him.*

*This time he gets it, and he nods a bunch, mulling it over in his tiny old man hick brain.*

*"You great warriors are welcome to anything you want here if you can slay this beast for us. Wine, women, food, a radical boom box, you name it," He says.*

**He didn't say anything about a boom box.**

*Whatever man, I'm just trying to liven things up a bit, but if you want an accurate portrayal of events you got it.*

*"Verily I doth willingly slayeth the beast thusly and betwixt thee lands yonder, verily I reckon again thy troubles be at an end," I say to the guy.*

*"Crikey that's tip top mate! What what!" he says back to me.*

**Never mind, I liked it better the first way.**

*Of course you did, those people talked like assholes, my version is way better.*

*So, we agree to go kill the dragon and that guy said we could have some pretty bitchin' stuff if we pulled it off. He told us there was a suspicious cave up on the mountain a ways away from town and that was probably a good place to look. I told him it was a shit place to look cause who wants to live in a shitty old cave, especially a badass dragon? But I'm not an expert on dragons so I said fuck it and we went up to his stupid cave.*

*By the time we get there it's dark again, and I don't want to fight a fucking dragon in the dark, it just seems like bad luck.*

*I tell Poncho, "Fuck fighting a dragon in the dark man, them sons of bitches are crazy."*

Poncho doesn't say anything, cause he's a stoic mother fucker, he just starts a fire around the corner from the cave, so the dragon can't see it. Poncho murders us up some animals and we fry them up on the fire, mix that with the wine I stole from town and we had a pretty good night.

I'm not sure how the dragon didn't hear us shouting and carrying on, but he didn't. Must have been deaf or something, which was good news. If it was an old dragon it probably would be way easier to slay.

In the morning we get our shit together to go kill this stupid thing. Poncho has his big ass axe all dulled up, which is the opposite of sharp, and pretty stupid if you ask me.

**It's more of a challenge that way.**

Sure it is buddy, doesn't explain why you took off that leather shirt thing, seems like fighting a fire breathing fucking dragon you'd want a shirt on.

**Armor is cheating.**

Whatever man, shirts aren't armor. And dragons are made of armor, so you can stick to being crazy and all burnt.

So Poncho just has pants and a dull axe. That's the front line of this little assault. I on the other hand had a shirt on, and a big rock.

"So here is the plan," I tell Ponch. "You go in yelling and making a racket and such, I'll sneak around the back and smash his head with a big rock. Dragon killed and we get a radical boom box. And if you aren't too burnt up I'll try to dump some water on you or something. That should fix you."

Poncho grumbles at me and heads into the cave, I have to move quick to keep up, he is as fast as a marsupial when he's itching for a fight.

Problem was though, when we got in there we saw no dragons, just some guy sitting in a big comfy chair reading a book. Poncho was so shocked that he forgot to yell and make noise, so I couldn't enact my part of the plan.

Reacting quickly to the new plan I move in front of Ponch, diplomacy was never his strong suit.

"Hey you shitty fuck face, let's fight!" I say to the guy.

He looks at me over his glasses and smiles. That's when I figure it out, dragons can turn into humans. This was our chance, we could take him out before he got all big and fire breathing.

"Go Poncho! Get him before he changes!" I yell to Ponch. But he doesn't move, idiot.

**It wouldn't have been fair.**

*Fuck fair man, the guy was a dragon, plain as day. I mean come on, the place was littered with loot, gold and weapons, you name it and he had it. I know he had some virgins hiding around there also.*

**There were no virgins.**

*Dammit Poncho, whose story is this? Plus I know you're a virgin because Glen told me.*

**That's a lie.**

*Whatever, now fuck off. I am trying to tell people how you wrecked a dragon.*

*But Poncho doesn't move, he waits for the guy to stand up. I make for cover cause this cave doesn't seem big enough for a dragon and I don't want to get smashed into the wall when he changes. Poncho just stands there looking at the guy.*

*"I didn't expect you to come so early," The guy says.*

*"It's not that far of a walk from town man," I tell him from behind my safety rock.*

*"You know what I mean, I didn't expect this for at least a few hundred more years," he says.*

*"Well times up dude, you don't even have a few hundred seconds left," I said. I was pretty proud of that*

*one too, but this asshole doesn't even chuckle. Some people just don't recognize a killer line when they hear it.*

**I thought it was pretty funny.**

*I know you did man, that's why we make a good team. Then the guy rushes Poncho and he slams the end of his axe into the dragons nose. He starts bleeding everywhere and cursing, but he still didn't turn into a dragon.*

*This is when I really started to get nervous, this guy might be the worst possible thing in the world.*

*A fucking dragon vampire!*

*They can only turn dragon at night, but they are super strong and they have to kill other dragons for food. It is the single most terrifying thing in the history of time.*

**Dragon vampires aren't real.**

*Not after you killed that one, you may have saved the planet that day. Maybe the universe.*

*We had one advantage though, he was stuck in human form and that meant Poncho had a chance.*

*They fought like two tempests colliding, one like a big half naked tempest with a dull axe, the other like a kind of old looking tempest with a robe on. It was nuts. The dragon came rushing at Poncho again, blood all shooting out his nose like fire, but Poncho sidestepped and bashed him on the back of the head.*

*The dragon didn't fall this time though, he stumbled a little, but stayed up. He eyed Poncho like a tiger, like an old looking tiger in a robe would eyeball a moose, a half-naked moose with a dull axe.*

**Holy shit, you have the worst analogies.**

*Fuck you man, you want to tell this story, No? Then please shut up.*

*So then the dragon pulls out a dagger from his sleeve, it looks pretty sharp. Poncho is in trouble now, but he waits, like a half-naked dull axe having statue. The dragon attacks, he rushes forward, feints left, ducks and comes up with the dagger point headed straight for Poncho's exposed chest.*

*Then Poncho head butts him and the dragon crumples to the ground limp, like an old looking jellyfish wearing a robe. Then Poncho smashes the dragons head into the stone with his axe.*

*After that we went back to town and we were heroes. Until the guy Ponch beat up the first day we were there woke up from his coma. Then they decided that maybe we should go someplace else. So we did, fuck those guys anyway, should have let the dragon eat them.*

**At least the let us keep the boom box.**

*Yeah, that thing was radical.*

# Breakfast

You haven't lived until you've woken up in the backseat of your own car covered in puke, using someone else's bloody battle axe as a pillow, all while sleeping on a bed of empty beer cans that you cannot know for sure who actually drank. Imagine that, and then imagine that situation in front of a shitty road side diner and you have just experienced my morning. Plus I really hate breakfast. The sun is never brighter than when you wake up unsure of where you are or how you got there.

When I finally fell out of the backseat and brushed as much of the puke off my coat as I could manage I noticed Dirt waving at me through the window with a stupid grin and a fork supporting a healthy amount of pancakes. I stared at him stupidly for a moment, my hung over brain attempting to decipher how glass worked, and made for the door.

The diner was your typical greasy spoon, not a place you would ever eat at by choice, but when drunk or recently drunk it was heaven. If you liked breakfast anyway. Everything looked sticky and it smelled like hell, my stomach was in no mood for this type of assault and almost revolted. I gained control over my urge to vomit and went to sit down with Dirt and Poncho.

They were sitting in a booth opposite each other and I unconsciously opted to slide in next to Dirt after seeing how poorly Poncho's mass fit into the seat. Dirt had a spread of virtually every breakfast food in front of him, all partially consumed. Poncho had one empty plate that no doubt had held a large portion of meat.

"About time you got up sleepy head," Dirt said past a mouthful of awful.

I managed a grunt of pure misery. Poncho nodded.

"I need you to talk some sense into Ponch here, he has gone balls out crazy on this one."

"About what?" I asked reflexively, I doubted I really wanted to get involved in their shit so soon after my back seat slumber.

"Poncho says pancakes are gross," Dirt said with over exaggerated disbelief and spitting food across the table.

"Pancakes are gross," I mumbled.

"Do you kiss your mother with that filthy mouth? Seriously that filth coming out of the two of you fucks' mouths is ruining my breakfast." Dirt seemed honestly upset.

"I just don't like breakfast." Another mumble slipped out.

"Da Fuck you say Frank?" Dirt said while standing up on the seat of the booth. "Did Poncho put you up to this shit? Seriously Frank, tell me you actually like breakfast or I will pour this syrup in Poncho's beard and right down your lying throat! I am seriously going to fuck both of you clowns up with syrup."

"Dirt, I am really hung over and I am just not a big fan of breakfast." Although I am not sure if I said that because I don't like breakfast or if I really wanted to see him pour syrup down Poncho's beard.

"Okay, so you assholes hate the only meal where it's acceptable to dump maple syrup on literally everything on your plate. Maple syrup is the second greatest invention in the history of ever, an entire countries economy is built on harvesting and selling it! Seriously go to Canada and start saying crazy shit like that, it is fucking illegal. They will throw you in syrup rehab. Oh, that is assuming that the Royal Canadian Mounted Police Officer that responds to the locals beating the shit out of your blasphemous syrup hating cock holster doesn't beat you to death first," Dirt said to the chorus of morons actually cheering for his speech by the time he finished. "Frank, chug that fucking bottle of syrup or I will never talk to you again."

"Promise?" I replied over the drums in my head.

"That is it. You fucks have pushed me over the line."

I had a hard time keeping track of what Dirt was saying at this point, but somewhere between telling me that he was going club me to death with a maple branch and explaining how he would have a moose drenched in syrup violate me, Poncho casually pulled a beer from somewhere and slid it across the table to him.

"Dirt, sit down and drink your beer. We don't need another hostage situation. This isn't Canada and they don't care what your reasons are here," Poncho said while cracking open a beer.

Dirt promptly sat down and shotgunned the impeccably timed beer. "Your right Ponch, maple syrup is kinda overrated anyways."

Poncho slid another beer across the table to me and I yet again fought the urge to vomit.

"It'll make you feel better Frank," Dirt said polishing off his can and tossing it behind him with a flourish. I shook my head grimacing as a response. Dirt took this as an invitation for a free beer and snatched it up.

"What exactly happened last night?" I asked.

"You really don't remember?" Dirt replied digging back into his food.

"I remember going to a bar, talking to a guy, then you guys killing all those guys."

"That about sums it up," Poncho said.

"Yeah man, but don't forget the part where I beat Clove in darts!" Dirt added.

"What happened after that?"

"Nothing special, you passed out, we drove around a while and came here," Poncho said unhelpfully.

That was all I was going to get out of them in the way of a straight answer so I decided to leave it. They probably just did something ridiculous anyway.

"So did you have anything planned for after breakfast?" I wasn't sure I wanted to hear the answer.

"We are going to go see Lonald with you," Dirt said shoveling more food in his mouth.

It was a surprisingly direct response, and I hadn't been expecting it.

"Why?" I asked. It was all I could manage.

"Do you really need me to explain it?" Dirt took my blank stare as a yes and sighed. "Well we helped you with your thing last night, which you would surely have been killed if you went by yourself. So we figure that Lonald will see what a good team we all are and let us come work for him on a regular basis."

"Couldn't you just go to him by yourselves?"

Dirt scoffed and looked away, irritated by some unknown slight. Poncho chuckled a little and took over.

"We had a small... disagreement a few years back and we weren't sure if he would still be mad. We had to get back in his good graces before we showed again. Just to be safe."

I had a hard time believing that these two ever thought about safety before doing anything. But then again, Lonald did have a small army of goons at his compound, I guess even they had their limits.

"So you guys have been using me to get back in his good graces? Has this whole thing been a setup?" I asked feeling a little hurt.

"Not at all Frank, we were just doing our own thing. We never knew he would want to hire you and give us this opportunity, it is a happy coincidence though," Dirt said.

Bullshit. It had to be, but it didn't really matter. No matter the reason I was in this to the end.

"It's not bullshit Frank, you'll see when we get there," said Poncho.

I sighed, defeated once again. "When do we leave?"

Dirt wiped his mouth on his shirt and said, "Right now!" Then he hopped out of the booth and ran for the door.

Poncho slid out and walked after him. I noticed that neither one had left money on the table and had no intention of doing so. I considered leaving money, but judging from past experiences I doubted anyone would notice. I got up and walked to my car not feeling the least bit guilty for not paying.

The drive to Lonald's was quiet. Dirt appeared to have slipped into a food coma and Poncho wasn't much of a talker anyway. I relished the quiet and the chance to let my guts relax. Before long we had pulled up to the gate to Lonald's estate, it opened as soon as my car got close and I drove up to the house. While on the long wooded drive Dirt and Poncho roused themselves from their lounging, they looked unnaturally alert.

I understood why when we approached the house, every member of Lonald's army had a gun pointed at us. The gunmen didn't move or issue any commands, so I shut my car off and kept my hands on the wheel. Maybe they would just kill Dirt and Poncho, it was wishful thinking, but it was all I had.

Poncho did nothing other than stare at them, and to his credit even that made a few of them back up a couple of paces. Dirt's tactic was different, he climbed out the back window of the car and started yelling "Parley!"

Over and over while running around the car. I braced for the hail of bullets, but it never came, I made a mental note to never attempt this maneuver, despite Dirt's success with it.

The fact that they didn't shoot after all his sudden movements led me to believe that they had been instructed not to shoot. This was a small comfort, as having a gun pointed at you is never fun.

Then Poncho got out of the car and I was sure they would fire, if only out of reflex, but again it didn't happen. Poncho leaned on the car hood and crossed his arms letting everyone present know he could care less. Dirt continued to circle the car.

"Parley! It's the law of the sea! You have to parley with us! Parley!"

On his next pass in front of the car Poncho stuck out his arm and clothes lined him. Dirt's feet kept going until his whole body was parallel with the ground, then he fell, flat on his back.

"Par..." Dirt broke into a fit of coughing, "ley."

If they didn't shoot after this they weren't going to, so I got out and leaned next to Poncho. I doubt I looked nearly as intimidating, but I was sure the association was enough. Dirt stood up and dusted himself off, he looked like he was about to start running again, but Poncho shook his head and he settled down.

Just about the time things were at peak awkwardness Lonald came outside, he gestured for the goons to lower their weapons and smiled. It dawned on me that this was all for show, he had no intention of killing anyone, he just wanted to show us that he could. This guy was more devious than he made it seem.

"Hey Lonald! Been a while!" Dirt said waving. "Parley!"

Lonald frowned in the judgmental way a parent might when presented with a disobedient child, he looked more troubled than angry and I guessed that was a good thing. I couldn't help but wonder what had transpired between them; surely something trivial that time had blown out of proportion.

"I have to say," Lonald said dramatically. "I never thought I'd see you guys again."

Dirt did his best to look hurt. "Did you think we would hold a grudge about you betraying us and leaving us for dead? Clearly you don't know us that well. I mean that is literally ancient history."

This came as a shock, I just assumed that they had somehow screwed Lonald over, not the other way around.

"If I had a dime for every time someone left me for dead I would have...." Dirt trailed off and looked at Poncho while alternating between holding up seven or eight fingers. "But that is just from you Ponch, how many other people have left me for dead?"

"Are you counting people who left you for dead when you were drunk or not?" Poncho asked nonchalantly.

"Both."

"Well more than eight I guess and less than the cost of a good whore." Poncho answered seemingly happy with his cleverness.

"Right then, so more than eight times and less than the cost of good whore," Dirt explained incredibly happy with his cleverness.

"Well, now that we have settled that unfortunate display of basic arithmetic and lack of simple etiquette, I would like to offer my most sincere apology for my past transgressions. We were all different people then," Lonald said while performing an apologetic bow.

"No worries, Ponch burned your house down that one time," Dirt said.

"Which time was that?" Lonald questioned seemingly agitated again.

"Just the once! How about we leave the past in the past and celebrate the future with a drink?" Poncho answered before Dirt could make things even worse.

"Well said my large friend, let us enjoy an evening of drink and conversation," Lonald said while ushering the lot of us into his mansion.

"Sold!" Dirt exclaimed while running past the confused guard and through the front door. Poncho followed shortly after, at this point the guard decided he was no longer needed at his post and entered the house as well.

"I worried for your safety Frank, I might have gotten an hour of sleep last night. You really should have called ahead, especially when arriving with mixed company. I expected more of you, and expect more in the future, friend," Lonald said while putting his arm around me and leading me into the palace he called a house.

"Sorry?" I said, not sure what else to say.

"Don't trouble yourself Frank, so long as they remain civil you have nothing to worry about," Lonald said in a way that really meant, if things go south I would be the one to pay.

Considering how well I was getting to know those two I've never been more unsettled in my entire life.

Lonald led me back to his study a short distance from the entrance where Dirt and Poncho had already made themselves at home. So far off to a bad start, Poncho was drinking liquor straight out of a crystal decanter and doing nothing else in particular. Dirt had again managed to find beer and was roaming around the room fiddling with anything he came across. These guys were going to get me killed after all, not from monsters and psychos, but from upsetting a tidy rich person's sense of manners.

Lonald was unperturbed however and gestured for me to have a seat.

"Gentlemen," Lonald said addressing Dirt and Poncho. "Have a seat and we can get down to business."

Poncho moved closer, but made no indication that he would be sitting. Dirt came over from whatever thing he was breaking on Lonald's desk and flopped himself down into the seat next to me spilling beer on the expensive looking leather. I cringed internally waiting for Lonald to signal the hit squad to take us out. But he didn't seem to notice, maybe he really was the nice guy he had always appeared to be and I was just being paranoid.

I did notice that he didn't offer me a drink this time, maybe he was mad after all. It was hard to tell with him, he just sat down and smiled his nice guy smile.

"So what can I do for you fellows? Our mutual friend Frank is already in my employ, I assume you want a finder's fee or some other ridiculous demand for me stealing him away from you?" Lonald asked. "I certainly couldn't let him go under any circumstances if that is your aim." He added for good measure.

"Frank can dance if he wants to, we are his friends and if we don't dance he can leave his friends behind," Dirt replied.

"What?" Lonald and I said at the same time.

Then the most terrifying thing I had seen so far happened, Poncho started laughing uncontrollably. Even Lonald looked startled.

"Frank can do what Frank wants, we don't want him back," Dirt said with assertion.

Poncho was still trying to regain his menacing composure and was actually wiping tears from his eyes from laughing so hard. To Lonald's credit he bounced back quickly.

"So what do you want then?" He asked cautiously.

"Oh nothing much," Dirt said slyly. "We just want in on the action."

This came as a shock, these two didn't seem like the type to work for anyone, ever. I was sure something else was going on, but I didn't have a clue what.

"You want to form a pact?" Lonald asked suspiciously.

Poncho had gained control of himself by this time and said, "In the manner of the old ways."

"If my memory serves me as well as it has in the past, I do believe that the two of you have never actually cared for the intricacies and politics involved in the forming of a pact," Lonald said with a certain amount of discomfort.

He seemed more intrigued than I had imagined. What could he gain from the two of them, sure Poncho was a force to be reckoned with, he was after all the scariest person I have ever seen, but Dirt was uncontrollable in a different way. Where Poncho's anger and demeanor might get you into a bar fight, Dirt's randomness was the exact opposite of everything that Lonald stood for.

"Too many failures can change a man's mindset," Poncho said in the most serene voice you could picture coming from a man his size.

"Well said Poncho, should we begin the pact ceremony tonight?" Lonald questioned while eyeing me.

"Frank's cool, he said something about loving to hang out on your porch earlier. Or something like that," Dirt chimed in. "Actually, Frank, go hang out on the porch. We have to apologize to Lonald for Poncho burning his house down, and he will never say how sorry he is with you being in the room. He does have an image to uphold, you wouldn't want to mess that up right?"

The only way I could respond was a quick head nod followed by a quicker exit. Whatever was about to happen I doubted that I wanted to see it, plus it was a really nice porch.

To my surprise, not even two minutes later a car pulled into the driveway. Even more to my surprise it looked just like my car. Before any of this actually sank in, Dirt rolled down the window.

"Shake a leg Franky, we have a big day tomorrow."

Before I could even figure out how Dirt made it to my car without me seeing him, let alone how the car was no longer right in front of the house where it was originally parked, Poncho and Lonald strode out the front door.

"Frank, I hope you found my porch most comforting," Lonald said as he clasped my shoulder affectionately.

"Hope we didn't keep you too long Frank, looks like Dirt is ready to rock already," Poncho said while pointing towards my car.

I did what any totally confused man would do, I gave a silly head nod to Lonald and went to sit in the backseat of my own car.

"Perhaps you should drive," Lonald said while shaking hands with Poncho.

Moments later the big man was pulling out of Lonald's estate with Dirt in the passenger's seat, while I sat quietly in the back seat more confused than ever. I fell asleep in the backseat before we got out of the driveway, woke for a few seconds when we got to my house, stumbled inside, and promptly fell back asleep on my couch.

# Road Trip

"Good morning, you fucking clowns!" Dirt exclaimed at seriously too early in the morning.

I sat up on the couch, trying to let the small amount of sunlight either lull me back to sleep or convince my brain to actually wake up. It was far too much sun for sleep to win, so I got up and was stumbling towards the restroom when Poncho's large paw grabbed my shoulder to steady me. For the life of me, I have no idea how a man so large managed to sneak up on me again.

"Time to have some fun Frank," Poncho said dryly.

"You've got that right buddy," I replied, seriously it's hard to be mad at someone as large as Poncho, at least to their face.

At this point Dirt was honking the horn to the tune of some song I have never heard, or it could have been a Dirt original.

Dirt stopped his horn melody when I was a few feet from my car. "Ponch, are you seriously going to let Frank beat you to the car?" Then he began his stupid horn song again.

"Frank, you should take a shower," Poncho said.

"What about Dirt, he is already in the car waiting?"

"We could sit in here for several hours before he finishes that song, until then he won't even notice we aren't actually coming," Poncho said with a sly looking smile.

I was relieved, two day old vomit and stale beer wasn't exactly the cologne I wanted to wear in public, and it didn't look like they were going to give me time to freshen up. I handled my bathroom needs quickly and went to the car; Poncho had beaten me much to Dirt's displeasure.

"Dammit Frank," Dirt said shaking his head. "I thought you had him this time."

Poncho grinned, they were both in good spirits this morning, and it was contagious. Despite everything that had happened since I met these two I found myself smiling and looking forward to what came next. This made me nervous about the state of my sanity though, but I pushed the feeling aside and basked in the moment.

I got in the backseat of my car, I was starting to get used to it. Dirt passed me a partially consumed box of donuts and a coffee, I almost wept at the kindness. No matter how much I don't care for breakfast food, donuts were a different story, they are like dessert that you can eat first thing in the morning.

"So where are we going?" I asked past a mouthful of Boston crème.

Dirt's mood shifted, he let out a long grumbling sigh and muttered something at the steering wheel. I looked to Poncho for an answer.

"We have to go pick someone up," Poncho said not sounding happy either.

"Who?" I asked, my curiosity roused.

"Our babysitter, Lonald's second-in-command watchdog, sent along to make sure we don't backstab him or something," Dirt all but shouted.

I started to ask who again, but Dirt's ramblings were not yet done.

"We are Dirt and Poncho, what is he thinking? We are men of our words, how could he think we would do a thing like that?"

"He is doing it because we haven't exactly seen eye to eye in the past," Poncho answered. "He doesn't trust us."

"Doesn't trust us? What have we ever done to him?" Dirt said shaking his fists to the sky.

"Well," Poncho began.

Dirt wasn't going to let him finish. "Besides burning his house down, besides fighting all his dudes that one time, besides that other time when you kept sneaking onto his estate and punching all his horses, and especially besides all those years we refused to talk to him. What does he have against us?"

"You stole his hat once too," Poncho added helpfully.

"Oh shit, I forgot about that. I bet that's it, he thinks this is all an elaborate ruse to steal his hats," Dirt said scratching his scruffy chin in thought.

I cannot stress enough that he said this in no way sarcastically, he was dead serious, and that didn't worry me at all. Which worried me.

Dirt started driving, having accepted that Lonald had a person watching him to protect his hats. Not that I had ever seen Lonald wearing a hat, but maybe that was because he was afraid they would be stolen.

"So which one of his goons is he sending?" I asked.

"The worst one, a mean, hateful monster of a person," Dirt stated gravely. "She is more horrible than you can imagine."

"She?"

"Neph," Poncho said.

"She's pretty," I said before I could stop myself. I should've taken a longer and colder shower.

Dirt almost crashed the car spinning his head to stare at me in wide eyed horror. "Pretty?" he shouted.

I was embarrassed now, but my path was committed. "Well yeah," I stammered. "She is a little cold, though."

Poncho chuckled.

Dirt's outrage quickly passed and turned into something worse. "Frank has a crush!" he exclaimed. "Frank and Neph sitting in a tree." He seemed to have forgotten the next part and improvised. "D-I-S-E-M-B-O-W-E-L-E-D! Cause that's what she would do to you if she got you into a tree Frank. I've seen it."

I took this as another one of his ridiculous stories, until I noticed Poncho nodding in agreement. That made me nervous.

"Wait," I said, a thought forming. "Neph is Lonald's second-in-command?"

"Has been for a long time," Poncho said.

"So, are they together?" I asked meekly.

"Yeah dummy that's what second-in-command means," Dirt said laughing.

"I think he meant to ask if they are together in the biblical sense Dirt," Poncho said.

"Well I guess they could be, she might be one of his followers or some shit like that, but people haven't done that sort of thing in a long time. Honestly you should know better Ponch."

Poncho sighed pretending he wasn't enjoying Dirt's feigned ignorance. "He wants to know if they are fucking."

"Oh, why didn't you say so?" Dirt said. "Probably."

I was a little disappointed, but it was for the best. Her being one of them meant bad news, although Dirt seemed unsure, so there was a chance. A chance for what I didn't know, I guess I'm just a hopeless romantic.

They were relatively silent as we drove to pick up Neph, and before long we pulled into a vacant parking lot.

"This is where we are picking her up?" I asked confused. I was expecting Lonald's house, or anywhere else really.

"That's what he said," Dirt said referring to Lonald.

I scanned the emptiness for Neph, there was nothing here, not even a stray bum. As I was looking around trying to spot anything the opposite car door opened and Neph sat down next to me. I jumped a little, there was no way she could have been hiding and she damn sure wasn't there a second ago.

"Let's get this over with," Neph said unhappily.

"Oh yes, let's," Dirt complained. "This is going to be a barrel of laughs." He started driving, grumbling to himself.

"That reminds me, where are we going and what are we doing anyway?" I asked, attempting to break the ice.

True to form Dirt forgot about Neph and took a deep breath in preparation for what was surely going to be idiotic.

"Lonald wants us to go kill a Frankenstein."

I waited for the punch line, or at least more of his usual gibberish. But it didn't come.

"Didn't you say Frankensteins weren't real?" I asked.

"They aren't," Neph said unamused.

"Well not the kind you are thinking of, they are more like a big dumb guy that's real hard to kill. Like Ponch, only uglier," Dirt grinned.

"That hurts," Poncho countered with little reaction.

"They are nothing of the sort," Neph said trying to shut this conversation down.

Dirt was unaffected. "Yes they are," he said defiantly.

"It's a gross generalization," Neph argued.

"So this Frankenstein isn't a big ugly dumb guy then?" Dirt fired back.

"Well, in this instance he is. But that doesn't mean..." She was cut off.

"Frankenstein!" Dirt shouted, thumping the steering wheel victoriously. "He has bolts in his neck, stitches all over, hates fire and kills for fun and profit with a samurai sword."

"None of that is true." Neph was apparently not used to arguing with Dirt.

"Prove to me that it isn't then."

"You know I can't prove any of that right now." Neph was running out of ground.

"Then I win! Shut your face lady!" Dirt said with a little hostility.

She looked as if she wanted to continue and even looked at me for help. I was honored, but realized that there was nothing I could do.

"It's best to just drop it, if you don't he won't stop," I told her.

"Yeah I won't!" Dirt said turning the radio on, presumably to drown out his new nemesis.

Everyone accepted this as quiet time and we rode for several hours listening to music I am pretty sure Dirt recorded himself. It was so entrancing that I have no idea how long we were in the car. When we left the city Dirt shut the radio off and I finally came back to reality and guessed it was ok to talk again.

"Where are we going?" I asked genuinely curious.

"We are going to kill a Frankenstein Frank. Haven't you been paying attention?" Dirt replied.

"Of course-" I started to reply only to be cut off by Dirt who was not quite done.

"Of course you have, I got us some rooms set up for tonight," Dirt said.

"Why on earth would we need rooms for tonight?" Neph questioned.

"To sleep in! Ponch I don't think she knows what rooms for the night mean," Dirt said clearly humored.

"I know what rooms are for. But this is only a six hour drive. You do realize that there are substantially more than six hours in a day right?" Neph asked with no small amount of sarcasm.

"Of course I know that, there must be way more hours in a day than six. Ponch, how many hours are in one day?"

"More than six," Poncho explained.

"See, we both know that shit. I hope that you are satisfied Neph," Dirt said.

"Delighted. However, if we are only driving six hours and both of you scholars agree that there are way more hours in a day, why the fuck did you get us rooms for the night?" Neph asked, clearly annoyed.

"I wouldn't expect you to understand so I will spell it out for you. There are three awesome reasons we are getting rooms tonight. One, I have some stops to make. Important shit that you could never understand. Two, everyone knows that Frankensteins are slower in the morning hours. Three, staying in rooms is tons of fun. They have little cold boxes that are always full of little beers and shit," Dirt explained.

"When would you ever need a little beer?" I asked.

"Goddammit Frank, sometimes it's nice to try new things!" Dirt said obviously frustrated.

This was the most information we were likely to get out of him, in an unspoken agreement we let it drop. We drove a while more in silence, the scenery passing by in the usual boring flat way it does in the middle of nowhere. After a few more miles of quiet we pulled up to one of the most run down gas stations I had ever seen. I didn't think they still had pumps anywhere that didn't have card readers on them, but here I was looking right at one.

Dirt stopped the car at the pump and hopped out.

"Fill it up guys, I got an errand to run," He said leaning through the window.

Poncho and Neph didn't move, so it was up to me. I got out and started filling up the tank. Dirt had disappeared behind the station, I decided that his errand must have been either steal beer, or use the bathroom. Both seemed equally likely with him, hell it was also likely that he was around back riding a dinosaur for all the sense he made.

When the tank was full I went in to pay, I briefly considered buying snacks or drinks. At least until I saw the layer of dust covering everything inside, there was no telling how long it had been since someone actually purchased something from this hell hole. I paid for the gas and retreated to the car where Poncho and Neph hadn't yet killed each other.

We waited for several minutes and Dirt still hadn't returned. Poncho didn't seem bothered, but Neph was starting to fidget, she wasn't the type to wait I wagered.

"What is he doing?" I asked also getting a little impatient.

Neph scowled and muttered to herself. Poncho shrugged. I found myself missing Dirt's ability to tie a group together. Receiving no answers from them I waited, and as soon as I had made peace with waiting he came strolling out of the front door with a duffle bag over his shoulder grinning like usual. He tossed it in the trunk and took his place behind the wheel. I almost forgot how odd it used to be that he could open the trunk without the key.

"What the hell were you doing?" Neph asked angrily.

"It's a secret," Dirt smirked. "Only one more stop before little beers time."

"I can hardly contain myself," Neph filled the silence.

I was sure this would turn into another ridiculous argument, but Neph let it go while Dirt turned back the way we had come from. At least I am pretty sure it was the way we came from. After Dirt pulled a u-turn ten minutes later I was just starting to be a little annoyed at myself for not saying anything when Dirt stopped the car, grabbed the duffle bag and placed it behind the no u-turn sign before the pull-through. If I had learned anything about Dirt it was never to start a rational conversation with him. Ten minutes later we passed the ancient gas station and were once again heading towards 'Frankenstein' or whatever Dirt and Poncho decided to call the mark.

I must have fallen asleep in the car because when I woke up Dirt was once again nowhere to be seen. Neph looked like a caged animal and Poncho was sitting on the hood of the car throwing rocks at the ancient car wash sign. I decided that we would likely be here for a while and joined Poncho at stoning the dilapidated sign.

"How long have I been asleep?" I questioned the vw flipper.

"Well Frank, we have been here for at least an hour. I honestly don't know how long you were sleeping before we arrived though," Poncho said earnestly.

"And Dirt?" I questioned.

Poncho didn't answer, just gave me an odd look that looked a lot like he had no idea.

I sighed and started chucking rocks at the sign, it was oddly satisfying and the challenge of hitting certain parts kept us entertained for quite a while. When we were in our sixth round of 'who can get a rock in the hole first.' Neph got out of that car and wandered off kicking the ground and muttering. Poncho and I exchanged glances and shrugged, then went back to our game, it was getting pretty intense.

Hours later Poncho was beating me 16-3, but I think he was sandbagging. I was about to go for the winning rock and put my score up to four when Dirt finally showed up, looking a little worn out.

"Let's roll out," Dirt said wearily.

Neph looked like she was about to explode, but managed to refrain and sullenly got back into the car. The rest of us followed suit and we were quickly on our way down the road again, just as the sun was starting to set.

For once Dirt didn't seem very talkative and it had been a long day. I think we were all ready call it a night. Time passed and before I knew it we pulled up to a shady looking motel.

"Home sweet home bitches," Dirt almost yelled waking me yet again.

As Dirt pulled halfway onto the sidewalk outside the motel office I managed to get my eyes somewhat adjusted to the now dark sky. The darkness enveloped me with its too familiar warmth. Once again I was on the path to salvation. That was probably just the night-madness setting in. I don't do well without a real night's sleep. I was almost too tired to realize that Dirt ran back to the car to jump in and put it into park. I guessed I was not the only one who had a long day.

"Whew, that was fucking close Frank. I don't think I could explain that happening again. Shit they would probably ban me forever," Dirt laughed.

That being said Dirt hustled past me into the office and hit the service bell about fifty times, and I am pretty sure it was in the tune of the theme song to one of those stupid daytime game shows.

Stumbling over himself, the attendant entered the room and placed the service bell under the counter while Dirt was in the second frame of the song again.

"Well, well, well," the walking grease fire of an attendant said looking us all up and down, only to focus on Dirt.

"My man! It would appear that you are still in short supply of shampoo out in these parts," Dirt said smiling.

"Clever as always, you have a bit of nerve coming here again," the grease fire said while turning on the no-vacancy sign.

"Cletus that is no way to treat an old friend. We need four of your best rooms friend," Dirt explained.

"Well, we have two rooms. However, I'll lose my job if I give one of them to you. By the way, my name still isn't Cletus."

"You look great Cletus! Plus the rooms aren't for me," Dirt grinned.

"Great, if you mean that I look like I cannot stand long enough to take a shower because some asshole ran me over while taking out three of our best rooms...." Cletus started only to be cut off by Dirt.

"Fuck yeah that's what I meant. I thought you were dead after that shit," Dirt laughed to himself. "Seriously, that was one crazy night."

"Oh yeah, crazy is right for sure. I would have been dead too, but luckily I didn't bleed to death because someone parked a dump truck on my leg." He was getting angry now.

"See the nice things I do for my friends Cletus?" Dirt said proudly. "Now how about those rooms?"

"Sure thing, one-thousand dollars. Each." Cletus looked dead serious.

I felt the uncontrollable urge to get the hell out of there, but I was tired, and I was pretty sure Dirt could pull this off.

"That's cheaper than last time! You got a deal!" Dirt said slapping a stack of bills on the counter.

Cletus looked quite surprised, and a little defeated, but he took the money and handed Poncho some keys. Making sure Dirt didn't touch them, then limped into the backroom he came from.

"Is there anyone you haven't attempted to murder?" Neph asked.

"You are a rude lady, I just got us cozy rooms for the night just like I said I would," Dirt said indignantly.

"You also said you reserved them," she replied with venom.

"Basically I did, me and Cletus go way back. Didn't you see the deal he gave us?"

Frustrated Neph shook her head and walked outside, we followed after her. Poncho had been holding the keys and when we arrived at the matching rooms he handed one to me, unlocked his, went inside and closed the door.

I looked at Neph, secretly glad we had to share a room, but also terrified that she would gut me if got too close to her.

"You kids have fun! See you in the morning," Dirt said waving and walking back to the car. We watched him get in and drive off to who knows where.

Neph snatched the key out of my hand an unlocked the door, we entered into exactly what you would expect from a shitty roadside motel. Well it would have been what you expect if you were on your honeymoon, and poor. Everything was red and pink with cupids adorning virtually every surface, and the bed was shaped like a heart. Everything was dusty and held the stains of countless horrible occurrences. It also reeked of industrial cleaners, but even that couldn't wash away the lingering air of uncleanliness.

Neph surveyed the room with cold regard. "Don't even think about it Frank, throw some towels on the floor," she said crushing my hopes.

I sighed and grabbed some threadbare towels from the bathroom and tried my best to make bed on the floor without having to actually touch it. Neph didn't wait for me to get settled, just shut the lights off. I heard the rustling that I imagined was her getting undressed then the bed creaking as she settled.

"Stay on the floor," she said becoming still.

She didn't need an or else. I laid down on my makeshift towel bed and did my best to sleep, I was going to be hurting in the morning.

"Frank, get in the bed. Keep your clothes on and stay on the far left side. Take off your shirt and I will gut you in your sleep. If you come close to my side I will do much worse than that," Neph said without an ounce of humor.

"Can I take my shoes off," I asked meekly.

"Your choice Frank," Neph replied.

I left my shoes on as I climbed into the far left side of the giant heart-shaped bed, semi-praying to whatever deities were listening that I didn't shift in my sleep.

# Frankensteins

I was sure that I wouldn't get an ounce of sleep. I was convinced that if I actually nodded off I would somehow get to close to Neph and spend my last few moments of consciousness wondering why it was so cold in our honeymoon suite. Especially after the momentary terror when I first woke from an incredibly vivid dream.

The dream started out fine, more than fine really. I had managed the courage to finally tell Neph how I felt about her. She took it in stride. "Frank, I have always known how you felt."

"In my heart, I knew that to be true," I replied.

At this point in time I realize that Neph was no longer wearing her traveling clothes, or any clothes for that matter.

"Frank, ravage me you bad, bad boy," she teased seductively.

Just when things were starting to get interesting I noticed an odd warmth in my stomach. "So this is how love feels," I teased back.

I looked down to see my intestines being pulled from my insides into the night. Then I followed the trail of my intestines, which didn't hurt at all, right to Neph's awaiting mouth. She was eating my goods like fucking spaghetti.

Strangely enough, I didn't sleep all that well after that.

Back on the floor.

Sleeping on shitty towels.

Still fucking terrified.

Why couldn't I sleep in Poncho's room? He probably wouldn't wake me up to kill me. I am sure Dirt was having a grand ol' time, wherever he was.

It seemed that only moments after I had finally fallen back into a fitful sleep the door sounded like it was coming off of its hinges.

"Wake up and wash the sex juices off of your old ass Frank. Meeting in Poncho's room in ten," Dirt screamed from the other side of the door.

I dragged myself off the floor feeling every ache my body could produce all at the same time. I looked around groggily and spotted Neph coming out of the bathroom wrapped in a towel with the steam from the shower rolling around her, not wanting to let her go. As she ventured further from the door the warm mists fell to the floor, unable to sustain the chase, and willing to let itself die instead of lose her.

Morning brain makes you stupid.

"If I wanted you on the floor I would have left you there Frank," she said.

"But you said," I trailed off.

"You think I wouldn't warn you at least once?" she smirked.

I'm sure she would have broken something on me had I tried anything, but her smile made me curse my cowardice.

"You better shower, I'm curious to see what those imbeciles have planned," she said

I grumbled incoherently for lack of anything better to say and went to shower. I couldn't decide if Neph was messing with me or not. She wasn't nearly as cold as she had been the day before, and nothing had changed. I never could figure women out, immortal ones were probably way worse.

A few minutes later I was showered and waiting in Poncho's room. Dirt had called this meeting and he was late, I could barely hide my surprise. After seeing Poncho's room I started to suspect that the room I had stayed in wasn't the honeymoon suite. His room was decorated much in the fashion I would expect from a medieval themed restaurant. There were plastic weapons and shields all over the walls, and the wallpaper was supposed to look like stone. His bed shaped like a throne, covered red velvet and fake furs.

We were staying in one of those theme room sex hotels. Dirt's idea of a joke no doubt. I couldn't help but wonder what he was doing here the last time he visited. However, I did have a few ideas as to why he was now banned.

"About time." Neph grunted as Dirt strolled into the room.

"You know what Neph, I resent that," Dirt replied. "I have been out all night getting everything in order for the plan to be awesome."

"I am sure you have," Neph started, only to be cut off as Dirt tossed a large leather bag into her lap and exited the room again.

He returned a few seconds later, sat one bag on the ground beside him, and tossed a larger bag to Poncho. "Okay don't open them yet I have one more present," Dirt said while bouncing out of the room once again.

"Bam!" He almost screamed as he entered again holding a brown cowboy hat in his hand. "Frank this is for you. You need to wear this from now on."

I was about to ask why I needed to wear a cowboy hat for the foreseeable future when Dirt cut off my train of thought. He almost seemed to know when people were going to ask questions he didn't feel like answering.

"One at a time bitches. Poncho open your present first," Dirt said.

Poncho almost looked excited to open his bag. He pulled out a new black shirt and some new leather pants. They appeared to be the exact some style that he always wore. Next he removed the battle axe that he took from Clove's place and a handful of throwing knifes.

"Thanks Dirt, it's just what I always wanted. You brought me some of my old clothes and my axe," Poncho said sarcastically, although he did seem genuinely happy. "You can keep the throwing knives though, not my style."

"I'll do no such thing, I make the plans and the plans say you keep the fucking throwing knives," Dirt said stubbornly.

Poncho didn't fight and just set the knives off to the side, then set about polishing his axe.

"Your turn Neph." Dirt said with an evil grin.

Neph reluctantly opened her bag looking as if she expected it to be full of snakes. It would have been better if it were snakes, because the look on her face when she pulled out what appeared to be a child sized leather suit made even Poncho cringe. I couldn't tell exactly what it was, but it looked like it was supposed to be clothes of some kind. Neph carelessly threw it to the side and her expression softened a great deal as she pulled out two swords.

"Nice swords," I said before thinking. Poncho and Neph both looked at me like I had just smacked a child, not that they would be too offended by that. But you get the idea.

"This is a Katana, Frank," Neph said holding up the larger of the two. "And this is a Wakizashi," She said pointing the shorter of the two swords at me.

"Seriously Frank, swords?" Poncho almost seemed disappointed.

I mumbled something nonsensical to myself in order to avoid further shame for my lack of knowledge on sword types. Poncho shook his head pitying me and went back to polishing. Neph went back to her bag, finding one last item, it was a small bundle of throwing knives.

"I'm not using these," she said setting them aside. "Not when I have proper weapons."

"You'll do what the plan says and like it," Dirt snapped, then immediately started grinning again.

"Do I get a bag?" I asked.

Dirt looked at me confused, "I already gave you your thing."

"The hat?" I said holding it up, just in case he forgot.

"Yes the hat, why else would you have it?"

"Why would I need a cowboy hat?" I asked apprehensively.

Dirt threw his hands up exasperated. "Why wouldn't you need a cowboy hat Frank? That fedora sticks out like a sore thumb. I didn't want to hurt your feelings, but you look like an asshole in it too."

My world crashed down around me.

"Chin up Frank, everyone looks awesome in a cowboy hat. Put it on, Neph has a thing for cowboys," Dirt said winking, while performing the universal sign for blowjob.

"That is simply not true Frank, do yourself a favor and ignore almost everything that idiot says," Neph said.

"Hush now woman, lucky for you I didn't make sleeping with everyone you see in a cowboy hat a part of the plan," Dirt said with a devilish grin.

"Why people of a greater worth put so much faith in your plan I will never understand," Neph quipped.

"I said hush woman. Now go put on your sexy outfit, with those throwing knifes in the slots I had sewn on specifically for them, and tell Frank how sexy he looks in that cowboy hat," Dirt said on the verge of tears.

"Frank, it wouldn't make much sense for Neph to tell you how sexy you look in that desperado sun blocker if you're not going to put it on your head," Dirt said.

I put the hat on. Dirt kinda made it sound cool and there was the off chance that Neph actually did like men in cowboy hats. That and I think that most men secretly want to wear them and are just waiting for a real reason to do so.

Neph glared at Dirt, and if looks could kill hers would have done the job. Then she looked at me.

"You look very sexy in your cowboy hat Frank," she said through clenched teeth. She quickly turned and stalked into the bathroom to put on her sexy outfit.

I knew what she said was forced, but I already felt a whole lot better about myself, and may have even swelled with pride a little.

A few moments later Neph came back dressed in a skin tight leather suit like you would see on a sexy lady spy in the movies. I'm not sure how Dirt got her measurements, but it was the right kind of tight in all the right places.

She didn't look happy about it, and I had no idea why she let Dirt talk her into wearing it. It was almost as if she didn't have a choice, maybe Lonald had something to do with it. While these thoughts were going through my head I must have been staring a little.

"Frank, if you don't close your mouth a bird will go in there and do stuff," Dirt looked confused. "Pretty sure that's how that goes."

Neph was shaking with rage and her cheeks were flush with anger. I briefly hoped it was just slight embarrassment at my gawking, but the steel in her eyes squashed that thought.

"Let's get this over with," she said grabbing her swords as she stalked to the car.

Dirt exchanged a knowing glance with Poncho, this all seemed like a big joke to them. Poncho got up from his seat and headed for the door as well, cradling his axe like a newborn made out of glass.

"Aren't you forgetting something?" Dirt asked tapping his foot.

"I told you, I'm not using throwing knives," Poncho grumbled.

"And I told you to stick to the fucking plan man," Dirt replied. "So pick them up and bring them along."

Poncho sighed and grudgingly stuffed the knives in his back pocket. He looked like he had no intention of using them, but was just appeasing Dirt's madness.

Dirt looked at me and smiled, pleased that I hadn't taken the hat off. "At least someone here appreciates a good plan. Let's head out, I'll go over the brilliant details in the car."

With that we all got in the car and headed out to go kill a Frankenstein.

Nobody said much on the way to our destination, not even Dirt, which worried me. Poncho didn't speak much in the first place, and I'd bet my hat that Neph was too angry to talk, but for me I was just nervous. I found myself once again mixed up in a murder plot with absolutely no information about what we were doing or why. Unless I was supposed to believe all that stuff about monsters and immortals. The scary part about the monsters and immortals though, was that I was seriously starting to believe it. I couldn't come up with any other theories about these people and the things we were doing, not any that were grounded in reality anyway.

The other part that scared me was the fact that Dirt had planned this whole adventure and everyone else was completely on board with it. I was convinced we would all die in a freak car accident before we even got close to where we were going.

This thought died quickly as Dirt stopped the car about two blocks from a solitary house in the middle of nowhere.

"Is this the place?" I asked.

Dirt nodded his head, contemplating the old house.

"Why didn't we park closer?"

"You should know that about two blocks away is the perfect distance to spy on a house Frank," Dirt said dismissively.

I couldn't help but think he was mocking me somehow, but I ignored it. "Why are we spying?"

"We aren't spying, we are going over the plan."

I started to object, letting him know that no plan telling was going on, but I was cut off.

"It's the same thing Frank!" Dirt said.

Again there was silence while we waited for Dirt to explain his plan. I braced myself for at least a few minutes of nonsense before he just told us to bust down the door and kill anything that moved.

"Ok," Dirt said cracking his knuckles. "Operation Overflow begins now. Target codename is Frank."

"Um, that's my name," I said getting nervous.

"Yeah, that might get confusing when things get bad," Poncho added.

I noted that Poncho said 'when,' not 'if.'

"Fine!" Dirt said throwing his hands up. "The new codename is Brian, happy now?"

Poncho nodded and Neph continued to try setting Dirt on fire with hateful staring.

"Wait, does this mean that all the other jobs had codenames too?" I asked, realizing full well that I was getting just as bad as them at sidetracking conversations.

"Well of course they did," Dirt replied. "Now the plan is this..."

"What were they called?" I interrupted.

"God dammit Frank, stick to the present," Dirt was conflicted, I could see his desire to explain his current plan being beat out by his love of distraction. "The first one was called Operation Disco Inferno."

"What?"

"It makes sense Frank, didn't you hear how loud that music was?"

"So the inferno part is because you were going to burn the house down?"

"No Frank, inferno just sounds cool," Poncho interjected.

He had me there.

"So what was the werewolf job called?"

"Operation Whiskey Bottle Batting Practice," Dirt said.

There was no way they could have known that was going to happen, maybe they were psychic after all. Or more likely it had all been an elaborate plan from the start. But even more likely, he was making these names up after the fact to fuck with me.

"And the woman in the street?"

"Operation Crosswalk," Dirt said. "Granted it isn't one of our best titles."

It made sense at least, considering the book and what he told me the night before it happened, I didn't have a hard time believing it was real. Believing anything was getting to be a problem lately.

"Enough bullshit Frank, are you ready to listen to the plan for Operation Overflow now?"

I nodded, unable to think of anything else to sidetrack him with. I was just stalling anyway.

"Ok," Dirt started. "First part of the plan is Frank goes to the house."

"By myself?"

Dirt glared at me, indicating that I should be listening, not speaking.

"So Frank goes to the house, by himself, and knocks on the door. Codename Brian should answer, Frank tells him that he has a flat tire and wants to use his phone. Codename Brian will let him in to use the phone, which he will do, calling us to let us know he isn't dead. Then while Frank waits for the 'tow truck' to show up he will ask to use the bathroom. While Frank is in the kitchen he will unlock the backdoor and overflow the toilet. Then he will go back into the living room to wait."

"That's when Codename Brian will notice a distraction in the backyard and go to investigate. Where Poncho and Neph will kill him dead."

"How do you know there will be a backdoor in the kitchen?" I asked.

"Look at the layout of the house Frank, all houses like that have a backdoor in the kitchen. Shit, it's like you don't even understand planning sometimes."

"Ok, why do I need to unlock it if this distraction will make him go out that door anyway?"

Dirt stared blankly at me, as if I was the dumbest person he had ever met. I decided to press on with my doubts.

"And what does overflowing the toilet do?"

"I can't even deal with him right now Ponch, you handle it," Dirt said shaking his head.

"Do the plan Frank," Poncho said not looking at me.

It appeared that I didn't have a choice; I got out of the car and regarded the house. Dirt reached out the window and handed me a crumpled piece of paper. I smoothed it out and found a phone number, presumably the one I was supposed to call when I made it inside and wasn't dead.

I sighed and started for the house. I didn't see how my part in this plan had any bearing on anything. If the whole point was to lure him outside and kill him, why did I have to go in and unlock the door and stop up the toilet?

Before I could come up with a convincing argument to turn around I was at the door. I knocked, and a few seconds later a very large man answered. He was at least as big as Poncho, and extremely ugly. He wasn't half as scary as Poncho, but he was more than a little intimidating.

"Can I help you?" the Frankenstein asked. He was so soft spoken that I wasn't sure it had even come from him.

I was slightly taken aback, but recovered enough to continue the plan. "Uh, yeah. I got a flat tire a ways back and wondered if I could use your phone to call a tow truck."

"That's terrible!" the Frankenstein exclaimed. "Come in out of the heat and we can work something out, my name is Brian by the way."

Of course it was, I thought. "I'm Frank, nice to meet you."

"I love your hat Frank!" Brian said ushering me to a seat on the couch. "Can I get you a drink? I have some fresh squeezed lemonade I think."

"That would be great, thanks." This guy was way too friendly, it made me suspicious. "You mind if I use your phone quick?" I asked as he hurried to the kitchen.

"You know, I've got a bunch of tools, I could patch it up for you myself in no time!" he shouted from the kitchen.

"I couldn't possibly trouble you anymore."

"It's no trouble," Brian said returning from the kitchen with a tall glass of lemonade. "Don't get many visitors here very often, it would be my pleasure to help you out. I've got a jack, air compressor, and a patch kit just sitting around in the shed."

Brian handed me the lemonade and took a sip, it was delicious. I hadn't realized how thirsty I was until it hit my lips.

"Man that's good, thanks," I said.

"My pleasure, it's a scorcher out there today."
Brian paused. "That coat looks really cool and all, but isn't
it a little warm?"

I was wearing my trench coat as usual, and he
was right, it was way too hot to be wearing it. I couldn't
say why I was wearing it, it just felt right.

"Yeah," I admitted. "Old habits die hard I guess."

"Anyway Frank, I can have that thing fixed in no
time, you sure I can't help you out on this?" he asked
eagerly.

"You've helped more than enough, if I could just
use your phone I can get out of your hair."

Brian looked disappointed, but handed me the
phone with a sigh.

I dialed the number Dirt had given me and
waited. Brian sat on the couch and waited, it looked like I
was going to do some acting.

Four rings later Dirt answered sounding bothered.
"What?"

"Uh, hi. I need a tow truck," I said.

"No shit dummy, you stop up that toilet yet?"

"No, I didn't," I replied.

"Well what's the hold up? This plan has a tight schedule," Dirt said.

"Well it's out on old route four, down past the motel a ways," I said staying in character.

"I know where we are Frank, we are still in the car waiting for you to do your end."

"Yes, that's fine."

"You aren't making any sense Frank! Blink twice if you are under duress!" Dirt said frantically.

I nodded, pretending I was listening to the tow truck service, not acting like I was trying to figure out what the hell he was talking about. So I didn't blink.

"Whew, that was close. Go stop up that shitter already." Then he hung up.

"Ok, thanks. See you in a bit," I said into the phone to the dead air.

I handed the phone to Brian. "Thanks a lot."

"Seriously, it's no problem at all. Do you want me wait at your car with you?" Brian asked fishing for another way to help. "Those guys can take forever, and a little company can make time pass in a flash."

I didn't want to crush him any further, which felt odd considering I was in the process of facilitating his murder. So I lied.

"That would be great, but can I use your bathroom first?" I asked.

"Sure thing Frank, it's in the kitchen, right by the back door."

"Thanks again, you're a life saver." I was laying it on thick now.

I headed to the kitchen to find the back door right by the bathroom as Dirt had predicted. I considered unlocking it as the plan dictated, but I was pretty sure Brian could see me from the living room, so I bypassed it and went into the bathroom. If he was going to rush outside because of the distraction it was pretty unnecessary anyway. Inside the bathroom I had to stop myself about two seconds from flushing a hand towel down the toilet. There was no rational reason I could come up with for stopping up the toilet, so I washed my hands and went back to the living room. Brian was sitting on the arm of the couch ready to go.

"You ready Frank?" He asked.

"Yeah I think..." I stopped as I heard some cans banging around behind the house.

"Darn," Brian said. "Can you wait a minute Frank? I think the raccoons are back, shouldn't take a minute to chase those rascals off."

"Sure," I said. Some distraction I thought.

Brian went outside, unlocking the door on his way. So much for Dirt's plan.

About three seconds after Brian went outside I felt myself being hoisted up by the armpits. Curious, I looked around to see what was happening. It turned out I was being carried by two of the largest individuals I had ever seen, and they didn't look happy. They carried me out the backdoor toward the distraction as my confused brain made a futile attempt to form words.

Just about the time I had managed to make some defiant grunts we were outside. My transporters stopped dead in their tracks when they saw Brian staring slack jawed at a shed. The shed was engulfed in flames, this was the real distraction I guessed.

"Get away from there!" the slightly bigger one shouted.

Brian didn't respond, he was transfixed by the blaze.

Then Poncho walked out from behind the raging fire and deftly cleaved Brian's head with one swing of his axe.

The large creatures cried out in what sounded like anguish as Dirt and Neph came into view and stopped by Poncho.

"God dammit Frank, I told you to stop the toilet up. Can't you even do one simple thing?" Dirt said slipping behind Poncho.

"What?" I asked, only to be cut off by a violent shake from my captors.

"I didn't think it was already time," The bigger one said regaining his composure. "But you didn't have to start with the boy."

"Them's the breaks big fella," Dirt said shifting around behind Poncho and Neph.

"So be it," the less big one said.

"Plan B," Dirt shouted as jumped back a little from Poncho and Neph. His hands were full of the throwing knives they had put in their back pockets. In an overelaborate gesture Dirt spread his arms wide, knives splayed out like you would see in a movie, he whipped his arms forward, releasing the knives directly at me. I flinched and heard knives slapping harmlessly into the house behind me. Not feeling any knife wounds I opened my eyes and glanced around. There was one knife in the arm of the bigger one, the rest had apparently landed ineffectually behind us.

Poncho looked over his shoulder and I saw that one more knife had hit meat, the meat of his shoulder.

"This is why I don't like throwing knives," Poncho said calmly ripping the blade out.

"That's why it's plan B Ponch," Dirt replied.

Everyone was pretty distracted at this point so I made my move. I slowly reached into my coat and pulled out my gun from the shoulder holster. It was awkward, but I managed to fire across my body into the jaw of the less big one.

I didn't see how much damage it did as I screamed and it dropped me, it's hands flying to its jaw in pain. The bigger one dropped me a split second later and I fell on the ground lopsided and dazed.

"Neph take the lady with the jaw hole! Ponch you take the dad!" Dirt shouted.

The one I had shot had been a female? You honestly couldn't tell by looking.

Poncho casually walked toward the male and they squared off, sizing each other up. Neph didn't have the same warrior code and rushed the moaning female giant.

She moved with the grace of the wind, slashing violently at the thigh of the 'woman' I had recently shot through the jaw. She was majestic. She was a feather on the wind. She was leading the giant I had just shot right towards me...

"Neph!" I screamed about six octaves higher than I had intended. Are there even that many octaves? Nonetheless, I screamed like a little girl which surprisingly helped me catch a bit of my bearings. I rolled away from the two women in what I knew was a duel to the death. The other show tonight was between heavyweights, and it was enough to evoke my 'see what happens mentality,' seriously who needs 'fight or flight.'

Poncho seemed to be testing out the much larger foe. He was sending his brutal axe towards the body and legs of the Frankenstein with amazing speed, all while keeping himself out of range from a counter from the giant. This giant was easily a foot taller than Poncho, who before tonight was by far the scariest man I have ever seen.

The Frankenstein seemed to absorb the blows without serious hesitance, always moving forward with destructive blows from his massive arms. As fast as the giant seemed to move, Poncho was always one step ahead. Not only was he always out of the way of the blow, he seemed to have planned a perfect counter attack for each blow.

Right when it seemed that Poncho secured the upper hand the beast leapt away, I have never seen anything move so far in such a short amount of time, and

Frankenstein pulled a smoldering chunk of tree from the fire pit that brought poor Brian outside in the first place. Frankenstein charged at Poncho with a new found fury, he closed the distance of his leap in a few heartbeats.

Poncho no longer easily kept the beast at bay, he was losing ground at a rapid pace. Moments ago he was parrying attacks and delivering massive counter attacks, now he was barely able to keep the beast back. Even for someone who was a proponent of arson Poncho seemed to be overly wary of the burning stump. Right when I thought that nothing could draw my attention from the heavyweights I noticed Dirt running with two throwing knifes leveled at me.

"Throwing knifes, stupid face!" he bellowed.

The knives snapped free from his wrist with amazing speed, how was he so fucking terrible a few moments ago. I knew that my opportunity for flight was past, and that this was my time to die. I would have never guessed that Dirt would be my reaper, let alone with throwing knives. I wrenched my eyes closed, only to hear a terrible howl.

As I opened my eyes I saw Frankenstein swing his tree trunk at an opening in Poncho's guard. Somehow Poncho stepped back as the flaming trunk approached his head. As the beast followed through air, Poncho buried his axe into the beast's back.

Another terrible howl, the beast sent his trunk back towards Poncho with a backswing. Poncho ducked while extending his hand and grabbing the beast's arm as it passed him, exposing its entire chest as Poncho slashed down with the axe, held in his offhand, cleaving the Frankenstein from throat to midsection.

"Frank. Move!" Neph screamed. She sounded terrified.

She was obviously not faring as well against the 'lady Frankenstein.' I could not let anything happen to Neph. I would not sit still. I would fight this time.

I managed to focus on lady Frankenstien again and aimed my gun towards Dirt's throwing knifes, guess he wasn't aiming at me after all, lodged in the middle of the she-beasts back. I took the shot, shots for that matter, and hit the beast at least once. Another roar.

Neph used this distraction to land her short-sword, what did she call it, right through the neck of her foe. The lady Frankenstein stumbled slightly, but even the addition of a gaping neck wound wasn't enough to stop her completely. So despite the almost entirely missing jaw, and slew of cuts and gashes, and the newly added partial decapitation, she got back to her feet and glared at Neph, who was breathing pretty heavy.

Neph steeled herself for another clash, and I heard Poncho yell.

"Duck!"

I decided not to hesitate this time, and threw myself to the ground. When I looked up I saw Poncho's axe embedded in the lady Frankenstein's back, he must have thrown it. The multitude of wounds finally became too much to bear and she fell to her knees, Neph wasted no time and started hacking the rest of lady Frankenstein's head off.

After a few chops it hit the ground with a thud, I could have sworn it blinked a few times before the eyes rolled back. Probably just adrenaline confusing me though.

With the battle over it was eerily quiet, even with the remnants of fire still crackling from time to time. The only other sound I could hear was my own breathing, and it sounded ragged. I looked around and took in the battlefield, it was a gory mess. Everything between the house and the smoldering shed was spattered in blood, it was a gruesome sight. I added the contents of my lunch to battlefield for good measure.

Then I saw Dirt pissing on the embers of the fire he started and reality came crashing back.

"What the fuck kind of plan was that?" I shouted at Dirt pulling myself off the ground.

Dirt looked back at me and said, "In a minute Frank, I'm busy."

I threw up my hands in frustration and looked to Poncho for help. He was in the process of pulling his axe out of several inches of bone and meat, he just shrugged at me and yanked it free.

I turned my gaze to Neph, she was wiping the blood off her swords with what looked like a t-shirt. She also shrugged and went back to what she was doing. These people were absolutely no help.

I decided to give myself a quick once over to see if I was injured, and I was surprised that aside from a few bruises I was unharmed. Maybe Dirt's plan really had been okay, I was still alive after all.

"Plan B is always messy Frank, that's why you should have stuck with Plan A." Dirt said strolling towards me.

"How exactly was that Plan B, Brian came outside for your distraction didn't he?" I asked a little indignantly.

Dirt scowled at me, as if he was disappointed at my stupidity. "The plan was for you to stop up the toilet and unlock the door Frank, you did neither."

"And how does that matter?"

"God dammit Frank, it was the plan." He paused as if this would explain everything. I waited until Dirt sighed and explained. "It's like this, we knew there were three of them in there, and as you can see, they are somewhat gigantic. I decided it would be wise to kill them one at a time."

I waited some more, still not grasping what he was getting at.

"So you were supposed to stop up the toilet, which would have kept mom and dad Frankenstein tied up in the basement trying to avoid a shit flood."

That made a stupid kind of sense, at least as far as the last few days had been going.

"And unlocking the door?" I asked, sure that he had no explanation for this one.

"That was part one of Plan B."

I raised a questioning eyebrow.

"Fuck man, this is easy shit, do I really have to spell it all out?" He didn't wait for a response, just went into the run down I was sure he had been waiting to give.

"So Plan A was you stop up the toilet, Ma and Pa stay in the basement until they fix it and Baby is dead. Then one comes up to see what happened to the shitter and see the unlocked door, they go outside to investigate, get killed. Then the other one comes and gets killed too, or we went in and did the one left, that part was up in the air. But since you didn't jam up the shitter they didn't stay in the basement when Junior went outside and they heard the commotions from the distraction, so they head upstairs and see a handsome, cowboy hat wearing, Frank and get suspicious.

"If you had unlocked the door they would have just asked you where Brian was and you could have lied and stalled while one went to go see why it was unlocked, but since you did neither their naturally suspicious Frankenstein brains jumped into crazy mode and hauled you off.

"If you had stopped up the john and left the door locked it also would have been fine, they would have assumed Junior was inside fixing or breaking a toilet somewhere.

"So doing neither was more like Plan C I guess, and you could have been killed if I didn't have the Plan D throwing knives ready to go. That plan was also called, 'Plan Frank doesn't listen' by the way."

Now I was more confused than before, this all sounded like a whole lot of complete, made up on the spot bullshit.

"You mean to tell me that this whole plan was based around the toilet overflowing and the door being locked or unlocked?" I asked dumbfounded.

Dirt thought for a second and came to a conclusion. "Yes, Frankensteins always leave the doors locked. Always. Unlocked doors make them investigate, they can't help it. They are naturally very suspicious of everything."

"Wouldn't they have been suspicious about the overflowed toilet then?" I asked.

"No idiot, you see the size of those guys? They are always jamming up toilets."

"I see," I said. I really didn't, but I really didn't want him to explain the size of a Frankenstein shit to me, so I lied.

Dirt eyed me disbelieving. "Ok, then let's get the fuck out of here. Poncho you know what to do." Then he headed around the house in the direction of the car, Neph followed him at a fair distance.

I Looked over at Poncho, he had a burning branch in his hand and a terrible gleam in his eyes. As he walked into the house I made for the car as well, arson was never really my thing. I glanced back after a minute and saw Poncho tossing the dead bodies through the unlocked back door. There was already smoke coming out.

As I sat in the car waiting for Poncho to finish his grisly work I started to wonder if I might be working for the bad guys. It gnawed at me, and I couldn't shake the feeling that I was in for a rude awakening soon.

Poncho returned smelling like a camp fire, or a house fire more accurately. Dirt turned the car around and we drove off the way we had come. I looked back one more time at the receding house, there was black smoke boiling into the sky like a beacon that said, "Crime just happened here!"

I turned back to the road ahead and found myself a little excited thinking about what would happen next.

It was maybe the dumbest thought I have ever had.

# Distractions

The first dozen miles of the drive back were more than eye opening. I quickly began to realize that Dirt's plan did not start and end with the toilet or whether or not I locked a door behind Brian. As we passed the carwash we stopped at on the way to the battle scene, Dirt began laughing hysterically.

"Look who remembered their part of the plan everyone." Dirt barely got out in between laughter. "Oh, those stupid fucks. They are just so damn curious. Honestly it is kinda cute."

There were about three dozen giant men, and presumably women and children, standing around the outside of the last bay of the car wash staring at something inside. Dirt slowed down our escape to revel at his creation.

It was hard to make out at first, but it appeared that Dirt had completely decorated the inside of the last bay we passed with some sort of art exhibit. The entirety of the bay was painted in ridiculous patterns of neon colors. And from a giant sheet or piece of canvas hanging in the middle of the exhibit Dirt had painted "Live today only! Your favorite band!"

"Wait, who is the Frankenstein's favorite band?" I couldn't help myself.

"How the fuck would I know Frank? Don't you think I would have put that on the banner? Plus, do you really think they all have the same favorite? That would be stupid," Dirt got out between laughs.

"I think we should probably be on our way Dirt." Poncho added. We were going about five miles an hour at this point, while Dirt enjoyed his show. "Who knows how long our giants will wait."

"Right on, but those fucks are going to be waiting for their favorite band until tomorrow. Why do you think I left off an exact time fools." Dirt laughed while taking a last look at the 'stage' before accelerating once again.

After a few miles I decided to see if I could get any actual information from Dirt on this distraction he had spent so much time setting up.

"Why did you set all that up anyway? If they are all Frankenstein's wouldn't you want to kill them too?" I asked.

"That wasn't the job Frankie, we just needed them to not chase us down and kill us all. Ponch is kind of a badass, but even he couldn't take all of them at once," Dirt said.

Poncho gave Dirt a dubious glance and went back to scowling at the landscape, I was inclined to believe Dirt on this one, despite Poncho's obvious aptitude for killing.

"Chase us and kill us?" I asked apprehensively.

"Duh Frank, this is Frankenstein country, the place is lousy with them. And they have a pack mentality, if one goes down the others go berserk," Dirt said cracking open a beer. Where did he always get them from?

I had seen this berserk mode in person, the alleged Frankenstein's seemed relatively calm until Brian had been killed, then they went nuts. This lent some weight to Dirt's comment, which as usual worried me.

"So why not set up one of your distractions to just kill them all? It just seems to me that at some point you're going to have to deal with them anyway."

"It's not that simple Frank, there are rules," Dirt said unconvincingly.

"It isn't sporting," Poncho stated.

"So there aren't any rules then?" I asked thinking I was starting to sound stupid.

"Sportsmanship is a rule," Dirt said to his beer can.

"It's more of a personal thing than a rule, you can't force someone to be sportsmanlike."

This line of questioning appeared to be making Dirt uncomfortable. I was pretty sure I had just caught him on his bullshit and for whatever reason he didn't have a response.

I was winning.

"It's a personal rule," Dirt said perking back up.

So I wasn't winning, who was I kidding in the first place. I was enjoying our idiotic conversations now, and I had played right into Dirt's insane hands. I wasn't mad, he had obviously had much more practice at idiotic arguments than me.

"Fair enough." As usual I wasn't going to get any answers out of him. Although I did have a hard time accepting that Dirt had a sporting bone in his body.

We drove a while longer without any speaking. Unless you count Dirt snickering to himself between beers. At this point, I no longer worried that was drinking and driving. Drinking was just something he did and I am certain that he is incapable of actually getting drunk. I couldn't tell if he was still amused by his clever ploy to distract the horde of Frankensteins or if it was 'literally' anything else. This was Dirt after all and it was fucking impossible to tell. The silence still made me incredibly uneasy though.

Poncho and Neph were silent also, which was no surprise at all. I only mention it because the silence was so out of place. The car ride felt like one of those you take home after catching a movie with your friends. The kind where nobody can decide if they enjoyed it or not, when you know everyone is thinking about the same thing, but not saying a damn word. I doubt we were all thinking about the same thing with this crowd, but you never really know. Poncho was probably thinking about his axe and whether or not it was having a comfortable ride in the trunk. Neph was a complete mystery. She had changed out of her cat suit before I even got into the car after the Franken-'battle' and was back in her customary garb. She looked like she was asleep, which made sense after her battle with the Franken-lady. She had held her own, but took some serious hits from what I could tell while cowering like a little kid. I checked all of her visible areas to make sure she wasn't bleeding through her clothes though. Then I did a mental check of what the non visible areas might look like, they were also fine.

I was shaken from my musings by the sound of Dirt's snickering turning into hysterical laughter. I looked up to see what had been so funny and saw only the same barren landscape we had been driving in for what seemed like days. I scanned the horizon and spotted one thing that looked out of place, it was a pillar of smoke barely visible in the distance. I didn't know what was so funny about it, but again, with Dirt anything is possible.

He slowed the car to a halt and shut it off on the side of the road.

"What are you doing?" I asked.

"You have to shut your car off when you put gas in it, everyone knows that. It's the law," Dirt said getting out of the car.

I needed to stretch my legs a little and followed him, Poncho and Neph didn't move.

"You do know there isn't a gas station here, right?" I asked starting to think he may actually be drunk.

Dirt just frowned at me and opened the trunk, revealing two jerry cans filled with what was probably gas.

"We have to fill up now, there isn't a service station for a hundred miles Frank," he said pulling the gas cans out.

I was pretty confident that we were going back the same way we had come, and I was sure we had stopped at a gas station along the way. I didn't mention this to Dirt and he was busying himself filling up the tank. I disregarded the whole thing and just left him to it, no sense arguing with a madman they say. I got back into the car and waited.

Before long we were moving again and Dirt was whistling. I did some quick mental math and decided that the gas station we stopped at had to be close, then I looked back at the ever advancing pillar of smoke. My stomach dropped out and I got a very sneaking suspicion about why there weren't any service stations for miles.

My suspicions were proven correct when we went over a small hill and the gas station I thought we had passed came into view.

What was left of it anyway.

It looked like the entire place had exploded, but not being an expert on explosions it could have been a god damn meteor for all I knew. One thing was true at least, in the very recent past the whole place had been a raging inferno.

Dirt slowed the car and started laughing again, even Poncho and Neph stirred themselves to rubberneck. Neph glanced at the carnage and quickly closed her eyes again, clearly not impressed. Poncho on the other had looked like a kid that had just seen the first sign on the way to Disneyland.

"Cool," Poncho said in awe.

"What the fuck?" I asked.

Dirt answered with hysterical laughter.

"Did you do this?" I asked, pretty sure I already knew the answer.

"Duh," Dirt said.

"Why?"

"Distraction!"

"How is this a distraction?"

"Fire is pretty distracting, look at how distracted Ponch is," Dirt said gesturing at Poncho staring out the window still.

"What?" Poncho said, distracted.

"Ok, I'll agree that fire is distracting, but how is this helping us?" I asked.

"Fuck Frank, do I have to explain everything to you?" Dirt asked.

I waited for him to continue explaining, but he only stared into the rear view mirror waiting for a response.

"Yes?" I said.

Dirt sighed. "Well you know how all those Frankensteins are distracted at the car wash about their favorite band?"

I again waited for him to continue, but his question apparently wasn't the rhetorical type.

"Yeah."

"Well," Dirt continued. "When they figure out that their band isn't going to show up and that a few of them got murdered they are going to eventually decide to take vengeance on somebody. And that means they are going to hop into their pickup trucks and chase us down, or at least head to town and start fucking shit up. So when they head to the gas station and see that all their gas is burned up they are going to be pretty distracted by not having any gas and they won't be able to get anywhere."

"What about the ones at the gas station?" I asked assuming they were all dead.

"There aren't any at the gas station," Dirt said.

"Why?" I asked.

"I know you are new to all this Frank, but come the fuck on."

"Humor me," I said flatly.

Dirt sighed again and far more exaggerated, "When the Frankensteins at the car wash saw the sign about the band they called the Franensteins at the gas station to come see. So they are all at the car wash waiting."

That was about the dumbest thing I had ever heard. Or it would have been if I hadn't been dealing with Dirt recently.

"Ok," I said, about to crack open the truth about this. "How did the place explode then?"

"I swear you're getting dumber Frank. You remember that bag I dumped in the road?"

This time I decided not to wait for him to continue, "Yes, I..."

Dirt cut me off, "Well that was bombs in that bag."

"Where did you..." I started.

"I got it from a man dressed like a tree, I gave him a bag of money and he gave me a bag of blow shit up."

"A man dressed like a tree?" I asked.

"Mostly like a tree, I mean he didn't have branches and leaves and stuff. Just dressed like a forest."

I mentally tried to decipher what Dirt was misinterpreting this time and it dawned on me.

"You mean a soldier?"

"Probably," Dirt said.

Close enough, I doubt he could tell the difference between a military person and a gun nut dressed in camouflage. But where he got the explosives wasn't really what I was concerned about.

"If you left it in the road how did it end up blowing up the gas station?" I asked.

"Finally an intelligent question, as you don't know the nature of Frankensteins. What you may have gathered is that they are really polite, when they aren't tearing your arms off that is. So when one of them noticed the suspicious very heavy ticking bag in the road they felt the overwhelming desire to find its owner. But not right away, they have a business to run after all. So one of these morons took the bag and put it in the lost and found hoping that the owner would come back for it. And there it sat until they got the call about their favorite band coming to play and they left the very heavy ticking bag at the station. Then it exploded the whole fucking place," Dirt finished with flourish and made and explosion noise.

"What if they hadn't left?" I asked only marginally concerned.

"Well then they would be exploded Frank, that's what happens when things explode. But that wasn't going to happen because Frankensteins are really stupid and they really like their favorite band," Dirt explained.

"The favorite band that was never specified?" I asked just to make sure it was as dumb as it sounded.

"Yes," Dirt said proudly.

"So let me get this straight," I said. "On the way here you left a bomb for them to find and put in the station. Then when we got to the car wash you painted that sign about the band to get them all there instead of at the gas station. Then when we were fighting the other Frankensteins all the rest were at the car wash waiting and the gas station exploded so they couldn't follow us?"

"Yes," Dirt said nodding.

"Why weren't the ones we fought at the car wash?"

"They didn't like music," Dirt said.

"So this entire plan more or less hinged on the Frankensteins we were going to kill not liking music?"

"Yes."

"Jesus Christ," I said dumbfounded.

"Where!?" Dirt shouted.

"What?" I asked.

"I thought that guy was dead. Did you see him?" Dirt said looking around.

I was sure he was fucking with me now, it probably wasn't the first time one of us had uttered that phrase. When Dirt stopped his over acting and grinned at me in the mirror I realized that he had been. I guessed he was tired of this conversation and was making an attempt to derail it. I decided that I was fine with it, but I had one more question.

"So what do we do now?" I asked.

"First we go get hammered and clean up, then we head back to Lonald's and see what he has planned." Dirt said.

Well at least it should be interesting.

# A Fancy Dinner Party

True to his word Dirt managed to get us all hammered ass drunk that night. We got back to Dirt and Poncho's house that evening and Glen provided a large supply of beer, which we did our best to eliminate.

Even Neph stayed and drank.

She claimed it was tradition after victory and I wasn't about to complain. Most of the night is hazy, but I do remember seeing Dirt, Poncho, and Neph all drunk. I was fairly certain they couldn't actually get drunk, but there we were having a great time.

Neph left somewhat early, saying she had to go meet Lonald and discuss the mission. I was little upset that I wouldn't have a chance to chicken out on making a move on her. But it was probably for the best.

After much drinking and laughing, and even some singing, we all passed out.

In the morning I was surprised to find out that I wasn't nearly as hung over as I suspected I would be. I walked into the kitchen after waking up on the way too comfortable couch and saw Glen making breakfast.

"Good morning Frank!" he said cheerily. "How did you sleep?"

"Great actually," I replied. "I'm not even hung over."

"Well of course not, you don't get hangovers from victory drinking," Glen said with a wink.

"Huh, I didn't know that," I said, filing the question away for later.

"Have a seat Frank, I'll get you some eggs and bacon."

I started to protest on account of my not liking breakfast food, but it actually sounded really good. I settled into a chair and waited for breakfast, and my stomach started growling in anticipation.

"Where are the guys?" I asked trying to distract myself from hunger.

"Poncho is in his room, and Dirt ran out to do some errands," Glen said over the sound of cooking.

Errands, I thought. That was probably bad.

"What kind of errands?" I asked.

"Oh, who knows," Glen said placing a steaming plate of eggs, bacon, toast, and hash browns in front of me. "Best not to worry about it. Eat up!"

I doubted I could not worry about what Dirt was up to, but once I tasted the food I quickly did. I'm not sure what Glen did to that food, but it was amazing. I think I spaced out and before I knew it the plate was clean, and when I looked up wondering where it had all gone Glen placed another in front of me. Against my better judgment I set in with gusto. This time I slowed down towards the end and regained control of my senses.

Poncho had emerged from wherever he was and had sat down next to me, Glen put a plate in front of him as well. We ate in silence and by the time I was done I was stuffed to the gills. I leaned back and relished feeling completely content. Poncho was next to me eating like there was a fire in his belly and eggs were the only thing that could put it out.

When his plate got close to empty Glen just dumped more food on it between Poncho's bites. He didn't seem to notice. I was marveling at his ability to breathe while eating that fast, when Dirt burst through the door.

"What's up assholes and Glen!" he shouted.

Poncho and I grunted.

"Breakfast?" Glen asked.

"Not today man, I already ate," Dirt said sitting on the other side of me.

"Did you fill up on candy and schnapps again?" Glen asked disapprovingly.

"Schnapps is breakfast," Dirt replied defensively.

Glen only sighed, he had apparently lost this battle before.

"Frank go shower, we have a busy day ahead of us before we meet Lonald," Dirt said.

"We do?" I asked getting worried.

"Of course, idleness is the great destroyers hand basket they say!" Dirt exclaimed.

I was pretty sure nobody ever said that.

"I picked up some clothes from your house while you boys were on business yesterday, they should be in the bathroom for you," Glen said helpfully.

I showered and found that Glen had indeed been to my house. He picked some of my nicer clothes and had bought me new underwear. How did he know I'd been meaning to do that? There was a new toothbrush on the sink and I decided it was for me. Once I was clean and ready to go I headed back out to see what Dirt had planned to try and kill me today.

We got into my car and Dirt started driving, he must have had it cleaned while he was out, because all the blood stains and beer cans were gone.

"When are we going to Lonald's place?" I asked from the backseat.

"Not til later, he is having us over for dinner." Dirt said. "He is rich though, so he will probably serve us people or something stupid like that."

"Just because he is rich doesn't mean he eats people," Poncho said.

"Not every day they don't," Dirt replied.

"So what are we doing until then?" I asked.

"Let's just play it by ear," Dirt said with a chuckle.

That worried me.

We rode in silence for a few minutes before I decided to ask my next question.

"I've never seen you guys drunk before, why were you last night?"

To my surprise Poncho fielded this one. "It was victory drinking," he said simply.

That made about as much sense as it was ever likely to, so I let it drop.

After that we headed into Dirt's busy day. It consisted of the silliest shit I have ever heard of three grown men doing. We went to an amusement park where we waited in no lines. We played mini golf where Dirt got a hole in one on every hole. We went to a batting cage where Poncho hit a ball through the net. And the day went on like that until early evening. I was beat, but I'll be damned if I didn't have fun.

Dirt checked the spot on his arm where a watch would be and declared that we should head to Lonald's house for the fancy dinner party. On the way he stopped at a gas station and got a bag out of the trunk, and I started to worry again.

"More distractions?" I asked.

"Sort of," Dirt said unzipping the bag to show a tuxedo. "It's to distract people from your horrible fucking taste in clothes. Go put this on in the bathroom."

I did as instructed, expecting them to magic up some fancy duds for themselves while I was busy. It took longer than I had expected to put the damn thing on, it had been a while since I had to wear one of those things. When I came out I felt fancy, any asshole can wear a tuxedo and look good.

When I saw Dirt and Poncho I felt a little too fancy, they were wearing the same clothes as before.

"What the hell?" I asked.

"Oh, we don't dress up Frank, it's not our style," Dirt said.

"Of course it isn't," I said, slightly annoyed.

I got back into the car and we headed to Lonald's estate.

"What can I expect from this fancy dinner anyway?" I asked as we drove. "Besides eating people, that is." I was only a little worried about that possibility.

"Who the fuck knows. Rich people are nuts." Dirt answered. "Probably small amounts of food on a big plate with some disgusting sauce smeared around to make it look fancy."

"You're just spoiled by Glen's cooking," Poncho said.

"Are you telling me that you want to eat that rich people shit they call food?" Dirt asked.

"Well, no," Poncho said. That's why I brought beef jerky." Poncho pulled a dried hunk of meat from somewhere, maybe under the seat, and showed it to Dirt.

"Hmm, well don't be stingy with that thing if the food sucks."

"Is it just going to be fine dining and conversation?" I asked, still a little shocked at the size of Poncho's meat chunk.

"God dammit Frank, I don't know. Yes, there will be dancing and you will have to dance the tango with Poncho and kiss each other all night," Dirt said throwing his hands up in frustration. If I didn't know better I'd say he was nervous.

"Jesus, fine. I'll shut up," I said annoyed again.

"Don't worry Frank, I'm a better kisser than I am a dancer," Poncho said with no humor in his voice.

"And he is a fucking great dancer," Dirt added.

We drove the rest of the way in relative silence; the only noise was Poncho eating his hunk of dried meat.

When we pulled up to the house it looked no different than before, same amount of guards, same amount of ominous.

Dirt stopped the car by the fountain and we got out.

"Don't forget the meat," Dirt said.

"I ate it all," Poncho replied.

"Fuck Ponch!" Dirt shouted. "That was our only hope!"

Poncho shrugged.

Dirt sighed and we went for the door. It was opened upon our arrival by a butler with a sub machine gun strapped across his chest. At least Lonald wasn't paranoid or anything.

He ushered us into the dining hall that was about as opulent as you could imagine. There were giant crystal chandeliers, chairs that looked like thrones, the whole nine yards. It looked like there was seating for about a dozen or more people and the only one present was Neph. She was seated at what I assumed was the right hand of the head seat, and she was dressed in her normal, non-fancy clothes.

I turned to Dirt to complain some more and he just smiled and stuck the cowboy hat on my head. He must have grabbed it out of the car before we came in. I sighed again, not much I could do about it now.

The butler led us to our seats at the same end of the table as Neph, I was in the left hand seat to where Lonald was sure to sit, Dirt next to me, Poncho next to Neph. That seemed like a safer bet than letting Dirt close to her.

"Howdy Neph! Frank wore his cowboy hat for you," Dirt said cracking a beer. I don't know if it had been on the table or if he brought it with him. It didn't really matter anymore.

To my surprise Neph didn't stare daggers into Dirt, she merely raised her glass to us and smiled. I could almost see her will breaking down under the onslaught of my hat tuxedo combo.

"Lonald will be here shortly," she said simply.

"Figures, the host is always late to this kind of shit," Dirt said dismissively.

Shortly after Dirt had stuffed most of the silverware within his reach into his pockets Lonald appeared, also dressed in his usual clothes. Granted his usual clothes are nicer than any of ours, he was still under dressed compared to me. I was irked again.

"Welcome esteemed guests," Lonald said looking over us all, and stopping at me. "Or should I say esteemed guest instead?"

"Hi," I said blushing a little.

"My, my, Frank. I must say you look rather fetching in that hat!" Lonald said taking his seat.

"Thanks," I mumbled.

"Neph, Don't you think Frank just looks stunning in that hat?" Lonald asked.

Neph glared at Dirt, remembering the incident at the hotel when I first donned my new hat.

"Yes, he actually does," she finally said, with much less reluctance than I had expected.

"You put us all to shame with your fashion acumen Frank. We should all feel quite mortified with ourselves."

"Frank is classy as fuck," Dirt said.

"Quite," Lonald said unamused.

"I guess it's nice to dress up once and a while," I said.

"Indeed it is! Now we all know each other so we can forgo introductions. Please regale me with the events of the past few days while we wait for the main course," Lonald said.

"Didn't Neph tell you what happened?" I asked.

"Indeed she did, but it sounded like a rousing adventure and I'd just love to hear it again."

I spent the next few minutes telling Lonald how everything played out with the Frankenstein attack with Dirt interjecting nonsense facts throughout. When the food came it wasn't what Dirt and Poncho had feared, it was a roast suckling pig and it was fucking fantastic. While we ate, I finished the story with Lonald bursting out into laughter between bites. When I was done we had finished eating and we were just drinking. I think they call them cocktails.

"Superb, just superb! I wish I could have seen it all," Lonald said after lighting a cigar.

"Did we pass your test then? Are we hired?" Dirt asked breaking through the levity like a truck.

"Indeed," Lonald said.

"So what's next?" Dirt asked.

"Well let me be Frank," Lonald said.

I started laughing, remembering the first time he used that joke. Not that it was particularly funny, but I was a little tipsy. I quickly choked to a halt when I saw Lonald glaring at me, I guessed this wasn't the time for jokes.

"The thing is, I know you two are going to fuck me over. I don't know when and I don't know how, but it's in our nature. You two are up to something, I can feel it. As long as you know that I'll be ten steps ahead of you every second you are around we can work together amicably. And when you decide to turn on me I will crush you into dust," Lonald said gravely.

"Seems fair," Dirt said. "Ponch?"

Poncho nodded.

Then they all looked at me, if there was a plan to screw over Lonald I didn't know about it, but I was sure I was involved somehow.

"Sure," I said meekly.

"Capital!" Lonald said clapping his hands.

"So what's next?" Dirt asked again.

"What's next is right up your alley I should think," Lonald said with an evil grin. "I have a battle royal planned for this very night! I know you have all been victory drinking so it should be great fun!"

"Shit," I said. That sounded bad.

# Battle Royal Prelude

"Just what is a battle royal? Is it like a battle royale?" I asked while Dirt was driving us to what was likely my death.

"It's a big fight Frank, like a battle. A royal battle if you will, seriously who says royale?" Dirt explained.

"Yeah, I get that part. But why have one and how does it work? For that matter, why the hell do I need to be there?"

"We have them to fight, and it works like you fight a bunch and try not to die. You are there cause we can't have a two person team, that wouldn't make any sense. Shit Frank, it's pretty simple."

"God damnit, I mean why the hell is this happening?" I asked frustrated.

"Lonald is trying to kill us again," Poncho said.

"What?" I asked, more than a little shocked.

"He tried to kill you at that bar with Clove, he tried to kill us all fighting the Frankensteins, and he is trying to kill us now," Poncho explained.

"Stop being dramatic Ponch, he just trusts our skills to get shit done."

I had to agree with Dirt on that one, if he wanted us dead he could have had us shot any one of the times we were at his place, or probably anywhere else for that matter.

"Don't be stupid, you're the man with the plans, you know he is up to something," Poncho said.

"The plans ran out bro! There aren't any more god damn plans!" Dirt laughed out.

"Bullshit," Poncho said simply.

"So what is the plan then?" I asked.

"The plan is," Dirt paused, apparently forgetting he had no more plans. "The plan is to not die."

"Solid plan, but Dirt is still lying to us. If he tells us, or anyone, any of his plans they don't work as well, or so he says," Poncho added.

"Bullshit!" Dirt exclaimed, almost crying laughing.

"What is so funny? Do you honestly think I am getting out of this car to join a battle fucking royal without knowing what is going on?" I almost screamed at Dirt.

"Oh, calm down you two!" Dirt said in between laughter. "Poncho, explain the rules to Frank here. I'm not sure I can keep myself together long enough to get it all out."

"Okay, but first...what is so fucking funny Dirt?" Poncho asked in a tone that seemed serious even for him.

"I forgot my weapons," Dirt said swerving the car while not trying to control his laughter.

"Fuck," was all Poncho replied with.

At this point I was literally a second away from losing my shit. Why was it so funny the he forgot his weapon? And what are the fucking rules that he mentioned? Before I could calm myself enough to ask any questions without shouting at Dirt or physically grabbing him, Poncho spoke with a death tone to his voice, "You will have to ask him for them before the battle starts."

"Tell him the fucking rules Poncho, we are here. I have to ask for some weapons," Dirt said straight faced while stopping the car in the middle of the road. He jumped out of my car and headed towards an old field before anything else was said.

"So what are the rules then?" I asked Poncho hoping to sort some of this mess out.

"It's pretty simple really," Poncho said. "No guns, the only ranged weapon you will see is some asshole throwing whatever they have. It's pretty uncommon to throw a perfectly good weapon away though. Besides that it's just groups."

"Groups?" I asked.

"Yeah. Everyone shows up in their own little group. You don't kill people in your group, that's a rule."

"What makes it a rule?" I interrupted.

"Call it an ancient code I guess. There is another rule about groups, but it's a softer rule. Basically if you and another group team up you shouldn't stab any of them in the back," Poncho paused. "That one mostly sticks. Sometimes."

"So who is in our group?" I asked getting worried.

"Just you, me, and Dirt," Poncho said.

"How many are in the other groups?"

"Usually around more than ten."

I knew his math wasn't good, but more than ten was a lot more than three. This was sounding worse, and worse.

"And Lonald is in his own group with Neph and his goons?"

"Probably."

"But none of his guys will try to kill us?"

"Unless they do," Poncho said.

"Fuck," I said.

"Yeah, it's usually a good time. Lots of fighting, then when there is one group left or a few allied groups it ends and everyone gets drunk."

Before I could come up with anything else to ask Dirt opened the door and got back in with a sigh.

"Did you get the weapons?" Poncho asked.

"No, he knew I'd forget so he put them in the trunk for me," Dirt explained.

"That was nice," Poncho said.

"Yeah, he knows his stuff."

"Who?" I asked getting confused.

Dirt just laughed at me and started driving. I guessed I wasn't getting any answers to this mystery any time soon. Not that I had gotten many answers to most of the stuff going on that is. Maybe if I survived this battle thing I could fish the truth out of them once and for all. I had little faith in that, but it was worth a shot.

Not too far down the road Dirt stopped at an abandoned drive-in movie theater. There were cars parked all around the edges of the place and groups of scary looking people lurking around the outskirts. They were mostly separated from any nearby groups with the members looking for the most part angry. I spotted more than a few of the type Dirt would call Frankensteins, but the rest just looked like regular folks. Scary looking regular folks, but nothing supernatural.

We got out of the car and lingered near it, as most of the others were doing. Lonald's group wasn't far away from us, and he nodded when he saw us, then headed to the center of the lot, dodging the old speaker stands that littered the place. While he was making his way to the center, Neph headed our way. I wasn't sure if it was as an official ambassador or just to say hi.

"Hi," she said when she got close.

So saying hi, that made me happy.

"As the official ambassador between our factions let me just say good luck," she said with a casual air about her.

Shit.

"Yeah, yeah. Official reply and so on," Dirt said not standing on ceremony.

Poncho nodded.

"I thought you guys would have a few more members. Three isn't good odds with all these other guys here," she said surveying the crowd.

"You should know as well as any numbers mean very little," Poncho said.

"True," Neph looked like she was going to say more when Lonald reached the center of the drive in and started to speak.

"Welcome everyone!" Lonald said loudly but calmly. "You all know the rules, but for the sake of formality I'll be going over them shortly."

Everyone visibly groaned at this, I guessed they weren't the type to honor formality.

"But first," Lonald continued. "For anyone left standing I have a trunk full of very nice bags as a trophy for winning the night. I do hope that everyone honors the old codes and just has a really nice time tonight."

Lonald was cut off by the sound of shouting, everyone's eyes were drawn across the lot to one of the groups having a disagreement. I have no idea what started it, but one of the larger men started bludgeoning one of his fellow group members into the ground. The guy getting beat wasn't going down fast, but he was for sure going down.

"Ancient code?" I asked Poncho.

He shrugged, "More of a gentleman's agreement than anything."

The beating went on, Lonald tapping his foot impatiently for it to end, when I heard music coming up the road. It started faint and got progressively louder, and it sounded like death metal. All of the groups nearby looked around trying to spot it as well until the source rounded the old movie snack shack and parked next to us.

It was Glen in one of those little two seat smart cars. I'm not sure how he got that music to come out of that tiny car so loud, but by the time he got out everyone was looking at him.

Not just looking either, some of them had fear in their eyes, Lonald looked downright nervous. The goon that had been beating his teammate picked up his former victim and brushed him off, handing him his weapon back.

I was mostly worried, Glen was a super nice guy, he had no business here. He was more likely to get killed than me.

Dirt and Poncho nodded to him and he gave a big goofy wave back.

"Hi guys!" he said happily.

I waved and looked back to Lonald, he had cleared his throat loudly and continued to speak.

"So as I was saying, it's the different bags, the ones completely different from the previous bags. I repeat: Not the old bags." What he was saying made no sense, and he was gesturing frantically towards Neph.

One of his gestures was the universal sign for stop doing anything, that or he wanted her to cut someone's throat.

When she nodded to him he relaxed a little and got back into his ringmaster bit.

I stopped paying attention around then because Dirt had started rummaging around in the trunk and it broke me from my stupor. Before I looked away from the amassed killers I did notice that a lot of the groups had started moving closer to each other, and it didn't look like they wanted to fight each other anymore. It was almost like they were afraid of Glen.

But that was silly.

Dirt pulled Poncho's axe out of the trunk and handed it to him, he also pulled out a stick and a jug, which he sat on the ground.

"If I'm not allowed to use a gun, what am I supposed to do?" I asked finally remembering the most troubling rule.

"I've got that covered," Dirt said, handing me a battered baseball bat. "Use this."

The bat felt good in my hands, but I had the feeling I was being set up for failure. I decided to distract myself.

"What are you doing here Glen?" I asked.

"Yeah, what are you doing here?" Dirt asked accusingly.

Glen was dressed in a polo and khakis, and it gave me the impression that he wasn't there to fight. Maybe he was the caterer.

"Well I would have been here sooner, but I couldn't find my keys. I looked in all the usual places you hide them Dirt, but after they weren't on the hook by the door I just got all flustered. When I found them on the seat of my car I knew you were just trying to help, but you could have told me. I almost had a heart attack!" Glen said as politely as he says everything.

"That's a terrible excuse, you show up late listening to your crazy music dressed like a tool. You are a disgrace to the team, Glen," Dirt said.

"I'm really sorry guys, I'll get changed right away!"

Glen took off his shirt and started to fold it up neatly, I was surprised by what was under his shirt. Where I thought there would be the soft body of a cubicle rat was a chiseled block of muscle. He wasn't bulky like Poncho, but he was freakishly in shape. Neph gasped and backed away a few steps muttering to herself.

This was all very confusing to me.

Glen stripped down to his underwear, and slipped on the most ragged pair of pants I had ever seen. It looked like they had narrowly escaped a wood chipper only to end up in landfill for a few years before he found them. Once he had them on put his folded clothes inside the car and looked expectantly at Dirt.

"That's better," Dirt said.

Glen wasn't even wearing shoes.

"Good to see you again Thunderaxe," Poncho said as if he hadn't seen him this very morning.

When Neph heard this she all but panicked and started waving her hands frantically at Lonald. When he noticed her through his droning on about ceremony and whatever she made a series of hand gestures at him. His eyes got wide and he changed what he was saying.

"As a correction to before, it's the third bags. The bags that in no way involve doing anything. The very simple bags with no ulterior motives," Lonald said and jumped right back into his prepared speech.

Neph relaxed a little, but didn't take her eyes off Glen.

"What the fuck is going on?" I asked, properly angry now.

"Calm down Frank. Let's have a customary drink before we start and everything will be fine," Dirt said, handing Poncho the jug from the trunk.

Poncho took a swig and smiled. "He really came through this time." Then passed it to Neph.

She looked at it warily, but took a drink despite her peculiar nervousness. She smiled knowingly and handed it to me.

I decided that if I was going to be murdered I might as well do it drunk. So I took a strong pull, it was some kind of wine. Normally I don't like wine but this stuff was great, I was about to take a second drink when Dirt snatched it out of my hands.

"That's enough for you Frank," he said before helping himself to a hearty drink.

When he was done he handed it to Glen, who paused before drinking.

"You said you were going to bring me a weapon?" Glen asked timidly.

"You're looking at it," Dirt said with a mischievous grin.

Glen got an evil smile on his face and chugged the remainder of the jug, then smashed it to bits on the ground.

"I'll pick that up before we leave," Glen said, embarrassed.

Around this time I had planned to find out why everyone was so afraid of Glen, but my words got stupid.

"How come... Glen?" I slurred. I frowned, not sure what had just happened to my mouth.

"Shut up Frank, you drunk bastard," Dirt said laughing.

"M'not drunk," I said sounding very drunk. My mind still seemed clear, but I couldn't get any of that to come out right and my body was acting very drunk. I was sure I was going to die.

"Don't worry Frank, I'll look out for you," Dirt said, not reassuring me at all.

I attempted to say something else, but all that came out was grunts and I fell down. I looked out to the lot where Lonald had wrapped up his speech and was heading back to his goons.

Neph readied her blades.

Poncho hefted his axe.

Glen started a primal, terrifying yell.

"Just so you know, almost everything me and Ponch told you was a lie. If you live through this I'll tell you the truth," Dirt said grinning at me.

And the next thing I knew Dirt was lifting me to my feet and we charged into battle.

# ~Dirt~

## *The Thunderaxe*

*A while back me and Poncho were headed down a road in some place I forget. It was a pretty important road, basically the biggest road around. It led from some big city, through some other cities and ending in some shit hole city in Russia I think.*

**It was the King's Road.**

*That's right, the King's Road, up in the frozen north with all the big hairy Vikings and shit. I don't remember why we were on this road, probably trying to avoid the law because Poncho punched somebody's horse or something.*

**I never punched any horses on the King's Road.**

*Fine, arson then, you probably burned somebody's horses down. And of course it wouldn't have been on the road, if it was we wouldn't have been evading the law on it. Come on man, keep up.*

*So there we were, trudging down this road, I don't remember which direction, it doesn't really matter. It was cold, windy, rainy, and getting dark. I hadn't had a drink in hours and I'm pretty sure I was dying. Then I see a light in the distance, surely I've gone mad and started hallucinating my way to death in the slush. But I soldiered on, making for the mysterious light, perhaps it was our savior, or perhaps it was the cold light of oblivion.*

*We never found out which one it was, because it was a torch. A torch attached to an inn, which with any luck had large amounts of alcohol.*

*We entered the cozy establishment and made for a seat by the fire. It was your typical inn, scarred wood tables that were sturdy enough to be treated rough, animal heads nailed to the walls, and it even had a table full of ruffians being rowdy by the back wall. It was everything I could've hoped for, the only thing that could've made it better was a busty wench strolling over with two big ass tankards of ale.*

*Instead of a busty wench this guy comes over, he is an unassuming man, kind of hunched over like he just pissed on your shoes and not at all confident. I hated him right away.*

*"What can I get you?" he asks us.*

*"Beers," I tell him.*

*Now he looks even more sad, like I just punched his dog, I bet he didn't even have a dog to punch either. Nobody with a dog is that fucking sad.*

*"Are you sure? I just made a big pot of stew for those gentlemen back there, but they changed their minds and I'd just hate to see it go to waste," he says all fidgety.*

*I start to tell him to shut his mouth and that I'm not hungry and to shut up again, but Ponch shoves his stupid delicious looking ham fist in my face and nods at the guy. I try to tell him I wasn't hungry but Poncho doesn't listen, he just wants to stuff more food down his face.*

**You were chewing on a tree branch just before we walked in.**

*If I'm chewing on a tree branch that's my own god damn business, doesn't mean I was hungry either. It's good for rickets.*

**You can't get rickets.**

*I know, because of tree branches. It's really not that complicated, man. Plus, it keeps your breath fresh.*

*So a minute or so goes by and this guy brings us a couple of huge tankards, like way bigger than normal. I almost cried at the sight of it, it was majestic.*

*"I'm sorry friends, these are all I had left. I hope it's not a problem, I'll be right back with your stew." He starts to leave and Poncho starts to get all pissy like a little girl because he didn't tell us his name this time.*

*He gets all, "Hey friend, I didn't catch your name, friend." Then he starts cracking his knuckles and being all menacing and shit, while poor ol' 'who the fuck cares' starts getting all fidgety back.*

*"Oh, how very rude of me. It sure has been a long night. Folks around here just call me Glen now," so he says before he gets all scared off by Poncho's menacing.*

**He offered us stew and I asked him his name. You don't eat a man's stew without knowing his name.**

*By the time he brought the stew my mug was empty, it was something like three minutes for fuck sake. Then I saw Glen on his way back, I was about to tell him what I thought of his shit service, until I saw that in addition to the stew he was somehow balancing four massive tankards filled to the brim and not spilling a drop.*

*"I love you Glen," I told him. At this point I knew I could trust Glen for the rest of time, he was a miracle among men and just a fucking winner all around.*

*"Hey, it's my pleasure having respectable gentlemen in here for once," says Glen.*

*"Those guys aren't respectable?" I asked pointing at the ruffians in the back. They looked like a fun loving bunch, shouting and carrying on like they were. I couldn't figure out why Glen didn't like them, I just chalked it up to him being kind of a square.*

"Oh no! Those rascals are bandits, they come in here sometimes, drinking and getting rowdy. They just wreck the place and don't pay for anything. I tell you, the King's Road is no place for an honest businessman anymore. But look at me talking your ears off! I'll go fetch you some roasted lamb now that the stew has you warmed up."

"No thanks Glen, just beers for me," I tell him.

"Are you sure? It's been slow cooking all day, the meat is likely to just melt in your mouth."

Glen wasn't making it easy to say no, so I say, "No man, it sounds great, but I'm on a liquid diet."

"That's a shame, I used my special seasonings on it, I promise you that you'll never find better lamb on the entire King's road," Glen was desperate.

"Bring the whole thing," Poncho says slapping his money bag on the table.

Well, then Glen gets this smile on his face that you wouldn't have been able to scrape off with a bulldozer, and rushes to the kitchen.

"Why did you encourage him? Now we have to eat his stupid backwoods food and pretend to like it because he is so nice. I fucking hate you," I say to Ponch.

But he just shrugs like some kind of indifferent tough guy. So I make it my goal to finish all my beers *before he comes back, that way I have one up on him. But right about the time I polish off the second one Glen shows back up with a giant plate of meat and more tankards in his hand. This guy was too good.*

*He clears away the empties and the empty stew bowls, I didn't even remember eating it, and sets the meat plate down. It smelled ok, for goat.*

**It was the single best meal I had eaten up to that point.**

*Well yeah, it was ok.*

**Really?**

*Shit, fine, it was amazing. Cooking that good would get you burnt as a witch in most places, I can't even explain the explosion of flavors that danced across my taste buds that day. Miracle is the only word acceptable to describe this food. This meal has never been recreated just to make sure its memory can never be sullied by an inferior reproduction.*

*That being said, Glen watched us house the whole thing, big stupid grin all over his face. When we were done I realized I hadn't touched my beers while I was stuffing my face, and that's no easy task to pull off.*

*"Glen you are a fucking warlock," I tell him.*

*"You flatter me, but to be honest that wasn't even my best work. If you stick around 'til tomorrow I can try again, I'm sure I'll get it right next time," Glen says.*

*"If you cook anything better than this the earth will cave in around you and the sky will crash down on your head, jealous that neither can take part in this pleasure, the earth will destroy itself," Ponch says to him.*

*Always the dramatic type.*

**I didn't say any of that.**

*Sure you did, you just can't remember because you were deep in the throes of the meat sweats.*

*Anyway, Glen starts blushing and fidgeting again, then he says, "I'll go whip you guys up some pastries, I never get the chance to bake for people anymore!"*

*He scurried off before I could stop him, I probably wouldn't have though, this fucker could cook and I wanted more. Ponch looked like he wanted more too, his eyes were all rolled back in his head and he was just moaning a bunch. It was awkward as hell.*

**I wasn't doing any of that.**

*Yes you were, don't deny it. You wanted to marry Glen and have his babies after eating that goat. It was shameful the way you acted.*

*But to be perfectly honest it was really good and Glen seemed like a standup guy, at the very least he was an excellent server and cook. Just one of those things is enough to judge a person acceptable, but both is like finding a unicorn that pisses beer.*

**How many times do I have to tell you that horse wasn't a unicorn? And it definitely wasn't pissing beer.**

*You keep being a skeptic, that's fine, next one I find I'm not sharing.*

*Anyway, not five minutes goes by and Glen is back with pastries. I don't question why he was so fast, because I didn't really care. I tend not to question people bringing me more beer and fresh dessert as well.*

*It probably doesn't need to be said, but they were fantastic. Some kind of flaky crust stuffed with sugared up fruit, it was pretty bitchin' stuff.*

*Well, by this time me and Ponch are just leaning back, full as baby fat things just enjoying the warmth. I settled back and watched the ruffians horsing around with some game I couldn't decipher. It involved a lot of punching and arguing, it looked like a lot of fun, and I would have joined in, but I was content.*

**Which is rare.**

*Fuck you, I can be content whenever I want.*

*Glen cleaned up all our empties and plates the whole time wearing that stupid grin. While he was doing that he started to hum a little, which made him just seem absurdly cheerful. It was sickening.*

*I was contemplating what things I could do to push his buttons. Everyone needs their buttons pushed once and a while, it's good for the blood. Or maybe it is good for the brain, it's good for something at any rate. I had just come up with the clever plan of dumping beer all over the floor to see if that set him off when a group of different ruffians entered the inn.*

*They looked pretty much like the standard bandit types, just like the guys that were already there. But the way they eyeballed each other you could tell they were from different gangs, or whatever they called them. I disregarded them because I found a fatal flaw in my plan to mess with Glen. In order to dump beer on the floor I would have to waste beer, it wasn't an easy decision to make. Maybe the hardest choice I never had to make. I didn't have to make it because Glen came back and he had a scowl on his face. Had he sensed my plan to spill beer and he was already mad? I didn't know, but somehow I had done it.*

*But Glen isn't looking at me, and that annoys me. He is looking at the ruffians, the new batch had taken a table a few away from the previous group, and they were quieter now. It looked like a fight was imminent, so dinner* and a show, what a good evening this was shaping up to be.

By the look on Glen's face I could tell he didn't agree. He just kept scowling and looking from one group to the other, he didn't even bring the new group any drinks. That just seemed rude to me, but I didn't own the place so fuck 'em.

The stalemate between bandit factions appeared that it would hold, because after a few minutes of silence they started to ignore each other. The new group waved to Glen and he reluctantly brought them some beers. He didn't bring them the big ones like me and Ponch had, even though he claimed to be out of regular sized ones. I am sure he gave us the big ones because he could recognize VIP's when he saw them and broke out the good china. These bandit goons got the shit cups.

When both tables of goons had fresh drinks the noise picked up again. Glen came back to our table and stood, not saying anything. Which again, I found rude.

"What's up your ass Glen?" I asked him. "Those guys punch your puppy or something?"

He fidgeted some more and said, "Nothing like that, I just can't help but feel like trouble is coming."

"Trouble isn't anything to worry about, they can fight it out between themselves, and you'll be fine," I tell him.

*"I don't like trouble, I wish they could just get along," Glen says, twisting his rag up.*

*This guy was really nervous for some reason. I couldn't figure it out, it was an unspoken rule that no matter what sort of banditry you are involved in you never hurt a good innkeeper. And even if tonight was just a fluke Glen was still one of the best innkeepers I had ever seen. There was no way these guys would hurt him. They probably just didn't want to fight each other in the cold.*

*Then out of nowhere a small tankard goes flying from one table to the next, spilling beer all over one of the bigger goons. Shit almost got real after that, they all stood up and started yelling and staring each other down. But this wasn't the kind of offense that would get solved by posturing; blood would be spilled for sure.*

*The next thing I know Glen is over there between both groups trying to break them up. Poncho was interested now and he leaned forward to get a better look. He always knows when a fight is coming, but he rarely stays out of it. There were a lot of them, that's why I assume he was chicken this time.*

**There were only less than ten of them per group.**

*That could be anywhere between two and eighteen.*

**That's what I said. Less than ten per group, child's play.**

*Whatever, at the time I didn't know why Ponch was hanging back, but in retrospect it makes sense, because Glen murdered almost everyone in that room except me and Ponch.*

*It started when they shoved Glen away from them, the mutual agreement to not harm a good innkeeper staying strong. But Glen didn't appear to want to get away from them, he was determined to stop this fight, but they weren't in a listening mood.*

*The fists started flying and it was a full on brawl in a matter of seconds. Nobody had drawn weapons yet, but it was getting heated and blood would be flowing soon. When you've seen a few bar fights you can tell these kinds of things. Glen was trying to interject, but they just kept shoving his dumb ass back out of the fray. Finally he just stands there, shoulders slumped in defeat. He looked sad, but I was happy he stopped attempting to break up a good brawl.*

*But then he grabs a stray axe off the floor and starts swinging.*

*"This is a family establishment!" he yells at the top of his lungs. Then the axe goes plowing into some poor saps neck and he dies.*

*Everyone in the place stops, Glen pulls his bloody axe out of that guy and stands there breathing heavy. The goons all look at each other and the come to a decision, kill the innkeeper instead. They start gathering their weapons and surrounding Glen.*

*"I asked you rascals to break it up, now this had to happen. If you promise to be civil from now on you can drink for free the rest of the night," Glen tells them.*

*Shit was escalating and I even started to get up and give him a hand, but Poncho stops me with a hand on the shoulder.*

*"Just watch," He says.*

*I don't argue with Poncho when it comes to fight stuff, so I sat down.*

**You do nothing but argue about fight stuff.**

*Well this time I didn't so you are wrong, I'd explain to you all the reasons you are wrong about a lot of things, but this story just started to get good. So shut your mouth please.*

*So there he is, the seemingly meek innkeeper who happens to be gigantic, surrounded by one to seventeen bandits, and just about to die. He doesn't look worried, and neither do they, also neither do we. Glen was pure resolve by now, he set his jaw and waited. It was very intense.*

*The bandits did some quick bandit math and decided that there were more of them than there were innkeepers. So a few of the braver ones rushed Glen, and* then they were dead. I don't know all the fancy fight words like Ponch does, but two guys ran at Glen and he moved around a little and cut the first one in the side, right under the ribs where it's soft. That was it for that guy. The second one was still coming and not terribly worried about his pal, or maybe it was one of the rival guys, pals for now anyway. This guy starts yelling, probably he forgot we were indoors and we could all hear him just fine, and takes a swing at Glen. But now Glen isn't where the blade was aimed, he was off to the side again burying his axe into the guys back.

That's how the scout party died, the rest were much more spectacular. Realizing that three of them were now dead they decided that caution with carefully planned overwhelming force was the key. At least that is what I suspect, because they came at Glen in as big of groups as they could manage in the tight space.

The problem for the bandits was that Glen was never where he was supposed to be, he was always stepping just out of the way of all those blades coming after him. And every time he was out of the way he was killing a guy, then he was moving and killing another guy. It was amazing, he never stopped moving and never stopped killing.

**It's how berserkers fight.**

Yeah, those guys are rare, they never last long. But Glen must have been the king of berserkers, he was so *calm before he went into his killing trance that you couldn't ever believe he was death on legs. I hate to admit it, but this guy was the only person I've ever seen more at one with a battle axe than Poncho.*

**I wholeheartedly agree.**

*So a few minutes of Glen killing and moving goes by, the only sound is yelling and the dull thud of Glen's axe cleaving flesh and bone. It was pretty gross; Poncho on the other hand was pretty much drooling. It was sad how much he wanted to have Glen's babies.*

**I wasn't drooling and I didn't want to have his babies.**

*I'll give you half on that one, you pick which half.*

*After a while there was only one guy left, and he didn't look excessively keen on going toe to toe with Glen. Glen looked like a maniac, he was covered in blood and his eyes were blank, like the stare you get after eating too many tacos. This guy is shaking pretty bad and almost drops his sword. It looks pretty bad for him as Glen starts walking up to him.*

*The guy drops his sword and falls to his knees when Glen gets within axe distance of him and starts weeping like a baby.*

*"Please don't kill me!" he whines. "I'm sorry we got in a fight! I'll do anything if you don't kill me!" It was pretty sad.*

*Then the craziest thing happened, Glen didn't kill him. He just helps him off the ground and brushes some chunks of his buddies off the guys shoulder. His demeanor appeared to have returned to his normal boring guy thing too.*

*"That's all I wanted, a simple apology. Do you want some soup and a hot drink to settle your nerves young man?" Glen asks him.*

*This guy starts crying even more now, it's unsettling, and he nods assent to the soup and drink.*

*Glen leads him to some back room, the whole time the guy is repeating "I'm sorry" and "Thank you" over and over.*

*Now I'm getting upset though, during all this fighting Glen didn't refill my beer, and it was getting low. This service was great right up until my beer got low, the food was good, the show was good, despite the ending, but an empty drink was unredeemable.*

*Then a bloody hand slaps a fresh tankard down in front of me, mother fucking warlock this guy was.*

*"I'm sorry about those guys. Some people have just the worst manners," Glen says transferring equal*

*amounts of blood from his hands to his apron and back again.*

*"No problem Glen, it has been one hell of a night. You fucking warlocked this beer on me. That is impressive for any innkeep," I tell him.*

*Poncho nods at him, Glen nods back. Probably some kind of stupid warrior code bullshit, I would have bet money they were going to kiss on the mouth any minute. I would have lost that money though, because they didn't, unless they did it when I wasn't looking, which was likely.*

**We didn't kiss on the mouth.**

*Oh, so just not on the mouth then, that's fair. Don't tell me the details of you guys and all your kissing, none of my business really.*

*Glen seems a little relieved that we had decided to forego litigation in recompense for our psychological damage incurred during the aforementioned bloodbath. Not that it was a proper bath, just in the sense that there was a lot of blood, so much that you could have taken a bath in it.*

*All of a sudden Glen slaps his head and groans. "Rats! Now I have to clean this mess up. This just isn't my day."*

*"You could just burn the place down," Poncho says with that pyro gleam in his eye.*

**I'm not a pyro.**

*Pyro means you like to start fires dummy.*

**Oh, then yeah, pyro works.**

*"I couldn't do that! It's such a nice building, it would be a shame to burn it. I'll just have to take them out back and sort it out in the morning," Glen says, heading towards the corpse pile.*

*Then Poncho gets up and walks over there too. "I'll help," He says.*

*"I couldn't ask you to do that!" Glen replies all mortified.*

*"I respect a good fight. I'll help," Poncho tells him.*

*Glen reluctantly accepts the help and they survey the pile deciding how to start.*

*"I'll supervise," I tell them. I wasn't about to start carting bodies around for no reason, not with a drink in my hand.*

*So Poncho and Glen start carrying bodies out the back door, Poncho hauling two or three at a time and Glen with one. It went fast, and pretty soon they had hauled all of the two to eighteen bodies outside to rot in the subzero temperatures.*

On the way back from carting the last body Glen brought me a fresh beer; we were pretty much best friends by then. After that he picks up a mop and starts to clean up the bloody mess all over the floor.

Needless to say things got boring around then, no more jolly bandit types, just cleaning. That was until the surviving bandit came back from wherever he was having his stew and puked on the floor. The sight of his friends' blood all over the floor was too much to take. What a waste of stew that guy was.

Glen rushes over to him and helps him to a seat by the fire. "You just sit here and look at the fire, you've been through a lot, just take it easy."

The guy nods and sits down, Glen drapes a blanket over him and heads back to his blood mess.

"Follow me," Poncho says out of nowhere and gets up.

I follow him, because it might be something neat, and I didn't have anything better to do. He leads me to the back door and we go outside.

"What the fuck is out here? The cold? Seen it, not impressed," I say.

Ponch points at the pile of dead guys.

"I've seen piles of dead guys too, this isn't even close to the biggest one," I say.

*Ponch shakes his head and points harder, I'm not sure how someone points harder but he was doing it.*

**You just needed to look harder.**

*You could have said that you know, not just pointing at stuff all the time. Use your words sometimes, it's pretty amazing what you can do with them.*

**You have more than enough words for the both of us.**

*Fair enough pal.*

*So I look at the bodies some more and I realize that there is something under the pile. I look closer and I see that it's a different, older pile of dead guys, a whole bunch of them. That's when I notice the full scale of what I'm looking at, the entire back of this inn is littered with frozen corpses. Hundreds of them.*

*One thing was for sure, this place was going to stink come spring. Also another thing, Glen was either a fucking badass, or a god damn psychopath serial killer. No matter which one he was it was very impressive. It was hard to tell, but they all looked pretty much like bandit corpses, so at least he was a good guy.*

*As we were surveying the corpse garden Glen had planted, Glen came outside to dump his mop bucket.*

*"So many ruffians roaming the roads these days, it's impossible to run a nice business. All I want is a place*

*where people come in, stay warm, have a drink and a bite to eat, but these rascals keep trying to ruin it. I warned each and every one, they just don't listen. I don't blame them though, it's probably lack of parenting," Glen says calmly.*

*"So you killed them and dumped them out here?" I asked. I was a little stunned by this whole thing, which doesn't happen often.*

*Glen looks ashamed and says, "Well they didn't give me a choice really, I didn't want to hurt them, but they wouldn't calm down."*

*"Wow." That was all I could say.*

*"Running a business isn't easy, you've got to break some eggs to make an omelet they say," Glen says, washing the blood off his hands in the snow.*

*"Can you make us omelets?" I almost shouted in Glen's face.*

*"Sure, everything is cleaned up, I'll freshen your drinks and whip up some eggs. Have a seat." Glen opens the door for us and we go sit down.*

*Glen shows up with more beers and some pretty awesome looking omelets not five minutes later. He is the best living thing I had ever met.*

*The surviving bandit had shaken himself out of his shock when he smelled the eggs and shambled over. As luck would have it, Glen had made the bandit and himself one as well. We all sat down drinking beer and eating eggs, it was perfect.*

*"Are you going to keep running this place with all the ruffians around?" I ask Glen between mouthfuls.*

*"I don't know, I really don't know anymore," he says.*

*"Hmm, well if you want out you can come with us," I tell him.*

*Poncho almost chokes on his eggs, because he is a great big idiot that never learned how to be surprised by things.*

**You never let people come with us. It was shocking.**

*I let people come with us all the time, they just usually die soon after so you forget them.*

*Glen is also shocked though. "Why!? What good could I be to traveling adventurers like yourself?" he asks.*

*"Hey man," I tell him. "You can cook, you are quick with a drink and you can handle yourself in a fight. What more could we ask for?"*

*"Well if you'll have me, I'd be honored. I don't think I'm cut out to be an innkeeper," Glen says.*

"It's settled then!" I say and we all clank mugs together.

"But what about this place?" Glen asks, clearly having second thoughts.

"He can take over," Ponch says pointing at that guy who wasn't dead.

That guy cowered under Poncho's direct acknowledgement of his existence. "Yeah, I'll turn my life around and run the best inn I can!" he says.

"That work?" I ask Glen.

"That's how I started here, works for me," Glen says.

We spend the rest of the night there drinking and staying warm. It was a good night, and in the morning we headed back out onto the road, this time with Glen in tow. He immediately started whistling, I wasn't sure if it was annoying or not.

"What was the name of that inn?" Poncho asks.

"Oh, the sign fell off years ago, but the gentleman I inherited it from called it The Thunderaxe."

"Neat," I said.

Then Poncho starts muttering to himself. "Thunderaxe, I like it."

"Glen and the Thunderaxe. That works for me," I added so Ponch couldn't steal the last word.

**I wasn't trying to steal your last word.**

Stop it!

**Stop what?**

Seriously Ponch, stop it! Last words, the end.

# Battle Royal

Luckily it only took a few steps into the charge to get my feet back under me, I hadn't been looking forward to getting killed while I was curled up on the ground drunk off my ass. I still felt a little off, a little like I was watching myself do everything, or maybe I was just thinking faster than I was acting.

While we were running towards certain violence, time seemed to slow down and I could hear Glen shouting.

"Poncho take the biggest guy, I'll handle the next biggest! Dirt and Neph on rear guard! Frank, try not to die!" Glen shouted, right before he and Poncho annihilated the outer ring of the biggest group of bad guys.

It looked like a chainsaw hitting a butter sculpture, or what I imagine that would look like. It was just blades swinging and blood spraying. I'm not sure what Glen did to defend himself from the blades coming his way, but by the time we breached the defensive perimeter he had an axe in each hand. Then it was carnage, Poncho and Glen cut a swath of destruction into the heart of them.

Rear guard consisted mostly of just staying close to our frontal assault and keeping goons from blindsiding one of them. Neph darted in and out cutting down stragglers and would be opportunists as the situation arose, while Dirt did whatever Dirt did.

"Did you stretch before we started Frank?" Dirt asked while smashing the teeth into a man's head with his staff. "Cause if you cramp up shits gonna get rough."

I didn't have time to answer because one of the stragglers came at me, I barely had time to bring my bat up and smack him in the face. This seemed to daze him a little and reflex took over. I beat him in the face and head until he went limp on the ground. It was the most disgusting thing I had ever done.

I promptly threw up.

"Fucking gross Frank," Dirt said dancing away from a swinging blade and countering with a smashed nose.

Oddly when I got done battle puking I felt better, and I had quickly come to terms that it was kill or be killed. And I didn't want to die all that much so I steadied myself and started swinging.

Having never been in a medieval style fight like this, I didn't really know what to expect, but it turned out to be pretty simple.

Find a guy that you don't know, then kill that guy. I wasn't the best at killing, but there was enough chaos going on that it seemed almost easy. Not as easy as Poncho and Glen made it look though, they had pretty much mopped up anyone over six feet tall and had started cutting down the rest. Their battle mentality seemed to be start at the biggest and work your way down.

It seemed like only seconds had passed when everything got quiet, there were still the sounds of fighting but they sounded distant. I assumed that I was mortally wounded and it was a side effect of dying. When I looked around though, all I saw were bodies and four blood spattered people standing amongst them.

We had killed the entire group of people already, there were still plenty others around, but they were keeping their distance.

I threw up again.

"It's not over yet Frank, pull up your big boy pants and fuck some dudes up," Dirt said attempting to swing his staff around like in the movies and dropping it in a pile of dead guy.

Then there was shouting again, at first I thought we were under attack again, but it was Glen. He was beating the blunt end of one of his axes against his chest and screaming like a mad man.

"Glen is gone," Poncho said.

Then Glen took off at a sprint to the closest batch of fighting, still screaming.

"Kill 'em all Thunderaxe!" Dirt shouted after him.

"I got his back, stay with Frank," Poncho said before he took off after Glen--or Thunderaxe.

They both hit the group much like before, but this time Glen looked a lot more unhinged, he was moving faster and far more carelessly. I guessed Poncho just didn't want him getting hurt, but his method of watching his back was just killing people. Pretty much exactly like he was doing.

"Should we follow?" I asked.

"Safest place to be," Dirt said running the opposite direction towards different fighting. "Neph, watch Frank!"

"Move!" Neph shouted.

I did, and we ran right to Poncho and Glen.

This group of bad guys was smaller than the previous one, but much tougher. I decided it was probably because not everyone followed our team's philosophy, and killed the weakest first, and since they had already been fighting each other the better fighters were all that was left. I almost got tagged once or twice, but I managed to fend off the attacks with blunt force in the form of a bat.

That was until a fairly large well-muscled fellow came at me. He didn't fall for my 'yell in terror while lashing out with my bat' tactic. So I had to improvise, I wasn't sure how blocking worked in practice, but my theory was sound. When he swings his sword at me, swing the bat out and hit it, or maybe that was a parry. Who knows, it worked. When I had smacked the sword away from me the last time I tagged him in the nose with the butt of the bat and when he was stunned I beat him into the ground.

It worried me that I wasn't too bad at this, but I was also pretty happy to not be dead. I guess it balanced out.

I didn't know where Dirt had run off to, and I didn't really want to tangle my mind up with it so I focused on what was in front of me. Which was also nothing I ever wanted to see, so much blood and death, and the smell. The smell was worse than I could have thought.

Poncho and Glen had continued cutting their way around the battle field, killing each enemy they faced a little slower each time. I wasn't sure if it was because they were getting tougher, or my comrades were getting tired. Either way they were still the most destructive thing around.

Neph and I followed in their wake finishing off the wounded and taking on the stragglers, she was much quicker than me and probably saved my life a dozen times, but I managed to help her avoid grievous injury on a few occasions. My method for that was to smash in the back of anyone's head that I thought she may not have seen in time to defend herself against. I wasn't sure if she needed the help all that much, but when I got a few head nods and even a smile, I knew I was a beast among men.

Then I got knocked down and almost killed. Something blunt hit me in the shoulder blades and I slammed into the blood soaked concrete, rolling to my back just in time to stop a club from crushing me into mush. With a combination of rolling and bat deflection I managed not to die right away. I frantically looked around for help, but Neph was busy fighting two angry looking men with scimitars.

I couldn't get up, and I was running out of ways to defend myself when the pummeling stopped. His club dropped to his side and he fell to his knees, revealing Dirt behind him with a cracked staff.

"You can't sleep here Frank, that guy tried to kill you! I broke my stick on him," Dirt said throwing the broken staff away and helping me to me feet.

"Thanks," I said brushing some of the gore from my tuxedo and grabbing my hat off the ground.

"Don't change the subject, you owe me a new stick," Dirt said, crossing his arms.

The battle looked to be winding down some, with pockets of resistance rallying together to make runs at the now back to back Poncho and Glen.

"Where were you?" I asked, changing the subject.

"Helping Lonald and his guys," Dirt said poking through the dead bodies, presumably looking for a new stick.

"How are they doing?" I asked.

"They're all dead I think," Dirt said, he was looking through a wallet and pulled out some cash and a library card. He stuffed them into his pocket and ditched the wallet.

"What?" I almost shouted.

"Yeah."

"Is Lonald ok?" Neph yelled appearing at my side.

"Nada chicka." Dirt did not look very upset.

"Shit," Neph and I said at the same time.

"What happened?" she asked, not looking as upset as I would have assumed.

"I'll tell you after the fight, there's still dudes around to kill!" Dirt said, excitedly running for a few steps before stopping to pick up what looked like a new staff.

"Hey Frank, you still owe me another one. This one is shit."

We ran after Dirt, filing the Lonald comment away for later, towards a much smaller group than the previous ones. I was starting to think this fight would be a blowout, until we got close that is. These guys were about as bloody as we were and looked like they had been killing just as many people as we had been. There were about five of them and they had just finished decapitating someone before they turned around to face us. Poncho and Glen were nowhere close, it looked like we were on our own this time.

Dirt ran in first swinging his stick like a madman, it was easily deflected throwing Dirt off balance. The bigger man wielding a two handed sword quickly advanced on the now off-balance Dirt.

I didn't see what happened next because Neph jumped in front of me to block an incoming attack. Then we were all in for the fight of our lives.

"Fuck!" I heard Dirt yell at the sound of breaking wood. I guess it really was a shitty stick.

Then I hit the ground again.

And this time I was bleeding.

It took me a second to realize what had happened, apparently when Neph pushed the guy she was fighting away from her, he hit me blade first in the arm, and we both went down.

I didn't have time to fully examine the wound, but my arm still moved and we both scrambled to our feet. I assumed we would square off and start fighting, but as soon as he got his feet under him he charged weaponless at me, catching me in the gut with his shoulder.

We hit the ground again, him wailing at my face with his fists and me barely soaking up the blows with my arms.

This went on long enough to decide I didn't like it very much and lifted my hips when he was in mid swing, throwing him off balance and landing on top of him. He tried to pull me down to his face, I think to bite me, but I bashed my forehead into his nose, crushing it.

His hands went limp enough for me to start raining down elbows on his face. I learned this from tactic from a few school yard brawls. Elbows hurt way more than fists, it just doesn't look as fancy.

He stopped moving soon after and I grabbed a short sword off the ground and put it through his neck to stop his resisting.

I raised my head to try and see who was going to try and kill me next. What I saw instead was Neph being beaten back by two men who had her on the defensive. I reached over, found my bat, and dragged myself to my feet, feeling the cut on my arm a lot more. The two goons didn't see me get up and I wasted no time charging the closest one.

He had his back to me and I swung for the fences, the fences being the back of his knee that is. He went down with a yelp and I promptly beat his face to pulp. The other man looked my way when his pal yelled. It wasn't long, but it was enough for Neph, and the next thing I saw was his head rolling across the ground.

We were in the clear for the moment.

Dirt now had a stick in each hand, I guessed it was the one he broke not that long ago and was pummeling the man he had broken it on. I didn't know how the fight had gone, but he was winning now, and with a flourish and a completely unnecessary backwards spinning swing, broke his opponent's neck.

There weren't any more bad guys in the near vicinity, and I could see some on the outskirts running away. It looked like we had won the night.

I glanced around until I saw Poncho. He was helping Glen back to the car, they were done fighting too it seemed.

I was relieved, and a little nauseous, but I didn't have anything else to puke up. We headed back to the car as well, avoiding the dead bodies that littered the ground.

I wasn't sure what I was supposed to feel about this, but one thing was for sure. I was glad to be alive.

We passed Lonald's body on the way. He was surrounded by his body guards and they were all cut up pretty bad.

Neph shook her head and sighed, that was the extent of her mourning period as she continued on.

I looked at Dirt and he just shrugged, even he seemed ragged after the fighting.

When we got back to the car Poncho was sitting Glen down against his ridiculous little car. They were both covered in blood, which I expected after the way they were fighting. But I looked closer at Glen and noticed that a lot of the blood on him was coming from the giant slash across his abdomen.

"I see London, I see France! I see Glen's guts all over his pants!" Dirt shouted pointing.

I threw up again.

# Poncho's Battle Royal

Why does Lonald insist on telling everyone the rules when no one ever listens? I imagine he just loves being the center of attention. The rules are always the same, except when the Thunderaxe shows up, and then who fucking cares. I will follow the lunatic around to make sure he doesn't take a killing blow. Dirt can worry about keeping Frank upright, he's good at that. No, that won't work. Neph will keep Frank upright. He will be fine. Dirt's plan will work, whatever the fuck it is.

Finally this fool Lonald is done wasting air, show me where we are headed Thunderaxe. To glory and the sweet smell of victory. Hell yeah, looks like Ol' Thunderaxe is going for the two coward groups who think two is better than one. What is the honor in joining up to even the odds? Won't matter.

Thunderaxe is shouting something. Could be important, but who cares. I will just follow his lead to these Sallies, numbers are stupid anyways.

Me and Thunderaxe rushed the unsuspecting fools in their big cluster and started killing them. Glen got three right away. By the time I was on four he had five. When he got to more than five I was also at more than five.

But when he got to more than ten I was still at less than ten.

This won't stand. I stepped up my killing and we got around to even. But there were way more than more than ten guys here. Maybe more than one hundred, but less than one thousand.

One thousand is less than one hundred. Right?

By the time we are done with this I'll have no idea how many we killed.

I could ask Neph.

No, that isn't safe. I'll ask Frank. He won't notice. If he says there are more than one hundred I'll say I killed half of one hundred, and Thunderaxe killed less than half of one hundred. That would probably be believable.

We stopped and Thunderaxe lost his mind, I tell Dirt I'll watch him.

Slashing and killing, blood everywhere. Everything just looks red. Where the fuck are Dirt and Neph? One of them better be watching Frank.

Then Thunderaxe gets hurt, more red, we finish killing and I help him to the car. He will be fine, Thunderaxe is a hard man.

# Dirt's Battle Royal

## *(That he single handedly wins)*

## *(By himself)*

*What a shit way to start a battle royal, Lonald up front flapping his gums and Frank trying to take a quick power nap on the cement. That or he couldn't handle good booze. I'd be mad about it, but these things always turn out fun, and all the extra dumb shit is never enough to spoil it.*

*I pick up Frank and drag his ass into battle, good thing he gets his feet under him or I would have left his sleepy-ass behind. Probably would have gotten picked off by some asshole in less than a minute.*

*And go figure, Glen and Ponch head for the biggest group of bitches they can find. Glen yelled some crap I didn't care about and they run into a wall of dude meat. They did ok, if I had been there it would have been way better, but someone has to watch Frank's back.*

*We start fighting when we get there and Neph is jumping around stabbing people in what some would call a shameful way to fight. Frank just stood there. He probably had a cramp or something.*

"Hey Frank, stop being a useless member of the team and fight!" I yell at him. "Also you should eat more protein so you don't cramp up so much. It's bad for your bones and things." At least it was something like that.

After I say that Frank beats the fucking face off a dude with his bat, it was pretty badass and I felt a little pride in my young protégé. Then he puked all over and my pride spattered on the ground much like his food.

"Fucking gross Frank," I say to him, countering three simultaneous attacks and expertly breaking all their noses to death. I wasn't even trying either.

I killed about seventeen guys after that, pretty much just smashing parts of their faces in with my stick. People underestimate how useful a stout bit of wood is in a fight, then when their teeth are inside the back of their heads they rethink how dangerous sticks are. It also helped that I'm like the best guy with a stick there is.

Ask anyone.

We fight for a while more, no real highlights to speak of. That is except for this one dude that I fought, he was nine or ten feet tall if he was a day. He also had arms the size of Poncho's. And I don't mean his arms were the size of Poncho's arms, I mean that is arms were the size of Poncho himself. Each arm was a Ponch.

Well it was the most terrifying thing I had seen in almost a week so I attack the shit out of him. It wasn't *easy though, he was fast. Like really fast. I almost couldn't catch him he was so fast. But he was fighting the Old Dirty One, and he didn't have a fucking chance.*

*Then I realize, it's not that he's fast, it's just that he's swinging his Poncho's around so fast I can't get close to him. I devised a plan that was sure to work. When this mountain person swung his tree at me.*

*Oh yeah, he was using a tree as a weapon, like a whole tree.*

*He swings the tree at me and I jump on top of it and run at his face. This scares the shit out of him and I bash him in the face. This is when I realize that this guy is also stupid as shit, 'cause he thinks I'm still on the tree and drops it, assuming that his face is safe from my wrath now.*

*But I'm not there. I'm on his shoulders choking him to death with my stick. It takes a while for this guy to die, but I'm no quitter. When he finally stops twitching I get up and spit on him for good measure.*

*Someone must have forgotten to tell him that I'm the best guy with sticks.*

*When that's all over it looks like most of the nearby fighting is done, or it better be because Frank is puking again. He must have filled up on tacos when I wasn't looking.*

I yell some inspirational stuff at him, like "Chin up!" and "Soldier on!" Then I do a super awesome move with my stick and he is impressed to the point of not wanting to be a pussy anymore.

Glen starts freaking out around then and runs off. Poncho states the obvious that Glen is deep in the throes of bloodlust and offers to do whatever, who cares.

I yell some stuff after Thunderaxe and he is motivated by it, I'm the best at this shit.

Neph and Frank run off after them, after they ask some dumb questions anyway. I say I have some stuff to do and I go the other way. Those lovebirds need some alone time, and the best kind of alone time is surrounded by people that want to kill you and killing them. They would probably ask me to marry them, or at least be the best man. Best man fits better, because I'm the best.

Now that they were gone it was time to enact my brilliant plan. It was called: Operation Stab, Stab, Stab. Not my best name, but the core idea was solid.

I run over to Lonald's group to see what they are up to. His goons are doing a good job of killing, but they simply aren't in the same caliber as Team Dirt.

I kind of expected Lonald to be surrounded by his guys drinking a glass of sparkling wine or something, but he was in the thick of it fighting his ass off. It had been a *while since I had seen that fucker fight, but as I recall he wasn't too shabby.*

*Not that it would help him.*

*I run up all, "Hey, I am that super awesome dude from dinner nerds." They know who I am, and if I might say are super fuckin' stoked that I am there to help those Sallies out so I add a little, "Hey you fucks, get your heads in the game. Go kill those fucks over there!" They totally run the fuck off to do what I told them because I am too awesome to ignore. Then Lonald's dumb ass finally finished wrecking some clown, which was well done by any standards besides mine, and I give him the ol, 'hey I'm about to fucking make your Momma wish she would have given you a I am immune to getting stabbed by the Dirt Man gene, when she brought your dumb ass into the world' nod.*

*Needless to say, he was seconds away from pissing all over his fancy clothes when I pointed my staff at him. We had done this dance before and he still had two left feet when I was his partner. While he was still fucking about like a lost cat, seriously those little shits get really lost and just fuck about, I toss him my staff and while the stupid shit takes his eyes off of me to catch it I close the ground before he knows what is going on and give him the ol' stabby stab stab before he knows what is what. I am the best at plans.*

*Not even Poncho knew I was hiding daggers in my sleeves. Oldest trick in the book, the book that I wrote. About plans and having knives in your sleeves.*

*Nailed it.*

*So I had this awesome part of my plan where I make fun of Lonald for getting wrecked by me, but then I notice that the stupid fuck is already dead. That fool wasn't even good at getting killed while leaving enough time for The Dirt to explain why. Fuck it.*

*Nailed it again.*

*Back to the plan. As I am running up to tell Poncho that Lonald's days of pretending to pull our strings are done I notice Frank and Neph in a badger of a tuff. I know that I should just run past them, so they will be tougher in the long run, but part of me can't stand other clowns beating on friends. I give the old staff a twirl, for the effect, right before I smash it into Frank's attackers face. He fell like bricks, but the force of my perfect stroke broke my staff.  Fucking Frank, that was totally his fault.*

*He actually had the nerve to question where I had been, probably because blood covered Neph was standing beside him. So I work my mystique and just tell them I was helping Lonald. But they don't stop with the questions so I tell them that Lonald was taking a long nap. Surprisingly they took it pretty well.*

*I decide they are fucking aces from this point on and grab another staff off of the ground and head for the last group. I have awesome luck, but this staff was shit, so I tell Frank he still owes me one.*

*Like I said, the first clown I smack with my new stick used his face to break it in half. Being the dude that I am, I just roll with it and enjoy having two smaller staffs to wreck some faces with, until I caught up with Poncho and the Thunderaxe.*

*I fight this guy for a while, toying with him like a housecat with two small staffs would. The guy is pretty good, but I wreck him pretty fast. Problem was, when I got done wrecking him to death the fighting was over. Any survivors must have run off after they all shit in their pants seeing me lay waste.*

*Oh well, more assholes to kill another day.*

*Good news though, Frank was still alive! He was bleeding a little, but he'd be fine. Frank is a tough cookie. Boo to Neph still being alive, that would surely make Frank's day, but I was hoping she wouldn't make it.*

*She doesn't like me, and that just won't do.*

*We head back to the car and Glen is bleeding all over himself. I say a witty comment about it and Frank throws up again. We should take him to the doctor after this. He might have food poisoning.*

# Aftermath

"Fuck, what happened Glen?" I asked after wiping what little puke I had left from my mouth.

"Oh, I got a little careless out there and let some rascal scratch me up. It's nothing really," Glen said just as happily as usual.

"I can see your insides Glen," I said fighting back the dry heaves.

"Honestly Frank, you'll make me blush worrying like this." Glen poked some of his guts back into the gaping chasm on his belly. "See? It's fine. Really."

I wasn't convinced.

"He is tougher than he looks," Poncho said. "He is a warrior."

"Warriors still bleed to death and... and whatever happens when your insides are on the outside!" I shouted.

"I insist that you stop worrying Frank," Glen said seriously.

"Yeah, bask in the glory of a fight well won!" Dirt said excitedly.

Bask? I was surrounded by the criminally insane.

"It was a good fight, how many guys do you think there were Frank?" Poncho asked.

"What?" I asked, somewhat relieved to have any distraction. I thought about it and came up with a rough average. "I don't know, like a hundred and fifty maybe."

"That's what I thought," Poncho said pondering. "That means I probably killed around half of a hundred. Thunderaxe got less than that."

"Half of a hundred?" I asked.

Dirt started laughing like a crazy person. "You know you can't count Ponch! Why even try?"

And I'll be god damned if Poncho didn't blush a little.

"I killed more than he did," Poncho said sullenly.

"No you didn't! He was a madman out there, he probably killed like twice as many dudes as you," Dirt said laughing.

"No, we were pretty close I think," Glen said. "Plus I lose some points for getting this." Glen poked his wound.

I wasn't sure how he was even still conscious with that thing, let alone poking it.

"Fair enough," Poncho said before breaking out into a coughing fit, and promptly coughing up at least a gallon of blood.

"Oh shit! Are you ok?" I asked, not sure how he could have been that injured and nobody noticing.

"It's not mine..." Poncho said trailing off.

"Fuck! Did you get turned into a vampire? I'll stake you brother, just let me do it before you turn evil," Dirt said brandishing one of his staff chunks.

"I'm not a vampire."

"Then why do you have so much blood in your undead belly?" Dirt asked inching closer.

"Battle. Things happen. I don't want to talk about it."

Dirt backed off a little. "Ok. For now. But when the change happens you know I'll end your suffering."

Poncho nodded, but he had a slight smirk on his face, as if watching Dirt try would be fun.

"I got the bags," Neph said with an armful of Lonald's bags.

She must have gone off while we were talking, I'm not surprised I didn't notice, what with all the blood and being bone-tired from the battle.

"Throw them in the trunk and we'll head out," Dirt said.

"What about Glen?" I asked.

"Don't worry about me, I'll meet you guys there. Shoot, I might even beat you home," Glen said continuing to bleed on himself. "Someone has to clean all this up."

"Glen," I said gravely. "I think you might die if we don't get you to a hospital."

Much to my surprise everyone including Glen started laughing.

"Thunderaxe is a fast healer," Dirt said wiping tears from his eyes.

"What the fuck is so funny?" I asked getting mad. Glen was too nice a guy to let die like this. I could even look past his insane bloodlust when we were fighting and see that he was a good man. I didn't want to see him die.

"I promise you Frank. I'll be fine, you just need to get out of here and get a shower and relax. I'll meet you there. Promise," Glen said.

It started to dawn on me that when Dirt said they had been lying to me the whole time it might be on a lot larger scale than I thought. I never put the pieces together that he was one of them either. Maybe he could heal through this.

"You still owe me some answers," I said to Dirt.

"I know Frank, and I'll tell you everything at Lonald's house."

"Lonald's house?" I asked. I assumed we would go back to my house or Glen's.

"Yeah, he died and we won. So we get all his stuff," Dirt said.

"Is that one of the rules?" I asked.

"Probably, who knows? Nobody listens to that shit," Dirt laughed.

We looked at Neph, she was the closest thing we had to an official party and it seemed she would know the answer.

She shrugged, "Seems fair to me."

"Ok, we head to Lonald's house and drink all his beers!" Dirt said.

"I doubt he has beers," Poncho said.

"Shit. Glen can you pick up beers on your way?" Dist asked.

"No problem, I'll grab some pizza too if you guys want," Glen said.

"Shit yeah!" Dirt exclaimed.

I think I was starting to fall full force into their madness now, because what I was about to say to a dying man was pure nonsense.

"Aren't you going to get your car all bloody?" I asked Glen. He seemed like the clean type.

Glen actually winked at me, hole in his belly, guts on the ground, he winked at me. "I put some plastic on the seats just in case, now you guys quit lollygagging and get going. I'll be there with pizza and beers before you know it!"

"Yeah!" Dirt shouted.

I really hoped that I would get some straight answers out of these assholes this time.

As I was about to get into that car Neph stopped me. I was sure she was going to hurt me somehow, but when she looked me in the eyes and planted a peck on my cheek, I all but melted. God damn I'm a big softie.

She smiled and got in the car.

I surveyed the battle field, a nice man bleeding to death by his silly car. A man that seemed nice was already dead, and we were going to raid his house for snacks. And I'd killed several... several who knows what? They sure as hell weren't human, and I sure as hell had no idea what was going on. But one thing was for sure, it was a lot more fun than taking pictures of cheating spouses. I can't really like this, but I do.

I got into the car and we drove away.

One way or another I was going to see this through to the end, even though it would likely kill me.

I think we might be the bad guys in this story, and I think I like being the bad guy.

# Resolution

Not long after the fight we were at Lonald's house sitting in his den with some drinks. After a short disagreement with the armed guards littering the mansion Neph managed to convince them that she inherited everything. I didn't think for a second that it was true, but when she assured them that they would still get paid they decided that who their boss was didn't really matter.

I was dreading the supposed answers that Dirt had promised me as much as I was looking forward to knowing them. If the truth was half as crazy as the lies they told, I was in for an interesting night. But for the moment I was satisfied simply enjoying being alive with an ice-cold, fancy, rich-guy drink.

Neph had bandaged my wound in the cold efficient manner I was used to, but she was surprisingly gentle at the same time. It wasn't too deep, but it was starting to hurt a little. It made me a little proud to have a battle scar, but irritated that Dirt and Poncho looked completely unharmed.

We had been sitting in silence for a few beers, I was exhausted and attribute my laziness to that. Neph was scowling in the corner, but she looked less hostile than usual. Only slightly though. Poncho was sitting in Lonald's chair pounding beer after beer and looking at nothing in particular. I was sure I didn't want to know what was going on in his head.

And Dirt. Dirt was talking, but he was doing it on the far side of the room to a stuffed boar's head. He was speaking in hushed tones and laughing like they were old friends. I should have been worried, but his behavior no longer shocked me.

I was about to start with the questions when I heard the door open, and a few seconds later the man we had left for dead walked in smiling like a mad man, with arms full of pizza.

"There is some more beer in the car, I'll grab them as soon as I get you guys fed," Said Glen, who should be dead, but looked as healthy as ever.

I found that I could no longer contain myself. "How the fuck are you alive? I saw your guts leaking out on the ground!" I shouted.

Glen blushed and looked at the ground shuffling past and setting the pizzas on a table. "It wasn't as bad as it looked," he mumbled.

"Yeah," Dirt added. "You know how belly wounds are, they look way worse than they really are."

"His guts were coming out," I said flatly.

"That's not as bad as you'd think, you can just poke them back in and sew it all shut. Problem solved," Dirt explained as if it all made perfect sense.

"I heal fast," Glen said sheepishly. "I'm sorry if we didn't explain properly, it was quite rude. I can't apologize enough Frank, but it just wasn't as bad as it looked. Honestly."

"I suppose that's about as much sense as I'm going to get out of this. I'll chalk it up to you guys all being some kind of crazy immortal psychic monster killers," I said.

"That about sums it up pal," Dirt said.

"So now we just continue to fight all these alleged monsters until we save the day forever?" I asked more than a little sarcastically.

"Yep," Dirt replied grabbing a slice of pizza.

"Bullshit," I said. "You promised me answers."

"I think we just settled it all didn't we?" Dirt asked innocently.

"Dirt," Poncho said sternly.

"Fuck, fine. What do you want to know?" Dirt said throwing his hands up in defeat and losing most of his toppings on Lonald's bookcase.

I had way too many questions I needed answers to, so I decided to start from the beginning. "Were those guys really monsters? I mean in the sense of vampires, werewolves, Frankensteins and so forth."

"Yes," Dirt said.

"No," Said Poncho and Neph.

"Turncoats!" Dirt shouted.

"Come on man, we owe him the truth," Poncho said.

"It is the truth, I think," Dirt said sullenly.

"They were like us," Poncho said.

That made sense at least. Sort of anyway.

"Ok, so what exactly are you guys?" I asked

"Crazy immortal psychic monster killers," Dirt said. "From space."

I looked to Poncho to clarify, but the answer came from Neph.

"We aren't really sure," she said.

Poncho nodded and Dirt scoffed. It wasn't really the answer I'd been expecting, but it made the most sense.

"Why am I not surprised about that?" I asked half to myself.

"Because of clues probably," Dirt stated.

"Why do you all fight each other all the time if you don't know what you are?" I asked.

"Why do humans fight each other all the time? It's not like you know where you came from either," Neph said.

I started to formulate an answer, but Dirt cut me off.

"And don't say any of that shit about God because you can't prove it, and evolution is just a fancy faceless god invented for people who don't believe in magic. Which is totally real by the way," Dirt said.

That kind of shut down any retort I had in mind no matter how nonsensical it was.

"Fair enough," I conceded. "But you guys kind of make an ordeal out of it, with your codes and battle royals and stuff."

"We are immortal, it's a little different," Poncho said uncertainly.

"If you are immortal, why kill each other?"

"There can be only one!" Dirt shouted.

I looked to the others for the sane answer I hoped one of them would supply, but all I got was shrugs.

"Seriously?" I asked.

"Pretty much," Poncho said.

"Why?"

"Again, we don't really know," Neph said. "It's apparently how we are built."

"That sounds stupid," I said.

"You're stupid Frank, we didn't ask to be this way! Why are you so cruel?" Dirt exclaimed in the most over exaggerated way he could think of.

This wasn't exactly how I'd pictured this conversation going, but I didn't have all that many expectations to shatter in the first place. At least I was pretty sure that they weren't fucking with me.

"What happens when there is only one left?" I asked slowly.

The reaction I got to this question was unsettling. Everyone in the room stopped what they were doing and exchanged furtive glances before looking anywhere. Anywhere, but at me.

"What?" I asked getting nervous.

"Apocalypse," Dirt mumbled under his breath.

"Pardon?"

"The apocalypse happens," Dirt said louder.

"What?" I asked again, I was having trouble processing this information.

"Only for a little while though, It's not that bad really," Dirt explained.

"Not that bad?" I said trying to think how the end of days could be 'not that bad.'

"It's after that apocalypse that things get... interesting," Neph said.

"Interesting?" I said showing my superb control of complex sentences.

"Well it's..." Neph started until a thought popped into my reeling brain.

"Wait a second! How do you know that if none of you know why you kill each other or why you even exist?" I had caught them in a lie, and I was never more relieved that I was being lied to.

"That's why it's interesting," Poncho said crushing me.

"I'm going to need an explanation," I said stating the obvious.

"Well after the moon turns to blood and the dead rise it gets pretty hairy. Everyone has to fight to stay alive until the great serpent rises and consumes all the evil. Then consumes all the other stuff too. Then explodes," Dirt said.

"Or none of that happens and everything just starts over," Neph simplified.

"It might happen, it's not like we would know," Dirt sulked.

"What do you mean everything starts over?" I asked.

"That's it, everything stops and we start over at what we assume is the beginning of time," Neph said.

"Which is super annoying, you know how hard it is to teach the dawn of man how to make beer?" Dirt exclaimed.

"Teaching them how to use fire isn't a treat either," Poncho added.

This was all too much to handle, it was too farfetched to be even close to real. But they were being far more earnest than usual, except Dirt anyway.

"So everyone dies, then the world starts over and you all fight to the death again?" I asked just making sure I had the facts right.

"Yes," Poncho said.

"Why?"

More shrugs, it was like dealing with children.

"Ok," I said licking my lips as if the extra moisture would make me want to vomit less. "Why did you need me?"

Shrugs again.

"God dammit. That's not good enough, I need answers!" I shouted.

"I was on the outside of their little plot so I really have no idea. I can tell you that Lonald didn't know either, he just thought that these two had some diabolical plan to kill him and that you were somehow the key," Neph said.

"I'm just a man, how would I be the key to anything?" I asked.

"Then why do you speak Chinese?" Glen asked quietly from across the room.

"What? I don't speak Chinese," I said.

"Pretty sure he speaks the same language we do," Dirt said.

"You guys don't notice it, you just understand and are understood in any language," Glen said.

"I don't speak Chinese," I said suspiciously listening to my own words.

"You don't notice it either, but you change tongues to fit the situation at a whim," Glen replied with a whisper.

"I think I would notice that Glen," I replied.

"But you don't," Glen replied a little softer.

"I call bullshit on that for now."

"Me too," Dirt added.

"Even if that were true why would that make me a candidate for any of this?" I asked.

Dirt and Poncho looked at each other and shrugged again. It was getting ridiculous.

"We don't know Frank," Dirt said after a few silent eternities. "You are just a strange dude and it felt like we needed you to help us."

"Help you what?"

"Win?" Dirt said sheepishly.

"How can you win if only one of you can be left?"

"Well we just turn on each other at the end and it's every man for himself," Dirt said.

"That's stupid, why does it matter who wins if everything just starts over?"

"I'm pretty sure if I win I can sort out what's going on. It's in the plan," Dirt said.

"What plan?"

"The plan to win dummy," Dirt laughed.

"None of this makes any sense," I said with my head in my hands.

"Now you know how we feel," Poncho said.

Neph nodded.

My mind was racing and I couldn't handle it anymore, luckily my stupid brain gave me a tangent to resolve.

"What was the deal with the crosswalk thing then?" I asked, maybe a little too harsh.

"We didn't want you to get hit by a truck," Dirt said.

"And how would you know that I would be hit by a truck? I assume the psychic thing was bullshit too."

"It isn't!" Dirt said defensively.

"It is," Poncho said. "When everything starts over everything more or less plays out like it did the time before that, and so on. So every time we recruited you to help us you would get hit by a truck, or something big, and die."

"I get hit by a truck every time the world starts over?"

"Eventually," Poncho said.

"Sometimes you don't even make it that far," Dirt added.

"Fuck you guys. This shit isn't funny anymore," I almost screamed.

"Frank, Poncho is known to be very honest," Neph added softly.

"Not good enough," I replied.

"Frank, Poncho cannot tell a lie," Neph glared at me. "You should have figured that out by now."

"Poncho, is that the truth? Will you answer whatever questions I have?" I asked.

"No Frank, I don't know all the answers," Poncho replied.

"Fuck that Poncho. You know what I am asking. Can you lie about a question when you know the answer?" I asked.

"I don't know Frank," Poncho answered again. "If I don't know the answer to something, I might think I know the truth and tell you a lie accidentally. I would think it's the truth and you thinking I can't lie would make you think it was the truth. It would be a huge mess and help no one. And it's not like I have to answer every question I'm asked, I'm not under some magic spell that makes me only speak the truth no matter who asks it. That would be stupid and in no way useful. Lies of omission are perfectly acceptable as well. The only real truth I know is the truth of battle, kill or die, that's all there is. When you step onto a battlefield and breathe the air gazing at your enemies on the far side all waiting to kill you and everyone with you, then you know truth. Kill everyone or they run away and try to kill you another day, then you kill them that day. The easiest way is to kill everyone in the bloodiest way possible so that none of their friends consider trying to kill you in the future, then kill them anyway. It's the only truth I need."

That was easily the most I'd ever heard Poncho say in one sitting, and I was stunned into silence along with everyone else. The silence went on for a few seconds that dragged into what felt like forever until Dirt ended it.

"Yeah, and he can't even count good either!" he added jokingly.

Poncho glared at Dirt and broke into a beardy grin. "Counting never solved anything."

Dirt laughed and lifted his beer in salute, I found myself doing the same with a slight grin on my face. I was glad Dirt had this ability to break tension, without it things would get pretty heavy with all these professional killers in the room.

After I had some time to process Poncho's little rant I had a thought, "When you guys die you just wake up when everything starts over? Nothing else happens?" I asked.

"Nothing," Poncho said.

"That's pretty grim," I answered.

"You get used to it," Dirt said. "Nothing is way better than some things, sometimes."

That comment was far more bleak than I'd expected from Dirt, but expectations with him were kind of a waste of time.

"Does that mean the rest of you have magic powers too?" I asked.

"Glen heals pretty fast, that's kind of like magic," Dirt said.

Glen shrugged, not looking like he agreed all that much, but accepting it at the same time.

"So what's your thing?" I asked Dirt.

"Fuck if I know," he replied.

"That's probably true," Poncho said.

"Wakka wakka Ponch," Dirt scoffed.

"What about you Neph?"

"I'll never say," she said sternly.

"I think I hate you guys," I said.

"No you don't Frank, we are all best friends now," Dirt said.

"I'm not sure how I feel about that man," I said.

"You love it stupid, let's get super drunk and jump off stuff," Dirt said throwing an empty at the bookcase.

It was the best idea I'd heard in a few days.

# Epilogue

So that's the first part of my story. I was constantly confused, lied to, and almost murdered. I'd be lying if I said I didn't enjoy it, and I'd be lying if I said I didn't question every decision I made throughout.

*Bullshit Frank, you never even got close to backing out. You love this shit.*

Maybe I do, and that scares me more than anything else that occurred. The entire ordeal changed me in ways that would...

*Fuck me Frank, are you still telling this story? It's been going on for-fucking-ever. Just end it.*

It doesn't end like this though, this was just the beginning.

*Don't care, Frankenstein showed up and killed us all with a samurai sword. The end.*

How would we be talking if that were true? And I'm pretty sure it's called a katana.

*It's called whatever I say it's called.*

**It's a katana.**